BITCH CREEK

BRADY COYNE
NOVELS:

Death at Charity's Point

The Dutch Blue Error

Follow the Sharks

The Marine Corpse

Dead Meat

The Vulgar Boatman

A Void in Hearts

Dead Winter

Client Privilege

The Spotted Cats

Tight Lines

The Snake Eater

The Seventh Enemy

Close to the Bone

Cutter's Run

Muscle Memory

Scar Tissue

Past Tense

A Fine Line

Shadow of Death

BOOKS ON
THE OUTDOORS:

Those Hours Spent Outdoors

Opening Day and Other Neuroses

Home Water Near and Far

Sportsman's Legacy

A Fly-Fishing Life

Bass Bug Fishing

Upland Days

Pocket Water

The Orvis Guide to Fly Fishing
    for Bass

Gone Fishin'

OTHER NONFICTION:

The Elements of Mystery Fiction:
    Writing the Modern Whodunit

OTHER NOVELS:

Thicker than Water
    (with Linda Barlow)

First Light (with Philip R. Craig)

BITCH CREEK

A NOVEL

By William G. Tapply

The Lyons Press

Guilford, Connecticut

An imprint of The Globe Pequot Press

Tap

10 9 8 7 6 5 4 3 2

Printed in the United States of America

ISBN 1-59228-765-4

The Library of Congress has previously cataloged an earlier (hardcover) edition as follows:

Tapply, William G.
    Bitch Creek : a novel / by William G. Tapply.
        p. cm.
    ISBN 1-59228-435-3 (trade cloth)
        I. Title.

    PS3570.A568B57 2004
    813'.54—dc22

                                    2004048954

DEDICATION

This book is for
Keith Wegener and Blaine Moores and Jason Terry
and Uncle George and Uncle Woober (rest their souls)
and all the other men of Maine
who have taken me out on their boats and into their woods
and told me their stories.

Epigraph

"... they could hear the fire coming. It sounded like a freight train. ... they just had time to jump into the car and drive away before the fire burst out of the woods, setting the backyard field aflame. The house exploded. 'It just blew,' Ruth remembers. 'It just blew apart.'"

Joyce Butler,
Wildfire Loose: The Week Maine Burned

Acknowledgments

I am grateful to Rick Boyer and Vicki Stiefel, who read early drafts of the story and steered me right, and to Lilly Golden, whose tough love made it a better book.

Chapter One

A FEW MINUTES AFTER EIGHT in the morning, Stoney Calhoun heard the bell ding over the door, alerting him that someone had come into the shop. He glanced up from his fly-tying vise. A white-haired man stood inside the doorway studying the rack of Sage and Orvis fly rods against the wall. Calhoun returned his attention to the nearly completed fly in his vise.

A minute later, the man was standing in front of him. "What in hell is *that?*"

Calhoun did not raise his eyes. "Bunker fly," he mumbled, pronouncing it *bunk-ah*. He always thickened his Maine accent for out-of-state customers, on the theory that they found it quaint and charming. Actually, it was Kate's theory, but Calhoun guessed she was right. Out-of-staters, flatlanders, folks "from away"—and this old gentleman, with his pressed chino pants, shiny loafers, green polo shirt buttoned to the throat, and his distinctly Dixie drawl, certainly was from away—expected Downeasters like Stoney Calhoun to talk like the caricatures they'd heard in television commercials, and Kate

1

Balaban believed they'd be more inclined to spend money in her shop if the shopkeepers satisfied their expectations.

"Say 'ayuh' more, Stoney," Kate kept telling him. "You've got to practice. Go for taciturn. If you have the chance, tell 'em they can't get there from here."

Kate was the boss, so Calhoun tried to do it her way.

Without lifting his head, he noted that the man's hands, which rested on the front of the fly-tying bench, were deeply tanned and speckled with liver spots. He wore a Rolex on his left wrist. No wedding band. Professionally manicured nails, cut short and square.

Calhoun licked his fingers, smoothed back the saddle hackles and Marabou and bucktail and Flashabou of his bunker fly work-in-progress, then made a few careful winds of thread in front to lay it all back, taking his time with it.

Taciturn. Laconic. A local character. That was Calhoun.

Finally he looked up. "Georgia? Florida?"

The man's thinning white hair was brushed straight back from a high, deeply tanned forehead. He had big ears that stuck out almost at right angles from his head and penetrating ice-blue eyes behind steel-rimmed glasses, with deep crow's feet webbing from the corners. Calhoun judged he was pushing seventy. "Key Largo, actually," the man said. "How'd you know?"

Calhoun shrugged. "Wild guess." He returned his attention to his bunker fly. He pivoted the vise around so he could look at both sides of it, and then he whip-finished the head, clipped off the thread, and took it from the vise. It was nearly eight inches long, and about half that deep from belly to back. He handed it to the man. "Stick on a pair of big prismatic eyes," he said, "and she'll be done. Whaddya think?"

The man squinted at it. "It looks scary. What eats something like this?"

"Stripers." *Strip-ahs.* "You don't have striped bass in Key Largo."

The man smiled, showing either expensively capped teeth or a spiffy set of dentures. "No, we don't. But we have tarpon that weigh two hundred pounds, and they'd flee if they saw something like this thing coming at 'em."

"Menhaden," said Calhoun. "Pogies. Bunker. Same critter. Important baitfish hereabouts. They start showin' up inshore in late June—about now. By the middle of the summer they've growed up to a foot long or more. Stripers and bluefish love 'em. You ought to see the bunker flies we tie for August."

The man gave the fly back to Calhoun, then held out his hand. "My name's Green. Fred Green. And actually I was hoping to do some trout fishing. Brook trout. Natives, not stockers. I'm looking for someone who really knows the back roads and woods around here. A native. A real Mainer. Folks at the hotel recommended you."

Calhoun looked up. "Me?"

Green shrugged. "I don't know your name."

"Calhoun," he said. He shook the old man's hand. It was soft and uncallused, although his handshake was manly enough. "When were you lookin' to go?"

"Today's my only chance. I'm up on business. Figured I'd play hooky from the convention for a day. Always wanted to catch a Maine brook trout."

Calhoun leaned back in his chair and looked at Fred Green over the tops of the half-glasses he wore for fly-tying. "You want a wild brookie, you're gonna have to do some trekkin'. Anything close to the road's been fished out or ruined by hatchery stockers."

"Good," said Green. "That's what I want. I've done a lot of trekking in my life. Ever been to Argentina?"

"Nope," said Calhoun.

"I have," said Green. "Sea-run brown trout as big as your leg. What about Russia? Siberia's the new Atlantic salmon frontier. Accommodations are mighty crude in Siberia."

"Ain't been to Russia, neither," said Calhoun.

"I camped for a week beside a river in Alaska," said Green. "King salmon. Monster rainbows that ate mice and ducklings, mosquitoes in clouds that blocked the sun. Grizzly bears prowling through camp every night. You've been to Alaska, of course."

"Nope. Been all over Maine, though. Jackman, Mattawamkeag, Chesuncook, Rangeley, Seboomook." Laying on the Maine accent. "Yessuh. Done a bit of trekkin' in Maine." Calhoun shrugged. "Sounds like you're one helluva fisherman, Mr. Green. A six-inch brook trout gonna make you happy?"

Green grinned. "I don't care how big they are. I've fished all over. Keep track of all the native fish I've nailed. Brown trout in Bavaria. Salmon in Iceland. Dolly Varden in Alaska. I've caught every sub-species of cutthroat out West. Hiked clear to the top of a mountain in Nevada to get my golden. But I've never caught a truly native brook trout before. I figure, here I am in Maine, and at my age I may never get another chance."

Calhoun sighed, got up from behind his fly-tying bench, and went over to the counter. He flipped open the shop's logbook and pretended to study it. "You should've called yesterday," he said. "Kinda short notice."

"Today's my only chance," said Green. "There's a big tip in it for you."

Calhoun didn't need to look at the logbook. He already knew that both he and Lyle McMahan were available to guide. Kate, who had become something of a striped-bass guru in the past couple of years, had left before sunrise to take a couple from New Jersey up to the Kennebec.

Calhoun should take Fred Green trout fishing. It was his turn. Lyle would come over to mind the shop.

But the truth was, Calhoun couldn't conjure up any enthusiasm for leading Mr. Green on a tromp through the woods to one of the secret little spring-fed trout ponds he'd discovered in the woodsy Maine hills west of Sebago. It would be a day of pushing through alders and briars, slogging through marsh and swamp, lugging the lunch basket and both his own and Fred Green's rods and waders and float tubes, swatting blackflies, and stopping every ten minutes while this old Florida boy sat down to catch his breath.

Well, the full truth was that with the right company, that could be a helluva good day, Stoney Calhoun's kind of day. But he reckoned that Mr. Green would be mighty disappointed if all that slogging and sweating and scratching didn't pay off in a few trout, regardless of how hard the guide worked at it. None of his secret trout ponds was a sure bet in the middle of a sunny day in June, and Calhoun had had his fill of unappreciative clients.

Anyway, a man—even a fishing guide—didn't share his private brook-trout ponds with just anybody.

Calhoun had pegged this Fred Green from Key Largo as a blowhard. He knew it was a character flaw, but he judged people quickly and rarely felt compelled to reverse his judgment. He had no tolerance for blowhards, and he knew if he spent much time with Mr. Green, he'd inevitably cut him down with sarcasm. Kate always worried about Calhoun's sarcasm. Bad for business, she said, regardless of how thick he laid on the accent when he was doing it.

No, he just did not want to spend a day with Fred Green. He'd rather mind the shop, tie some flies, find some Bach or Sibelius on the radio, and be there when Kate got back to help her unload, and afterward they'd put their feet up on the fly-tying bench, have a Coke, and she'd tell him about her day's adventures with the folks from New Jersey.

Calhoun looked up from the logbook. "You're in luck," he said to Fred Green. "Lyle's available, and he's just the man you're lookin' for. Registered Maine Guide. He's lived around here all his life, knows every creek and pothole in York, Oxford, and Cumberland counties.

Anybody can catch you a wild brookie, I reckon it's Lyle. Stick you in a float tube, paddle you out onto a little pond. Like I said, pretty short notice. But I'll give him a call, see if he can shoot over and make a plan with you, if you want."

"Lyle," said Green. "I think that's one of the names they mentioned to me at the hotel."

"Lyle McMahan," said Calhoun. "He's got a good reputation hereabouts."

"You mentioned a float tube," Green said. "You mean a belly boat? One of those canvas-covered inner tube things you sit in? I've never done that. Are they safe?"

"Oh, sure," said Calhoun. "You'll enjoy it."

Green rubbed his hands together. "Well, it sounds good to me."

Calhoun picked up the portable phone and pecked out Lyle's number. Lyle McMahan, who was a graduate student in history at the University of Southern Maine, shared a big, run-down rented house in South Portland with an ever-shifting mixture of students and their boyfriends and girlfriends and assorted hangers-on. Calhoun couldn't keep track of Lyle's housemates.

This time a sleepy female voice answered with a muffled, "Yo?"

"Lyle there?" said Calhoun.

"Hang on, mister. I'll take a look."

A minute later she came back on the line. "He's coming." She paused. "Hey, is that you, Stoney?"

"Yep. Who's this?"

"It's Julia." She dragged out her name, giving it three distinct syllables—*Joo-lee-yah.* "Remember?"

"Sure," he said. "Of course. How're you doing?" Actually, Calhoun couldn't remember whether Julia was one of the several little athletic blondes who shared Lyle's commune, or the tall gal with the red hair.

"Doin' just fine," she said. "Well, here he is."

"What's going on, Stoney?" said Lyle a moment later.

"Got a job for you, bud," said Calhoun. "Mr. Green, here, up from Florida, would like to catch himself a gen-u-ine Maine brook trout."

"It's your turn, man. What's the story?"

Calhoun glanced up. Fred Green was standing in front of him, watching. "Good," he said into the phone. "Haul your butt right over here, son. Your client's itchin' to go. He's askin' for you personally."

"This dude another one of your rejects?" said Lyle.

"Ayuh. That's about it."

"I'm telling Kate that you're pullin' rank, old buddy." Lyle laughed. "Sell the man some flies. Tell him that story about how George Smith's wife got stuck on the toilet seat he'd just varnished. I'll be there in fifteen minutes."

Calhoun disconnected and looked up at Fred Green. "You're all set. He's on his way. How're you fixed for gear?"

"I hope you can rent me what I need," said Green. "I didn't bring anything with me."

"Lyle will set you up when he gets here," said Calhoun. He waved his hand around the little shop. "There's coffee in the back. Poke around. See anything you like, let me know. Twenty percent off all the clothing."

He went back to his fly-tying bench, dismissing Fred Green, feeling only a little guilty that he wasn't trying harder to sell something to the man.

Calhoun had tied two more bunker flies by the time Lyle breezed in about a half hour later. He looked up to catch Green's reaction. Lyle McMahan was a gangly six-and-a-half-footer with a wispy goatee, a hoop in his ear, and a ponytail that was held back with one of those rubber bands they use in restaurants to clamp shut the claws of lobsters.

If Fred Green had expected Lyle McMahan to look like a stereotypical Maine guide—red-and-black-checked shirt, bushy black beard, dead cigar butt clamped in his teeth, maybe—he didn't show it. He shook hands with Lyle and the two of them huddled for a few minutes. Then they moved around the shop assembling some equipment, and after a few minutes, Lyle lugged it out to his ancient Dodge Power Wagon and Fred Green followed along behind.

Calhoun watched through the front window as they stowed the equipment in the back. Then Lyle pulled out his gazetteer of topographic maps, which he kept under the driver's seat, and opened it on the hood of the Power Wagon. He and Fred Green bent over it, and after several minutes of chattering and turning pages and poking at it, Green with his forefinger and Lyle with a pencil, they lifted their heads and grinned at each other.

When Lyle came back in to make his entry in the shop's journal, he said, "Ol' Mr. Green and me, we're gonna have some fun."

Calhoun looked up and smiled. "Ayuh, I expect you will."

"He's actually a pretty interesting guy," said Lyle. "He's fished all over the world." He finished writing and dropped the pen on the counter. "He even knows a place."

"A place, eh?"

"Yep. This here's a no-lose proposition, Stoney. Someone told him about a top-secret hotspot, and I think we found it on the map." Lyle grinned. "He wants to try it. If it works out, I can just add it to my list. And if we get skunked it ain't my fault."

"You trying to pull a Tom Sawyer on me, sonny?"

"Nossir," said Lyle. "Mr. Green and I are gonna have us a helluva good day, and he's gonna lay a monster tip on me when we're done. Too bad, Stoney. You could've had it, but this here's my gig."

"Well," said Calhoun, "tight lines, then. You two lads go on, have yourselves a day."

CHAPTER TWO

CALHOUN HEARD KATE'S old Chevy Blazer coming a full minute before it pulled into the pea-stone parking area out front. He'd have to crawl under it sometime and give that tailpipe a few more wraps of duct tape.

He glanced at the clock radio on his fly-tying bench. Nearly six-thirty. She'd met the New Jersey folks at five in the morning. Another typical thirteen-plus-hour day for the fly-fishing guide.

Actually, he was a little surprised she hadn't kept them out there for a second go at the turn of the tide, which had come around eight in the morning, and would, therefore, happen again about eight in the evening. Kate knew exactly where the cow stripers holed up at the bottom of the tide, and more often than not, the clients yelled "uncle" before she was ready to quit.

He pushed himself up from his chair and went outside. Kate had backed her boat into its slot and was bent over the trailer hitch, cursing softly.

"Let me take a whack at it," said Calhoun.

Kate straightened up, put her hands on her hips, and arched her back. "Damn thing keeps jamming on me."

Calhoun gave the crank a few more turns, thumped it with the heel of his hand, then lifted the trailer off the truck's hitch. "You've got to hold your mouth right," he said.

"You've just got a way with machines," she said. "Too bad you're not so good with people. Hold it up here for me."

Calhoun lifted up the front of the trailer while Kate slipped a plank under its front wheel. Then he went to the side of the shop, turned on the outside spigot, uncoiled the hose, and brought it over to the boat. Kate opened the plugs and Calhoun hosed it down, first the inside and then the outside.

She scrubbed at some blood stains with the big boat sponge. "We had us a day," she said.

"Bet you did."

"They were on sand eels all over the mudflats the entire last two hours of the outgoing and well into the incoming. My folks couldn't throw much beyond the tip of their rod, but we dropped anchor there and they were sloshing and churning all around us for three solid hours."

"Schoolies?" said Calhoun.

"Mostly. But we had some fun."

"Any keepers?" *Keep-ahs.*

"I think Charlie had one on earlier, but she came unbuttoned before we got a real good look. You know that rip off the tip of the island?"

"Where the black dog always comes out on the dock to bark at you?"

"That one. This fish was lying there with her nose pointing at the rocks, and Charlie threw one of your bunker flies up into the wash. That old cow sucked it in, and Charlie hit her, and she hightailed it for Boston. He panicked, tried to snub her down, and—"

"Ping!" said Calhoun.

"Busted that ten-pound leader like it was a trout tippet. I think it must've got nicked on a mussel shell." Kate grinned. "I thought the poor man was gonna have a heart attack."

Calhoun always marveled at Kate's undiminished enthusiasm. She had owned Kate's Bait and Tackle for eight years and had been guiding for nearly five. Every day was still an adventure for Kate, and every client was a new friend. For a while, the first-time sports had tended to look at the ground and shuffle their feet and mumble when they realized they'd hired a woman to guide them. But it didn't take long for the word to get around: Kate Balaban had a nose for fish, a limitless repertoire of shaggy dog stories, and twice the stamina of any man. She could repair a dead outboard in the rain while her customized Boston Whaler bounced on heavy chop, she could cast a sink-tip line eighty feet into a ten-naut breeze, and she fixed an old-fashioned Maine shore lunch— an ice chest full of beer and fruit juice and soft drinks, fresh bluefish fillets (if they'd caught any, sirloin steaks if they hadn't) grilled over an open fire, with smoked oysters for appetizers, a big tossed green salad, slabs of extra-sharp Maine cheddar, fresh-baked bread from Sally's next door to the shop, and a wedge of Sally's apple pie for dessert.

Besides, Kate was a spectacular woman who didn't mind the fact that men liked looking at her. She usually wore her black hair in a long braid that reached almost down to her waist, and she knew how to apply subtle touches of makeup to emphasize her high cheekbones, her big black flashing eyes, and her wide mouth. Kate usually wore walking shorts, T-shirts, and sneakers when she guided, and after a few weeks in the sun her Irish half disappeared and she looked like a full-blooded Penobscot Indian.

She was an inch shy of six feet, most of it in her legs. In shorts, she never failed to stop Calhoun's breath. She looked about twenty-five, except for her eyes. Her eyes betrayed more troubles than anyone could ever accumulate in twenty-five years. Kate Balaban was, in fact, three years older than Calhoun, who was thirty-eight.

Her wedding band had failed to discourage more than one optimistic client, but Kate had a way of putting them in their place without offending them.

He helped her unload her gear from the back of the Blazer, and while she hosed the salt water off the rods and reels, he lugged the rest of the stuff into the shop. When she came in a few minutes later, he had a cold Sam Adams on the counter for her and a Coke for himself.

She picked up the beer, took a long swig, then bent to the logbook. "Humph," she mumbled. She looked up. "Where'd Lyle go?"

"He didn't write it down?"

"Nope. All it says here is: 'Mr. Green's secret trout pond.'"

Calhoun summarized his encounter with Fred Green from Key Largo and how he had turned the client over to Lyle McMahan.

"Well, hell, Stoney," said Kate. "It was your turn."

"The man seemed pretty pleased with Lyle, and Lyle was happy to get the job. He and Mr. Green seemed to hit it off. Anyway, Lyle needs the money more'n me."

"That's not the point. We've got a system here, and none of us are supposed to pick and choose our clients. I've told you that before."

"Sorry, ma'am." He shrugged. "I didn't like the man. What can I say?"

"You can say it doesn't matter whether you think you like him or not. You can say it's Kate's rule that you guide when it's your turn like everybody else." She shook her head. "Dammit all anyway, Stoney."

"I tied two dozen bunker flies and twice that many sand eels. Got to hear Van Cliburn play Beethoven's *Emperor Concerto,* then the Chicago Symphony did some Bartok. Sold one of those nine-weight Sage rods and an Abel reel, and a couple of ladies come in around noontime and damned near cleaned us out of those discounted Orvis shirts. You think you had yourself a good day? I had a helluva day."

Kate cocked her head and frowned at him. He grinned back at her. She fought it for a minute, then shook her head and smiled. "Sometimes you really piss me off," she said.

"Yes, ma'am."

"You are incorrigible."

"Ayuh."

"I don't know what I could've been thinking, hiring on a grouchy old shit like you."

"I never could figure it out myself," said Calhoun.

An hour before sunup on a June morning almost exactly five years earlier, Calhoun had been creeping along the muddy bank of a little tidal creek that emptied into Casco Bay just north of Portland. A blush of pink had begun to bleed into the pewter sky toward the east. The tide was about halfway out, and the water against the banks lay as flat and dark as a mug of camp coffee. A blanket of fog hung over the salt marsh, heavy with that rich mingled aroma of wet mud and decaying kelp and salt water and dead shellfish. Except for the squawks from a gang of gulls eating mussels along the high-water line and the muffled gong of a distant bell buoy, it was quiet and solitary and altogether peaceful, the way he loved it.

He was still nearly a hundred yards away when he spotted some nervous water along the edge of the eelgrass in the shallow water. He knew they were stripers, and he knew enough about stripers to guess that they could be big ones. He had a small chartreuse-and-white Deceiver tied to a long leader, and he went into a crouch as he neared the fish and began false-casting to the side so the shadow of his line wouldn't spook them.

His first cast fell a little short, but as he twitched it back, he saw a wake materialize behind his fly, and then came the swirl and he felt the fish close its mouth on his fly. He pulled hard with his line hand to set the hook, came tight, felt the live weight of a heavy fish, and swept up his rod. The fish bolted for the middle of the creek. Calhoun's reel screeched. He held his rod high and let the fish take line.

"Yeow! Whoopee!"

The shout came from so close behind him that Calhoun nearly dropped his rod. He jerked his head around. Sitting on a boulder that had been exposed by the falling tide, not twenty feet away, was maybe the most beautiful woman he'd ever seen. Big dark eyes, black braid sprouting out of the back of her pink cap, a wide exuberant smile, long tanned legs.

He opened his mouth to speak to her—he didn't know what he was going to say, but he figured, under the circumstances, she'd excuse him if it turned out to be something stupid—when his line went slack.

"Aw, shit," the woman said. "That was my fault. I'm damned sorry, mister."

Calhoun reeled in and examined his fly. The tip of the hook point was bent, and he remembered failing to check it when he'd nicked an underwater rock earlier.

He went over to her and showed her the fly. "*My* fault," he said. He bit it off and tied on another. He noticed that a spinning rod was propped against the boulder she was sitting on. "Catching any?"

"I've been following you since I got here," she said.

He smiled. "Nobody follows me without me knowing it."

"Hey," she said. "I'm an Indian. Been thinking of taking up fly fishing for some time. Sure looks like fun. Mind if I tag along?"

He noticed that she was wearing a wedding band. "Let's find us some more fish," he said, "and you can try it."

"I'm not much good with a fly rod," she said.

"We'll give it a shot."

So they walked the edge of the creek, following the ebbing tide toward the east where the sun had just risen behind a cloudbank, and she spotted the wakes first.

He handed her his rod.

"No," she whispered. "You catch 'em."

"Take it," he said.

"I'll screw it up."

"So then we find more fish. Go ahead."

She took the rod, bent low and crept into casting range, then began to work out some line. Her cast was sloppy and well to the side of the fish, but she twitched it back and Calhoun saw the wake turn. "Get ready," he whispered. "He sees it. Keep it coming. Wait till you feel him."

Suddenly the water exploded. "Hit him!" Calhoun yelled.

She hauled back on the rod, but it did not bend with the weight of the fish.

"Dammit!" she said. She pulled in the fly. "I was so excited I forgot to hang onto the line." She patted herself over her left breast. "My heart's thumping like that little two-horse outboard of mine." She cocked her head and grinned. "Okay, mister. That's it. I'm hooked. You've got to teach me."

So they stood there on the bank of the little creek while the tide ebbed and the sun burned off the fog, and Calhoun stood behind her, guiding her wrist and counting rhythm for her, very aware of the soapy smell of her hair and her slim muscular body close to his, and within half an hour she was casting as if she'd been doing it all her life.

Along the way she told him that her name was Kate Balaban— her maiden name, actually, which she went by—and how when her husband had gotten sick, she'd bought a little bait-and-tackle shop on the outskirts of Portland and was trying to run it all by herself. Walter—her husband—thought it was dumb and frivolous, and she guessed he was right, because so far she'd barely been breaking even, but she was determined to make a go of it.

Calhoun told her more than he intended to—that he was building a house in the woods outside the little village of Dublin, about an hour due west of Portland, and that he'd been released from the hospital in Arlington, Virginia, just three months earlier. He was okay now, he said, except for the deafness in his left ear, which the doctors had said was permanent, and the black holes in his memory, which they thought might be temporary, and the fact that he could no longer drink alcohol, which had something to do with the change in the chemistry of his brain and wasn't much of a handicap that he'd noticed.

Kate Balaban nodded when he told her this, as if he'd explained how he'd just gotten over a touch of the flu. She asked no questions, for which he was grateful. He had no appetite for telling her the whole story.

Finally she glanced at her watch. "Hell," she said. "This is fun, but I've got to get back and open up."

She reeled in, handed him the rod, and they trudged back to the parking area.

Calhoun leaned against the side of her Blazer while she stowed her spinning rod in back. She returned with a Stanley thermos and two mugs. She poured coffee, handed a mug to him, and leaned beside him. They sipped their coffee and gazed down on the creek, and after a minute, without looking at him, Kate said, "So, what're you doing for work these days?"

"Finishing the inside of my house. Moldings, cabinets, stuff like that. Then I've got the painting. Keeps me busy."

"Oh," she murmured.

"I don't have an actual job," he said.

"Planning on getting one?"

"Wasn't giving it much thought," he said. "Why?"

She turned to him. "I can't pay much right now. But I sure could use someone in the shop. I've been thinking of getting into fly fishing. Now that the stripers are back, it's really popular. You could help me with that. And I want to do some guiding. Landlocked salmon, smallmouth bass, trout. Saltwater, too, of course. I got my guide's license, but I'm stuck in the shop." She smiled at him. "What do you say?"

"You don't know me," said Calhoun.

She shrugged. "Oh, I guess I know you well enough. I'm mostly right about people."

No, he thought. I mean, you *really* don't know me.

~~~
~~~

They sat around picking at the leftover bread and cheese and salad from Kate's shore lunch for the folks from New Jersey while darkness seeped into the parking lot outside the shop. Calhoun sipped a Coke and Kate put away two bottles of Sam Adams beer, and finally she looked at her wristwatch and said, "Where the hell is Lyle?"

Calhoun shrugged. "On his way, I expect."

"He's a good kid," said Kate. "But damn, sometimes he just doesn't do things right. He knows he's supposed to—"

"He'll check in," said Calhoun quietly. "Probably found some trout rising when the sun got off the water. He'll have some stories."

"I worry," said Kate.

He reached over and covered her hand with his. "Lyle's a big boy."

"Tromping through the woods after dark, some old out-of-shape city guy with a bad ticker trying to keep up with him . . ."

Calhoun squeezed her hand. "I'll hang out, wait for him. You go on home, take care of Walter."

She turned her head and smiled at him. "You know, Stoney," she said softly, "most days, I really don't want to go home."

He nodded. "I know."

"You've got an hour's drive," she said. "You go on. I'll give Lyle another hour, and if he hasn't showed up by then, the hell with him."

"I'll stay with you."

"No," she said. "Please. I wouldn't mind a little alone time."

He nodded and stood up. "We've got no trips tomorrow, right?"

"Right," she said. "I'll open up. Can you come in around noon?"

"I'll be here, boss."

"Get going, then," she said. "And drive careful, you hear?"

CHAPTER THREE

CALHOUN HAD LEFT the hospital in Arlington, Virginia, where he'd lived for eighteen months, on a warm Thursday toward the end of March five years earlier. He had a cashier's check for twenty-five thousand dollars and a Visa card with his name on it in his pocket, along with the promise that money—enough so he'd never have to work—would be deposited monthly in the bank of his choice for the rest of his life.

Somebody obviously owed him a great deal, although when he'd tried to find out who and what and why, they always neatly changed the subject. Calhoun hadn't pushed it. He figured it might conjure up one of those memories that would be better left forgotten.

So he bought a secondhand Ford pickup truck and headed north. Even though he was a southern boy, he was drawn to Maine. It was irresistible. He couldn't have gone anyplace else. His brain fed him evocative, random images—the smell of seaweed and salt air and pine needles, the sound of night surf crashing against rocks, the taste of clam chowder swimming with bits of salt pork, boiled lobster dripping with melted butter, fresh-caught bluefish grilled over a beach fire, the feel of a smallmouth bass tugging against the bend of a fly rod, the sight of an October brook trout in full spawning regalia finning in a gravelly riffle, the silvery arc of a landlocked salmon leaping over a big gray lake.

He knew, because they'd told him that much—that he'd grown up in Beaufort, South Carolina, which accounted for his name: Stonewall Jackson Calhoun. He hadn't been able to figure out where the Maine memories came from. But they were there, and they were strong.

In the hospital he'd read E. B. White, those perfect little essays about living close to the rocky Maine soil, and he knew he'd been there, and he knew he'd read these essays before.

And when he'd read Thoreau, it was so familiar that he only need-ed to skim a passage once to be able to recite it. "I went to the woods," Thoreau had written, "because I wished to live deliberately, to front only the essential facts of life . . . I wanted to live deep and suck out all the marrow of life . . ."

Stonewall Jackson Calhoun, after being reborn in a Veterans Ad-ministration hospital in Arlington, Virginia, had been drawn to Maine, where a man could still go to the woods. He intended to suck some marrow out of his new life.

Maine. Powerful flashes of déjà vu, so vivid and evocative and dis-turbing that sometimes he had to sit down and blink the tears from his eyes. Dusty roads flanked by stone walls, sandy soil, blueberry burns, old cellar holes at the end of rutted cart paths now grown up in alder, meadows studded with juniper and clumps of poplar and gnarly old Baldwin apple trees, the roar of a flushing partridge, the flash of a whitetail's flag, sugar maples tapped with sap spigots, the aluminum roof of a barn covered with old tractor tires so it wouldn't blow off, Holsteins and Jerseys grazing in rock-strewn pastures, double-wide trailers sprouting twenty-foot television antennas, goldenrod growing through the rusted carcasses of dead automobiles, hens pecking gravel in the dooryards, blizzards and thunderstorms and September nor'easters, and always that honey-haired girl supine on an old brown army blanket, green eyes smiling, small naked breasts, reaching up to touch his face, murmuring something that sounded like *ayuh* . . .

Calhoun had not lost his memory. He remembered things, knew he'd seen them before. *Déjà vu.* His brain, in fact, sometimes felt like an electrical socket with too many plugs stuck into it, sparks flying, sucking the juice out of him. He was overloaded with memories, and many of them were quite coherent and complete, although they tended not to connect with each other. They were like clips of movies playing in his head, with him as both main character and audience.

There were other characters in these mental movies besides Stoney Calhoun himself. That bare-breasted girl on the blanket, laughing children, white-haired old women. But most of these others had no names, no identities. As hard as he tried to slow down the scenes and zoom in on the faces, he could not locate these characters in the tangled landscape of the first thirty-three years of his life.

The Maine memories were the strongest. So that's where he'd gone to start over again.

Calhoun always stayed up late and got up early. He resented every minute he wasted sleeping. He'd already lost big chunks of his life, and he'd be damned if he was going to miss anything else.

And, he didn't welcome the dreams.

So at five-thirty the next morning, Calhoun and Ralph, his four-year-old Brittany, were sitting side-by-side on a slab of granite beside the little spring-fed creek in back of his house, sipping coffee and waiting for the day to get going. He'd spotted two brook trout sipping mayfly spinners in the downstream pool. Ralph saw them, too, and he was trembling and whining and staring at them in the semblance of a point.

Calhoun scratched Ralph's ears and held out his coffee mug. "You aren't much of a bird dog," he said. "But you're dynamite on trout. We'll make a fishing guide of you yet."

Ralph took a lick from Calhoun's mug, his eyes never leaving the rising trout.

Calhoun did not bring clients to his private creek. It was his secret place. He'd showed it to Kate, of course, but he didn't allow her to fish in it. He had never tried to catch any of its trout, at least not with hook and line. He had caught dozens of them mentally and found it entirely satisfying.

He was gazing idly at the moving water, looking through the surface down into it, trying to watch how the trout behaved, when it happened again. A naked human body drifted downstream and stopped in front of him in the middle of the pool. It was facedown with its arms and legs stretched out, suspended there just off the bottom. Its fine, straw-colored hair was flowing out around its head, waving gently in the current. The body might have been a male or female, child or adult. Calhoun couldn't tell.

He looked at the body, no longer surprised when one of these visions decided to show up, but curious about it. He wondered where it had come from, what charred synapse in his brain had sent it out, what story it might've told him if he could follow it back to where it had come from. He wondered, of course, who it was, although, strangely, that did not seem terribly important.

It came out of his life before the hospital, he knew that much—one of those teasing fragments that seemed, at the moment, absolutely real. It brought him an overpowering feeling of sadness. It made him think that dying wouldn't be so bad.

He wondered if that body was his own.

He closed his eyes, kept them clamped shut until the image of the drifting underwater body disappeared from the insides of his eyelids. When he opened them again, the body was gone.

Calhoun sat there on the granite slab beside the little creek, watching the trout and pondering the peculiar way his brain worked. Then a picture suddenly appeared in his head. It was Kate with telephone pressed against her ear, tapping her foot and staring up at the ceiling.

This was another one of those spooky things that happened to him. He didn't know where it came from.

He stood up. "Come on," he said to Ralph. "Let's eat."

Magic words. Ralph took one last, longing look at the trout, then scrambled to his feet.

They climbed the hill to the little house and went inside. Calhoun picked up his phone and pecked out the number of the shop.

Kate answered on the first ring. "That you, Stoney?"

"Yes, ma'am."

"I tried to call you a few minutes ago."

"I know," he said. "What's up?"

"Lyle never showed up. I waited till after eleven."

"So call him up, give him hell."

"Well, duh," she said. "You think I'm stupid or something? I called his house. Woke up some girl, who wasn't too happy about it. She said she was up till two in the morning and Lyle never came home."

"He's not your kid, Kate. He's a grown-up man, and he can take care of himself."

He heard her blow out a quick breath. "Well, I know that. But this isn't like him, not checking in after a day of guiding. I'm worried, Stoney."

"Look," he said. "He probably stopped off somewhere with his new friend, Mr. Fred Green. They had some dinner, a few beers, and Mr. Green started telling stories about his angling prowess, all the great places he's been to, the trophies he's nailed in Costa Rica and Siberia. And maybe the waitress took a liking to young Lyle, said she'd sure like to show him her tattoos, and pretty soon it's closing time, and—you know?"

She sighed. "You're probably right."

"It's not even six-thirty," he said. "The boy's probably still all tangled up in perfumey silk sheets and bare legs somewhere. He'll be in. Then you can give him hell, both barrels."

"Bet your ass I will."

"Look," he said, "if it'll make you feel any better, I'll shoot on over, hold your hand."

"I don't need my hand held by any God damn man," she said amiably.

"'Course you don't," he said. "I was just about to scramble up some eggs for me and Ralph. I'll be along after, okay?"

"You don't need to. Be here at noon, like you're supposed to. I'll be fine."

"I know you will. I got nothing better to do."

She hesitated, then said, "Thanks, Stoney. Appreciate it."

He left Ralph in charge of the house, reminding him to bite all intruders in the ass, clean up the dishes, and split some firewood. "No swimming in the trouts' pool, either," he said.

Ralph, who was sprawled on the sun-drenched, east-facing deck, wagged his stubby tail without opening his eyes.

Calhoun climbed into his truck, bounced out over his quarter-mile dirt driveway, and headed for Portland. He hadn't admitted it to Kate, but he was worried, too. It wasn't like Lyle not to check in at the shop after a day of guiding.

He got there a little before eight. The CLOSED sign was hanging in the window. He used his key to get in and found Kate in the office in back, her feet up on the desk and the phone against her ear. She smiled at him and held up a finger.

"Do me a favor," she said into the phone, "and go take a look in his room, will you?" She glanced at Calhoun and rolled her eyes. "I *know* he likes to go fishing real early," she said, "but maybe you can tell if his bed's been slept in. . . . Well, now, thank you. I sure do appreciate it."

Calhoun took the chair across from her desk. "Trying his house again?"

She nodded. "Couldn't think of anything else. That gal I talked to earlier, I figured she was probably smoking dope all night, wouldn't have noticed if an elephant had come tromping through her living room, never mind Lyle. I think they party every night over there."

"Not Lyle," said Calhoun. "Lyle doesn't party. Like the gal said, he gets up early, and he's pretty damn serious about finishing his thesis."

Kate nodded. "That's just it. I—" She held up her hand and dropped her eyes, listening to the phone, nodding. "Yup," she said. "Okay, shoot." She fumbled for a pencil and jotted down a note. "Got it," she said into the phone. "Thanks . . . Sure I will. You, too."

She put the portable phone down on her desk. "She says Lyle's room's a mess like always, and no telling when was the last time he slept in his bed, since he never makes it. Seems he's been spending lots of nights away." Kate grinned. "Lyle's got himself a girlfriend."

"He never said anything to me about a girlfriend," said Calhoun.

"Some reason he should tell you?"

"Nope. Guess not. We men never talk about relationships."

"Well," said Kate, "that probably explains it. Her name is . . ."—she picked up the scrap of paper she'd written on and squinted at it—"Penny Moulton. Lives up in Standish. Ring any bells?"

Calhoun shook his head. "Like I said—"

"Right," she said. "Real men don't talk about relationships."

"Don't suppose you got a phone number for Miz Penny Moulton?"

Kate shook her head. "But that would explain why he didn't check back in last night. Any trout pond he and Mr. Green found would've been north and west of here, and Standish would be on the way back."

Calhoun nodded. "Which is why Mr. Green followed Lyle in his car. I noticed they took both cars when they pulled out of here yesterday. Lyle didn't want to drive him all the way back here, then turn around and head back to Standish. He might've mentioned to me what he was planning to do, saved you worrying about him. Gimme that phone."

Kate shook her head. "Stoney, you can't call the boy at his girlfriend's house."

"Why the hell not?"

She shrugged. "I don't know. Go ahead." She stood up. "Want some coffee?"

CHAPTER FOUR

LYLE'S GIRLFRIEND HAD HERSELF a good old Maine name, and Calhoun found nearly half a column of Moultons listed in the slim phone directory that covered Standish, Gorham, Windham, and the other towns and villages to the west and north between Portland and Sebago Lake. There was no Penny listed, but it wasn't hard to figure out that "Moulton, P." was a good possibility.

Calhoun couldn't understand why single women thought they could disguise their single-ness and their woman-ness by using their initial instead of their whole first name. He didn't know of any men who listed themselves that way in the phone book.

He pecked out the number for Moulton, P. on Kate's phone, and before the second ring a soft female voice answered. "Hello?"

"Penny Moulton?"

She hesitated, then said, "Yes, it is."

"I'm looking for Lyle McMahan," said Calhoun. "I'm a friend of his. Name's Calhoun. Understand he might be there?"

"Shit," she muttered.

"Miss?"

"I'm sorry," she said. "I thought you were him." He heard her blow out a long breath. "Listen, Mr. Calhoun. If you're his friend, the friendly thing would be for you to tell Mr. Lyle McMahan that his key won't unlock my door anymore—and I mean that literally as well as figuratively—so he shouldn't bother coming around. I don't take that kind of shit, you tell him, all right?"

"He's not there, I guess," said Calhoun.

"No, he's not. He was *supposed* to be, but he's not."

Calhoun glanced up. Kate was out in the shop fixing the coffee. He swiveled around in his chair, putting his back to her. "Look," he said to Penny Moulton, "I don't want to upset you, but I'm calling from the shop where he works. Lyle had a guide trip yesterday, and he never checked back afterward. We can't seem to get ahold of him, so if you have any idea where—"

"I don't know where he is," she said quickly. "Hell, I cooked dinner, sat up half the night getting madder and madder." He heard her sigh. "Now you've got me worried."

"Well, I'm sure there's no need to be worried," said Calhoun. "But maybe you oughtn't to be mad just yet, either."

"He called me in the morning, said he'd be around for supper. Lyle always does what he says he's going to do, you know? I mean, that's what I—I love about him. He's not like most men. You can depend on Lyle. Lyle says he'll be there at eight, he's there at quarter of. I mean, he loves his guiding, I know that, and if he gets stuck out on a boat or something and it's after eight, well, as soon as he gets ashore he finds a phone and calls. Last night he never called. And he never showed. I've been with men like that. Figured I finally found somebody different. Then, along about midnight, I figured I was wrong, figured Lyle was exactly like all the others . . ."

Kate came into the office, put a mug of coffee beside Calhoun's elbow, and arched her eyebrows. He shrugged and waved his hand. She nodded, then went back out into the shop.

". . . didn't sleep hardly at all," Penny Moulton was saying. "I had candles and wine and . . . You think something happened to him, don't you?"

"Lyle?" Calhoun forced himself to laugh. "Not likely." There was no sense in upsetting this girl. "You'd best not expect too much out of any of us guys, miss. Lyle's an awfully good boy, but none of us are what you'd call overly dependable, especially when there's fishing. Give him another chance. I expect he'll be full of apologies and have a good logical explanation, and he'll be extra sweet to you for a while."

"You really think so?"

"Yup, I do. When I catch up to him, I'll give him hell, and I suppose you ought to, too, when you see him. But I wouldn't go changing my locks."

"He *always* calls," she said softly.

"Well," said Calhoun, "men, you know?"

"You'll have him call me?"

"Count on it," he said. "And you too, miss. I expect you're the one he'll call first."

After he disconnected from Penny Moulton, Calhoun sat there holding the telephone and sipping his coffee. She was right about Lyle. If he'd had a date, he'd show up on time for it. If he couldn't, he'd call.

If he didn't call, it meant something *had* happened.

He poked out the number for the York County Sheriff's Office, gave the dispatcher his name, and said he needed to speak to Sheriff Dickman himself.

A minute later Dickman said, "What's up, Stoney?"

"Need some information," he said.

"When're we going fishing again, son?"

"You name it," said Calhoun. "But look. I was wondering if there were any accidents last night."

"There's accidents every night, Stoney. What's going on?"

Calhoun told him about Lyle's failure to show up at the shop and his broken date with Penny Moulton. "Only thing I could figure . . ."

"I've got a printout here somewhere," mumbled Dickman. "Hang on . . . Okay. Here we go. What'd you say that boy's name was?"

"McMahan. Lyle McMahan." Calhoun spelled it.

"Nope," said Dickman after a minute. "What kind of vehicle does he drive?"

"Old Dodge Power Wagon. Sixty-three, I think. It's sort of gray. Gunmetal gray, I guess you'd call it, except for the rust."

"Whoa," said the sheriff. "You saying this thing's over forty years old?"

"Yup," said Calhoun. "Pretty beat up on the outside, but those old Power Wagons are indestructible, and Lyle keeps it humming. It would've been full of fishing gear. Trout Unlimited, Ruffed Grouse Society stickers on the rear window."

"You don't have a registration on it, do you?"

"No."

"Well, there can't be a helluva lot of sixty-three Power Wagons left on the road. Hmm . . . Uh-uh. No Power Wagon on my accident report here. Not in York County any time yesterday."

"What about Cumberland or Oxford? He might've been up there."

"I don't have them right in front of me," said the sheriff. "I can check for you, if you want."

"Please."

"You want me to get back to you? I can pull 'em up here on my computer, but it'll take a minute."

"I'll hang on," said Calhoun. "If you don't mind."

He sipped his coffee, and several minutes later Dickman said, "Sorry, Stoney. Nothing in Cumberland County, nor Oxford, either."

"Well, don't be sorry. It's a relief."

"If I hear something, I'll let you know."

"I'd appreciate it."

"It'll cost you a day of fishing," said the sheriff.

"You got it. Just name the day."

Calhoun put the phone on the desk, stood up, and went out into the shop. Kate was at the front counter paging through the shop's logbook. She looked up. "Well?"

He recounted his conversations with Penny Moulton and Sheriff Dickman. "I don't know what else to tell you," he said. "I guess if something happened to him, the sheriff would know it."

"That's a comfort," she said. She shook her head. "I've been looking back through the log, trying to figure where Lyle might've gone yesterday."

"He said he was heading for someplace that Mr. Green knew of. Someplace new for him."

She sighed. "I know. It was just a thought."

"All we can do is wait," said Calhoun.

She looked up at him and smiled. "You know," she said, "I can sit for hours beside a stream and wait for the mayflies to start hatching and the trout to rise, and I don't have any trouble waiting for the tide to turn and the stripers to move up onto the mussel beds. Some things, I'm pretty damn excellent at waiting for. But I have a good deal of trouble waiting for a boy to show up when I just know goddam well something bad's happened to him." She shook her head. "What're we gonna do, Stoney?"

"Nothing we can do," he said.

Calhoun spent most of the morning taking inventory while Kate did some ordering on the phone. Every time somebody pulled into the parking area out front, Kate twisted around and peered out the window. Then she turned, looked at Calhoun, and shook her head.

A few customers came in, poked around, bragged about their angling prowess, tried to weasel secrets out of the shopkeepers, bought some flies.

At noon, Calhoun got into his truck and drove over to the new Thai restaurant at the mall for takeout, that spicy noodley stuff with baby shrimp and hunks of chicken that Kate liked. They ate it with chopsticks and washed it down with Coke, sitting on the front porch outside the shop.

Kate had a half-day guide trip in the afternoon. Her clients—a father and his twelve-year-old son who'd driven over from Rochester, New Hampshire—showed up around one-thirty. Neither of them had ever caught a striped bass before. This was the boy's birthday present. They were bubbling with eagerness, the father as much as the boy, and Kate put on a good show of enthusiasm, though Calhoun could tell that she was still preoccupied with Lyle.

He helped her get her trailer hitched up and her Blazer loaded with gear. The man, who turned out to be a plumbing contractor, climbed into the passenger seat, and the boy crawled in back.

Kate got behind the wheel and rolled down the window. "Don't wait around, Stoney," she said. "I plan to keep these fellas out through the bottom of the tide, see if we can't hang a keeper for the birthday boy."

"Tide doesn't turn till, what, after eight?"

She nodded. "It'll be late. Close up at six and get on home and feed Ralph."

"I'll leave you a note if I hear anything."

"I know you will," she said.

He stood there as she pulled away, the Blazer belching smoke and sounding like a motorcycle. Got to fix that damn tailpipe, he thought, before she gets a ticket.

Around five o'clock Calhoun heard a car pull into the lot. He glanced out the window and saw a green Ford Explorer with a light bar on top and the York County Sheriff's Department logo on the door.

A moment later Sheriff Dickman came in. "Happened to be in the neighborhood," he said. He was a short, barrel-chested guy with twinkling eyes and a sly leprechaun grin. The sheriff was close to sixty, but Calhoun knew he had the vitality of a man half his age. He wore khaki pants and matching shirt, a Stetson on his head, a badge on his chest, and a revolver on his hip.

"Hear something?" said Calhoun.

"Nope. Wondering if you did."

"Nope," said Calhoun. "Coke?"

"Sure," said Dickman. "Let's sit outside so I can keep an ear on the radio."

They sat on the porch. The radio in the Explorer squawked and buzzed through the open window. Dickman took off his hat and hung it on his knee. He smoothed his hand over his balding head and said he'd alerted everyone in his department, plus his counterparts up in Cumberland and Oxford counties and the state police, to be on the lookout for a gray-and-rust '63 Dodge Power Wagon that might've been in an accident, and he'd had one of his deputies call the hospitals. So far, nothing.

"Maybe you'd want to call his house again," said Dickman.

"No harm in that, I guess," said Calhoun.

He went inside, got the portable phone, brought it out on the porch, and dialed the number for Lyle's house. This time a young man named Danny answered. Nobody had seen or heard from Lyle, as far as he knew, and Danny had been there all day.

When Calhoun disconnected, he turned to the sheriff and shook his head. "He hasn't been home, and he hasn't been here," he said. "Something's definitely happened to him."

The sheriff shrugged. "I expect you're right. Don't know what else we can do. Something'll turn up."

"That's what I'm afraid of," said Calhoun.

~~~
~~~

Darkness had fallen by the time he pulled into his dooryard that night. He fed Ralph and heated a can of beans for himself, tuned his stereo to the classical music station out of Portland, and settled into his soft chair for an evening of reading. Ralph curled up on the floor beside him, strategically positioning himself so that Calhoun could dangle his arm over the side and absentmindedly scratch his ears.

Shortly after he'd come to Maine, Calhoun had bought a thick American Lit college anthology at a yard sale. The book was nearly two thousand pages long. It began with the diaries and poems and sermons of the first settlers—John Smith and John Winthrop and Roger Williams, Anne Bradstreet and Edward Taylor, Cotton Mather and Jonathan Edwards. It ended with some stories by Ann Beattie and John Updike and Bernard Malamud.

Calhoun was sure he'd read a lot of this stuff during the time of his life that was still fuzzy, all those years that he'd lived before he woke up in the hospital. He wanted to recapture it, to catch up on his education.

He'd been doing it slowly and chronologically, dipping into the anthology now and then, skipping nothing, not even the sermons of those early fire-and-brimstone preachers, keeping his place marked with a matchbook, no more than one writer in an evening of reading. Most of them, he figured, he'd never read before. But once in a while he had a hit—a flash of recognition, a certain knowledge that he'd read, and probably studied, one of these writers before. Hawthorne, Melville, Poe, Mark Twain, Sinclair Lewis, Hemingway, Whitman. The excerpts in the anthology led him to the novels. He read as many of them as he could find at yard sales. He'd liked these writers before, he knew, and now he liked them all over again. Some of the Walt Whitman poems, he only needed to read the first few lines to be able to close his eyes and recite the rest.

Now, after five years with the anthology, he'd read his way well into the twentieth century.

Tonight it was a Katherine Anne Porter short story called "Maria Concepcion." It sparked no memory flashes, but Calhoun rather liked it—liked Porter's clear, no-nonsense writing, the complexity of her characters, the irony in the story. When he finished it, he closed the heavy book and put it on the table beside him, dangled his hand, and gave Ralph a scratch.

He hadn't noticed when the radio station switched from classical to jazz, which meant that it was sometime after midnight. Calhoun laid his head back and closed his eyes. He recognized Miles Davis on trumpet, Red Garland on piano, John Coltrane on tenor sax. Bluesy, moody music, more déjà vu that brought Calhoun a flood of memory fragments which he didn't bother trying to sort out.

The first thing he'd bought for his new house—as soon as he started sleeping inside—had been an expensive stereo system with top-of-the-line Bose speakers. Pretty ironic for a man who was completely deaf in one ear and could not really hear in stereo.

He loved music, got a lot of those déjà vu rushes when he heard something from before. He wondered if he'd ever played an instrument. Figured he had. He expected that one day he'd pick up a saxophone or guitar or sit down at a piano and music would come bursting out of his fingers. Things kept happening to him that way.

That's how it had been the first time he'd picked up a fly rod after the hospital, and the first time he'd sat down to tie a fly. The memory was all there, in his brain and in his muscles, waiting to be let out.

He resisted sleep, thinking about Maria Concepcion, trying to analyze the story, wondering who he'd known before that Maria reminded him of. But he must've drifted off, because he jerked up when Ralph scrambled to his feet, scuttled over to the door with his toenails scratching the floor, and barked.

"Shut up, you," said Calhoun mildly. Ralph barked whenever a coon or a porcupine wandered into the yard. His ears were considerably sharper than Calhoun's.

Then he heard the grumble of the busted tailpipe, growing louder, coming up his driveway, pulling in outside, falling suddenly silent. A car door slammed. Soft footsteps on the deck, the rattle of the doorknob, the click of the latch.

Then Kate came in.

CHAPTER FIVE

KATE USUALLY PUT ON MAKEUP and wore a dress and stockings and jewelry when she came in the night, but this time she had on the same shorts and T-shirt she'd been wearing that morning.

It didn't matter. Kate always looked great.

Ralph's entire hind end was wagging. Kate knelt down to scratch his ears. She looked up at Calhoun. "Evenin', Stoney."

"Hi, honey," said Calhoun. "You're right on time."

Calhoun had started working for Kate Balaban a week after they met beside the tidal creek. At first he'd just waited on customers and tied flies in the shop, giving her a break and allowing her to guide clients occasionally. By September he was dickering with sales reps and building up the shop's inventory of fly-fishing gear and studying for his Maine Guide license.

Even during slack times or when they shared lunches on the porch, they talked only business. She never asked him where he had come from or why he seemed to be a man without a history, and he did not ask about her marriage.

Within a month, he realized he loved her. He tried not to dwell on it. Kate was married, and that was that.

She'd appeared at Calhoun's house for the first time one evening in early October following that first summer. He had a fire going in the woodstove and a Bach organ fugue was playing loud on his stereo when he heard a car door slam out in the dooryard.

He got up from his chair, took down the 12-gauge Remington autoloader from its pegs beside the door, switched on the floodlights, and went out onto the porch.

Kate was climbing out of her Blazer. She made a visor with her hand and squinted up at him. "You're not gonna shoot me, are you?"

"I was thinking of it," he said.

She was wearing an ankle-length white dress with a scooped neck and sandals with thin leather straps decorated with silver studs. Silver earrings dangled from her ears and a big leather bag hung on her shoulder. He had never before seen her in anything except jeans or shorts and T-shirts or men's flannel shirts. He liked how she looked in shorts. In a dress, she was just spectacular, and he stood there staring at her.

"Are you going ask me in," she said, "or are you just going to stand there with your face hanging out?"

"Come on in, I guess."

He held the door for her. She stood inside the doorway, and Calhoun saw his place as she probably did—the comfortable, messy home of a single man, one big open room with dirty dishes piled in the sink, walls hung with fishing and hunting prints, secondhand leather couch and chair, cheap braided rug on the pine-plank floor, fly-tying desk strewn with hackle necks and bucktails and scissors and bobbins, aluminum rod tubes stacked in one corner and a glass-fronted gun case in another, neoprene chest waders sprawled on the kitchen floor.

He returned the shotgun to its pegs, then went over to the stereo and turned down the volume.

"Place needs a dog," Kate said.

"I've been thinking of that," he said.

"Don't suppose a girl might have a glass of whiskey?"

He smiled. "I don't keep liquor. Can't drink."

She reached into her bag and took out a pint of Old Grandad. "All I need is the glass," she said.

He found a tumbler, rinsed it out, and put it on the round table in front of the big kitchen window. She sat down and poured a slug of bourbon. He sat across from her.

She lifted her glass to him, held his eyes with hers for a moment, then took a sip. She wiped her mouth on the back of her wrist, then smiled. "I thought I had this all planned out," she said softly.

Calhoun just sat there looking at her.

She took another sip. "Okay," she said. "Here it is, Stoney. We've got to talk."

"Sure."

She stared at the tabletop, shaking her head. "Shit," she mumbled. She looked up at him. "You aren't making this easy."

He shrugged. "I don't know what you want me to say."

"You could tell me I'm pretty."

He smiled. "Jesus, ma'am." He shook his head. "Sometimes I wish I could drink. You suck the breath right out of me, and that's the truth."

"Maybe I was mistaken, but I had the idea you might . . ." She took a sip from her glass, put it down, looked into it. "I guess I shouldn't have come here," she mumbled.

"Why don't you just spit it out," said Calhoun.

She looked up at him. "I'm trying, dammit." She nodded. "Okay. I guess I was wondering if—if you were feeling . . ." She shook her head.

"Feeling what, ma'am?"

"I wondered if you liked me."

"Hell, of course I like you."

"That's not what I mean."

He just looked at her.

She laughed softly. "Stoney," she said, "what I'm trying to say is, do you *love* me?"

He shook his head. "Truthfully, I'm trying very hard not to, ma'am. But I'm not having much luck at it." He smiled at her. "You know I love you."

She nodded. "Yes. I feel the same." She took another sip from her glass, then gazed down into it. "And for Christ's sake, will you stop calling me 'ma'am'?"

He nodded.

She looked up at him. "How would you feel about us being lovers, Stoney?"

"What?"

"I didn't say I wanted to make love with you," she said softly. "I mean, I do. But that's not it. I want you and me . . ."

"I know what it means," he said, "being lovers."

She cocked her head and held his eyes.

"I don't think so, Kate," he said.

She nodded. "Well, hell, that's all right." She let out a long breath, then lifted her glass and took a long swig. "I figured I might as well ask."

"You're married," he said.

"Yes, I am."

He shook his head. "I'm not into adultery."

"Me neither."

"Believe me," said Calhoun, "it's not that I wouldn't . . ."

"Wouldn't what?"

He shrugged.

She reached across the table and put her hand over his. "Listen to me, Stoney. They diagnosed Walter's MS four years ago this coming January. He hasn't touched me, or even hardly looked at me or said anything sweet, since that day. He resents my good health, resents the fact that I'm continuing to live my life, resents the shop. I'm not saying that I don't understand, because I do. And it's not that I don't still love him. I *do* love him. But he's stuck in that wheelchair just waiting to die, and I'm—"

Calhoun was shaking his head. "Doesn't matter," he said. "Just because he's sick and grouchy and you're not getting along—"

"What if I weren't married?"

"That's a dumb question," he said. "You're about the most—the most beautiful, the smartest, the most desirable damn woman I've ever known."

She smiled. "Can I tell you my idea, then?"

"I guess so. Sure."

"Usually," she said, "when a married woman has herself a—a lover—not her husband—everybody knows it except him. Everybody except the husband. They sneak around, and I suppose part of the excitement is that sneaking around, worrying about getting caught, worrying that the husband's going to find out." She shook her head. "I'm not into excitement, Stoney. At least not that kind. I love you and I want to be with you, and I don't want it to be sneaky and dirty. I was hoping we could do it the other way around."

"Are you saying you want to ask Walter's permission?"

"No," she said. "I just want to tell him. I want him to know. I want him to be the *only* one who knows. I want you to come over to the house, meet him, and I want the two of us to tell him we're going to be lovers. I want to assure him that we'll be lovers only here, in your house in the woods, and I want to assure him that nobody else will ever know about us."

"What if he says no?"

"I'm not saying to ask him. We'll tell him. You and I. It's got to be the two of us. I just want to be sure he understands. I mean, if you want."

Calhoun frowned. "This sounds cruel, Kate. It sounds like torturing the poor guy."

"You don't know Walter," she said. "You don't know how we are. He and I. We've always told each other the truth. It's the only way. It's how he'd want it."

"Then we ask him," Calhoun said. "We don't tell him. If Walter says no, then it's no."

Kate smiled. "I knew you'd say that. I guess if I didn't know you'd say that, I wouldn't . . . love you. Most men . . ."

Calhoun squeezed her hand. "When do you want us to talk to Walter."

Her dark eyes were solemn. "Tomorrow after we close up. Okay?"

"I've got one request," said Calhoun.

"What's that?"

"Don't ever dress like that around the shop."

"I thought you liked how I look."

"I do, ma'am. That's just it."

A wheelchair ramp led from the driveway to the side door of Kate's square brick house on the outskirts of South Portland. "He doesn't use it," she'd told Calhoun as she led him inside the night after her first visit to his place. "He never leaves the house anymore. He just sits in there watching TV, observing himself shrivel up, waiting to die."

The front room was dark except for the flickering blue light of the television. Walter was sitting in a wheelchair with a plaid blanket over his knees, and when Kate and Calhoun went in, he glanced up, nodded, then turned back to the television.

"Walter," said Kate, "this is Stoney."

Walter had dark, thinning hair and a sharp hatchet face. It looked as if his skin was stretched so tight over his bones that it might crack open if he smiled. "I figured," he mumbled, barely moving his mouth.

"We brought pizza," she said. "Turn that thing off and come eat."

Walter drank three beers and ate half of a pizza slice. Kate talked about the shop, about how the stripers were mostly gone for the season, about putting together a catalog and starting up some mail-order business, about how Stoney was trying to negotiate some advertising with Umpqua and Loomis, about how she was looking to hire on a couple more guides for next year.

Walter kept sipping his beer. He said nothing.

Then Kate cleared her throat and said, "Walter, Stoney and I, we need to talk to you."

Walter lifted his eyes and looked at Calhoun. "You're fucking my wife."

"No, sir," said Calhoun. "But I do love her."

"Of course you do."

"But we're not—"

"Why not?" said Walter.

"Kate's not that kind of woman."

"No, I don't suppose she is. What about you?"

"I'm not that kind of man, either."

Walter nodded. "Good."

"We wanted to ask you first," said Calhoun.

He looked at Kate. She gave him a little nod. He turned back to Walter. "We're asking your permission, sir. We want you to know how it would be. Sometimes your wife would come to my house back in the woods in Dublin, and she'd sleep with me and wake up with me and have coffee with me on the deck when the morning sun's on it. I'd share my little spring creek with her, and I'd like to show her where it bubbles out of the hillside up behind my house. Kate and I, we'd fish together and walk in the woods together and listen to music together and talk about books. And we'd make love."

Walter stared at Calhoun without expression for a long minute. Then he said, "Don't call me 'sir.'"

Calhoun nodded.

"It's Walter," he said.

"Okay."

Walter turned to Kate. "I worry about you," he said.

She began to speak. He lifted his hand off the table. "Let me finish," he said. "I sit around here all day, and maybe you think I spend all my time feeling sorry for myself. Well, I do. But I also feel sorry for you. I know what I am. I know what you've been living with." He turned to Calhoun. "I admire what you're doing."

"If it was up to me," said Kate, "I would've just told you. I wouldn't have asked."

"You think I'd say no?"

She shrugged. "I don't know."

"How could you know?" said Walter. "You've got this bitter, shrunken-up invalid on your hands, never says anything nice to you." He looked at Calhoun, then back at Kate. "Do me one favor, will you?"

"What?" she said.

"If anyone finds out about the two of you, you make sure they understand that I know, that I said it was okay by me, that"—he turned to Calhoun—"that I like this man. I don't want anybody thinking bad things about either of you."

Calhoun never knew when Kate would come to him. They didn't plan it or discuss it in advance, and he learned never to expect her. Not a night passed that he didn't wish she was with him.

But usually she wasn't. Sometimes several weeks elapsed between her visits. Sometimes she showed up two or three nights in a row. When she arrived, Kate poured herself some bourbon from the bottle she kept over Calhoun's refrigerator, and he had a Coke. They sat at the kitchen table, or, in the summer, out on the deck, where they could hear the creek gurgling and the nightbirds singing. They touched hands tentatively, were silent for long minutes, getting used to each other again.

Finally Kate would tip her glass until the ice cubes clinked against her teeth. Then she'd smile. "I'm kinda tired, Stoney," she'd say, and she'd stand up, hold out her hand, and lead him into the bedroom, where they'd lie together, their naked bodies pressed together, talking softly in the dark until they drifted off to sleep.

"I guess you've got no news on Lyle," murmured Kate. Her cheek lay on his bare chest and one of her long naked legs was sprawled over both of his.

He stroked her hair. "Sheriff Dickman came by after you left," he said. "And I called the house again. No news."

"I'm worried."

"Me, too."

She wiggled against him. "Hang onto me, Stoney," she said. "I want to be sure you're right here when I wake up."

He closed his eyes and sighed. "I'm not going anywhere, honey."

Ralph's bark awakened him. He didn't need to check his clock to know that the sun had not come up. Silvery predawn light oozed in through the windows, and somewhere out in the woods a gang of crows were having an argument.

"What's going on?" murmured Kate.

"Somebody's here."

He slid out of bed, pulled on his jeans and a T-shirt, took the Remington off its pegs, and opened the front door.

Sheriff Dickman was leaning against his Explorer, tapping his Stetson against his leg.

"Want some coffee?" said Calhoun.

"Wouldn't mind."

"Well, come on in."

Dickman jerked his head at Kate's Blazer. "Don't mean to intrude."

"Too late now."

Calhoun went back inside. The sheriff followed.

Kate, wearing one of Calhoun's flannel shirts and a pair of his baggy sweatpants, was padding barefoot around the kitchen, loading the coffeepot. She looked at Dickman with her eyebrows arched.

"I've got some news," he said.

"Lyle?"

He nodded. "They found his truck."

CHAPTER SIX

"WAS THERE AN ACCIDENT?" said Kate.

Dickman shook his head. He sat down and put his hat on the table beside him. "Lyle wasn't in the vehicle," he said.

"Where?" said Calhoun.

"The janitor noticed that old Power Wagon parked behind the grammar school out in South Riley last night," Dickman said. "They had a PTA meeting in the evening, and the janitor, guy named Russo, had to clean up, put all the folding chairs away, didn't finish up till nearly midnight. Taking his time, I expect. Time-and-a-half for those meetings. Everyone else had cleared out a couple hours earlier, but that old truck was still sitting there. He didn't recognize it, and there aren't a lot of forty-year-old Power Wagons around, so Mr. Russo called the sheriff's office up to Oxford County, and they passed on the word to me, which I got when I arrived at my office this morning. I checked the registration. It belongs to Lyle McMahan."

Kate looked at Calhoun with questions in her eyes.

"This janitor," said Calhoun, "he didn't recall seeing Lyle's truck earlier?"

Dickman shrugged. "I gave you all the news I've got, Stoney. Hell, it's, what, now, ten of six in the morning? I been up since four-thirty, but who else has? I haven't talked to anybody, and to tell you the truth, I don't know when I will. I don't see that we've exactly got a crime here to investigate, unless South Riley's got an ordinance against parking overnight in the school lot. Anyway, I've got no jurisdiction in Oxford County. Sheriff Bean over there, I doubt he's that interested in parking violations. If it's bothering somebody, they'll have it towed, so I left a message for them to leave that Power Wagon right where it is for now, figuring Lyle will eventually show up for it, or maybe you'd like to go over and pick it up for him."

"How do you take your coffee, Sheriff?" said Kate.

Dickman glanced at his wristwatch. "Actually, ma'am, I can't linger, much as I'd like to. I do have a travel mug out in my vehicle that I emptied on my way here, if you wouldn't mind."

"Fetch it," she said.

When Dickman went out, Kate looked at Calhoun. "I'm thinking about Walter," she said.

Calhoun nodded. "I'll talk to him."

Dickman was back a minute later. Kate filled his mug and Calhoun walked back outside with him. The sheriff climbed into the front seat of his Explorer.

Calhoun leaned his forearms on the roof and bent to the open window. "Want to explain something to you," he said.

Dickman smiled and shook his head. "Nothing to explain, Stoney. I don't deal in gossip."

"I know that, and so does Kate. I wasn't worried about that. But we made a promise to Walter. That's Kate's husband."

"I know Walter," said Dickman.

"He knows about us," said Calhoun. "Kate and I, we squared it with him before we—we started. We are discreet, Sheriff. But Walter, he figured sooner or later someone would—well, drop in, like you did. It's

48

important to Walter that nobody thinks we're going behind his back. He knows. It's okay by him. Walter and I are friends. He'd want you to know that."

"You don't have to explain to me, Stoney."

"Kate and I would prefer it was a secret," said Calhoun. "But it's never been a secret from Walter. That's all I'm trying to say."

Dickman nodded. "It isn't any of my business," he said. "Nor anyone else's, either." He turned the key in the ignition. "Meanwhile, I expect you're gonna take a swing by South Riley this morning."

"I expect I am. Lyle's about my best friend in the world, Sheriff. I'm a little concerned."

"Well, if he's gone missing, Stoney, we'll try to track him down. You know that. But there's no evidence of it."

"No," said Calhoun. "Most likely he's shacked up somewhere."

"You let me know what you learn." Dickman shifted into reverse. "Russo. That's the janitor's name. South Riley Elementary."

"Got it," said Calhoun.

After Dickman left, Calhoun and Kate took their coffee mugs out to the big maple rocking chairs on the deck. Ralph found a patch of sunlight to curl up in. "I'm thinking of building a hot tub out here," said Calhoun.

"That would be fun," she said.

The ground sloped away to the little spring creek, which funneled through the narrow place at the site of the burned-out bridge. In the slanting rays of the early sun, Calhoun could see a cloud of mayfly spinners swirling and glittering over the stream. They'd fall to the water soon, spent and dying after their reproductive efforts, and then the trout in the downstream pool would sip them from the surface.

"I don't get it," said Kate after several minutes.

"Get what?"

"Lyle. Why would he leave his truck in back of a school?"

Calhoun shrugged. "Maybe he was planning to pick it up after fishing on the way to Penny Moulton's place."

"But that was two days ago."

"That's a fact," said Calhoun.

"So why didn't he pick it up? Where was Lyle all day yesterday?"

"It's a mystery, all right."

"She lives where? That Penny Moulton?"

"Standish."

Kate shook her head. "Makes no sense." She turned and put her hand on Calhoun's arm. "Why would they leave Lyle's vehicle and not Mr. Green's? They stowed all the gear in the Power Wagon, right?"

"Yes, honey. I watched them do it."

"You think they parked behind that school, transferred all their stuff into the other vehicle? What kind of car was that Fred Green guy driving, anyway?"

Calhoun shut his eyes, trying to see it, to remember the glimpse he'd had of Fred Green's car through the shop's window as it followed Lyle's Power Wagon out of the lot two days earlier. "White," he said slowly. "New sedan. Ford Taurus with Maine plates." He opened his eyes.

She was shaking her head. "You are spooky when you do that memory thing. I mean, you can't remember your own parents, but you can remember a car you weren't even looking at."

"I looked at it," said Calhoun. "I just wasn't thinking about it. But I've got the picture here." He tapped his forehead with his forefinger.

"So what about the plates? Can you read the numbers?"

He closed his eyes again, then shook his head. "No. But it must've been a rental. All those rental cars are white, and there's Mr. Green, up from Florida, driving a car with Maine plates."

"Okay," said Kate. "So you're telling me that Lyle and Mr. Green decided to drive that brand-new rented Taurus sedan over old potholed dirt roads to some remote trout pond instead of taking Lyle's old Power

Wagon that already had their fishing gear in it? Could they even fit two float tubes in the back of a Taurus sedan?"

"I wasn't tellin' you that, Kate," he said softly. "It doesn't make much sense. But I expect Lyle will have an explanation."

"Well, damned if I can think one up."

Calhoun shrugged. "So Lyle's got himself a lady in South Riley. Maybe some pretty first-grade teacher. Met her there after school and they drove to her place in her car, shacked up for a couple days."

"He had a date with that Penny Moulton in Standish, didn't he?"

"Well, Penny Moulton sure thought so," he said.

"It isn't like Lyle to break a date."

"Now, Kate, honey, you don't know that. Lyle's a good boy. But he *is* a boy." He drained his coffee mug and stood up. "How about some pancakes?"

"What about Lyle?"

"I'll go look for him," said Calhoun. "But not on an empty stomach."

A little after eight, Kate gave Calhoun a long, hard hug, bent down to scratch Ralph's muzzle, climbed into her Blazer, and headed back to Portland.

Calhoun piled the dirty breakfast dishes in the sink, and then he and Ralph climbed into the truck. Ralph rode shotgun beside him. Calhoun had tried to persuade him to wear a seat belt, but the dog wouldn't hear of it. He liked to move around, poke his nose up at the crack in the window, stand on the seat making wet-nose smudges on the windshield, or curl up with his chin on Calhoun's thigh, making it damned awkward to shift gears.

It took about half an hour over the back roads to get from Calhoun's little house in the woods in Dublin to South Riley. He found the elementary school north of the village.

The small parking lot out back held a couple dozen vehicles— Isuzu wagons, Jeep Cherokees, new-looking Toyota and Ford pickup trucks, and one sexy little red Mazda. Calhoun figured they were pay-ing schoolteachers more than they used to, even in this little town in rural Maine.

Lyle's Power Wagon looked like a mutt in a dog show, big and cum-bersome, muddy and rusted and pocked with dents. It was parked at the end of the row with its nose facing the playground.

He pulled up beside it, told Ralph to sit tight, and got out.

The first thing he noticed was that all of Lyle's fishing gear—his rods and waders and float tubes and vests and lunch basket—were not inside. This suggested that they had moved everything into Fred Green's rented Ford Taurus and had not returned. If they had stopped here after a day's fishing, Lyle's gear would be in the back so he could return it to the shop.

He walked around the Power Wagon. It was mud-spattered, as if it had recently plowed through puddles. Calhoun recalled that they'd had a thunderstorm the night before Lyle had set off with Fred Green. The rain would have washed off old mud, and it would've made new pud-dles. So Lyle's truck had driven back roads after leaving the shop two days earlier. There were no back roads between Portland and South Riley, which meant they must have taken Lyle's Power Wagon when they'd gone exploring for Fred Green's secret pond.

Puzzling.

He tried the driver's door and found it unlocked. He bent in, reached under the seat, and found Lyle's DeLorme *Atlas & Gazetteer,* the big eleven-by-sixteen paperback book that contained topograph-ic maps of every quadrant in the entire state of Maine. It was Lyle's Bible. On those maps, Calhoun knew, Lyle had marked his prize grouse and woodcock covers, his secret trout ponds and streams, the hidden swamps and field edges where he knew he could find deer, the deep holes and the mussel beds and sand flats on tidal creeks and rivers where striped bass lurked on certain tides. Lyle circled those places on his maps with a black felt-tipped pen and gave them his own names—Stick Farm and Hippie House, Red Shoes and Arnold's Pasture, Suck Hole and Pipeline.

You could read Lyle McMahan's hunting and fishing life off those maps, and Calhoun knew that he treasured that gazetteer.

"This your vehicle, mister?"

Calhoun bumped his head on the roof of the Power Wagon as he whirled around.

A woman wearing a gray shirt and matching trousers stood there frowning at him.

"Jesus, ma'am," said Calhoun. "You startled me." He rubbed the top of his head.

She was nearly a foot shorter than Calhoun, a sturdy woman with iron-gray hair cut like an upside-down bowl, dark eyes, and a lumpy nose that looked as if it had been broken a few times. "Didn't mean for you to hurt yourself," she said. "I been watchin' for you. This ain't a public parking lot, you know." She dug her hand into her pants pocket and came out with a ring of keys. She held them to Calhoun. "Here. You oughtn't to leave 'em in your ignition, you know. Not unless you want someone to steal it. Which might not be a bad idea, come to think of it, considering the condition of that vehicle of yours." She jerked her head at Lyle's Power Wagon. "We ain't got crime, not like Portland or Bangor, but even out here in the sticks there's plenty of kids'd be happy to take your old truck for a ride, run over a few cottontails, see how many potholes they can hit before the bolts start poppin' out of it and the muffler falls off. Lucky for you I noticed it last night."

"Those keys were in the ignition?" said Calhoun.

"Yessuh. Could've been stolen."

When they parked in the woods, Lyle always locked up and tucked the keys under the left rear tire for whoever got back first. Even at the end of a long woods road, he never left the keys in the ignition. Lyle was not careless about things like that.

"It's not my vehicle," he said to the woman. "It belongs to a friend of mine. The sheriff told me I'd find it here. Was it you who reported it?"

She nodded.

"When did you first notice it?"

"I come back at seven-thirty last evening to set up for the meetin', and I didn't notice it then. When I come out—oh, it was close to midnight, after everyone had cleared out and I got the place swept up and the chairs put away—this old thing was here. Just this old bag of bolts and my truck. That's when I first saw it. Midnight, I guess. I grabbed the keys and called the sheriff, just to be on the safe side."

"This was last night?"

"Yes, sir."

"Was it here Tuesday?"

She shook her head. "Didn't notice it. Of course, I wasn't here in the evening Tuesday."

"And you didn't see who left it here."

"No."

"So he must've left it sometime between—what?—seven-thirty and midnight last night?"

She nodded. "About that. During that meeting."

"My name's Calhoun, by the way," he said. He held out his hand.

She took it. Her grip was firm. "Russo," she said.

"When you first saw this vehicle," said Calhoun, "was it full of fishing gear?"

She shook her head. "Nope. I looked inside, because if it had anythin' in it I would've locked her up. Nothing worth stealing that I could see. Prob'ly should've locked her anyway, but like I say, South Riley ain't exactly your high-crime area, and everybody's sleeping by midnight."

"I'm wondering," said Calhoun, "if yesterday, or the day before, Tuesday, you might've noticed another strange car parked out here. A white Taurus sedan, this year's model."

Russo shrugged. "Not that I recall. Miss Wilhelm—she's the music teacher—she drives a Taurus, but it's blue and it ain't that new."

"It might've been here until this Power Wagon showed up."

She narrowed her eyes. "You mean someone decided to swap this old truck for a new Taurus?"

"Something like that."

"Well," she said, "I don't remember any Taurus. Don't mean it wasn't here. But I don't miss much."

"I don't doubt you." He smiled. "Look, why don't you lock it up and hang onto those keys. This truck belongs to a friend of mine named Lyle McMahan, and I expect he'll be back for it eventually. He'll appreciate your letting it sit here until he shows up."

She shrugged. "It ain't doin' any harm, I guess."

"Well, thank you, Mrs. Russo." Calhoun turned to head back to his truck.

"Miss," she said. "It's Miss. That book belong to you?"

Calhoun held up Lyle's gazetteer. "No, it belongs to the guy who owns the Power Wagon. I'm borrowing it." He stopped. "Do me a favor, Miss Russo?"

"Maybe."

He fumbled in his shirt pocket and found one of Kate's business cards. He handed it to her. "If you feel you've got to have this car moved, or if anybody comes for it, give me a call?"

She squinted at the card, then looked up at him. "I guess I can do that."

CHAPTER SEVEN

WHEN CALHOUN GOT HOME, he put on more coffee, took his phone out onto the deck, and called the shop.

"Kate's Bait, Tackle, and Woolly Buggers," she answered.

"It's me," he said. "What've you got going on today?"

"Nothing particular. What's up? What'd you find out?"

"I was thinking I might take the day off, do some snooping." He told her about his trip to South Riley, finding Lyle's Power Wagon, and his conversation with Miss Russo, the janitor. "Figured it was about time I tracked down Mr. Fred Green," he finished.

"We should've done that yesterday," she said.

"Probably should have. But we didn't. So we'll do it today."

"I know you'll let me know what you find out."

"Sure will."

She was quiet for a moment. "Stoney?" she said softly.

"I'm here, honey."

"That was nice last night."

"It's always nice," he said. "And that's the truth."

After he disconnected from Kate, Calhoun went inside, poured himself a mug of coffee, found the Greater Portland phone directory, and went back out on the deck.

He looked up the number for the new Marriott down on the waterfront. It had the most rooms in town, so the way Stoney figured it, the probability was greater that Green had stayed there than anyplace else.

When the young man answered, Calhoun asked to be connected to Mr. Fred Green.

"What room, sir?"

"I don't know."

"Please hold." Calhoun endured about three minutes of what sounded like the Elevator Orchestra playing a slowed-down version of "Day Tripper" before the desk clerk came back. "I'm sorry, sir. No Mr. Green staying with us."

"Hmm," said Calhoun. "Wonder if he checked out yesterday or this morning. Could you look that up for me?"

"I'm really not supposed to—"

"This is Deputy Sheriff Calhoun, over in York County," said Calhoun quickly. "I'd appreciate your cooperation. Makes things easier for all of us, okay?"

The clerk hesitated a moment, then said, "Certainly, sir." This time the violins played "Everything's Up to Date in Kansas City." Surely an impressive repertoire. "No, sir," said the clerk a minute later. "I'm sorry. We've had no Mr. Green with us this week."

"There was a convention in town," said Calhoun. "Could you tell me where it was held?"

"All the conventions are held at the Civic Center, sir, but there have been no conventions this week. No conferences, for that matter. The New England Periodontal Association will be here on Thursday. That's our next one."

"No conventions or conferences," said Calhoun. "You sure of that?"

"It's my business to know about conventions and conferences in Portland, sir. Is there something else I can help you with?"

"No, thanks," said Calhoun. "You've been a big help. And I love your music."

"Excuse me?"

"Nothing. Sorry."

"Well, sir, you have a nice day."

"It's off to one helluva doubtful start," said Stoney.

Calhoun sipped his coffee, scratched Ralph's head, and gazed down to the creek. The mayfly spinners were no longer swirling over the water. The trout would be resting their bellies on the bottom of their pool where they could find some tasty stonefly nymphs to chew on until the sun got low and the next batch of mayflies began hatching and the evening caddisflies flew out of the bushes and started fluttering over the water.

He looked at the listing of hotels and motels in the phone book. There were dozens of them. Well, the hell with it. Green was staying somewhere, and maybe he'd misunderstood about the convention.

Now he wished he'd been friendlier to Fred Green, encouraged the man to keep talking, asked him some conversational questions. He might've learned something.

He started with the Abbott Motel and worked all the way down the list to the Zanzibar Inn, and after that he looked up the bed-and-breakfasts and called every one of them, too.

By two o'clock in the afternoon, Calhoun's only functional ear, the right one, was ringing, and his neck had a painful crick in it from cradling the telephone against it. He was convinced that Fred Green had not rented any kind of room in Portland or any of the surrounding towns.

And he had not been attending a convention or a conference, either, because several of the innkeepers he'd talked to had repeated what the young man at the Marriott had told him. There had been none in Portland that week.

Well, dammit, the man *had* rented a car. So Calhoun proceeded to call every car rental agency in the Greater Portland phone book. None of them had done business with anyone named Fred Green that week.

That's when Calhoun decided that Fred Green was not the man's name, and he further deduced that if Green—or whatever his name was—would lie about his name, he must've had an important reason to do so.

Then Calhoun decided it was time to be seriously worried.

He stood up, arched his back, and went down to his truck. He retrieved Lyle's gazetteer from where'd he'd left it on the dashboard, and as he was walking back to the house, Kate's image popped into his head.

She had a telephone to her ear and a frown on her face.

He went in and called the shop.

Kate picked up on the first ring. "Stoney?"

"What's the matter?" he said.

"Your phone's been busy for hours. I was concerned."

He told her about calling all the hotels and motels and bed-and-breakfasts and car rental agencies.

"But why would the man give a phony name?" she said.

"I'd say that's the big question, all right," he said. "I reckon he had somethin' to hide."

"And you think . . ."

"I'm thinking what you're thinking, honey. You're thinking that I sent Lyle off with a man who should've been my client, a man who had cause to lie about who he was. You're thinking that if I'd've taken Mr. Fred Green fishing myself, like I was supposed to, we wouldn't be sitting here worried about Lyle right now."

"Now, Stoney," said Kate, "I wasn't thinking that at all."

"Well, I am." Calhoun let out a long breath. "This is my doing, Kate. I was selfish and small-minded. Decided I didn't like the man. You've said it a million times. We don't have the luxury of selling stuff only to nice folks or guiding only people we like. We do business. Well, I didn't do business. I sluffed Mr. Green off to Lyle, and now we don't know where Lyle is."

"What're we gonna do?"

"Well, I don't plan to sit here on my ass for the rest of the day, I can tell you that. Guess I'll head back up to South Riley, poke around, see what I can shake out of the trees."

"I want to go with you."

"You stay put," he said. "Nothing you can do I can't do myself. Anyway, we've got several people who'll call the shop if they hear something. Wouldn't want to miss a call."

She sighed. "I guess you're right. You let me know what falls out of those trees."

"Of course I will."

After he disconnected from Kate, Calhoun opened Lyle's gazetteer on the kitchen table and flipped to Map 4, the one that included South Riley.

Unlike road maps, topographic maps, as their name implies, show topography—man-made as well as natural features. Each map is a rectangle—a quadrangle—which they call a quad. It represents twenty-five minutes of latitude and longitude, encompassing an area twenty-nine miles north-south by twenty-one miles east-west, on a scale of one-half inch per mile.

Calhoun, like many outdoorspeople, and especially hunting and fishing guides, consulted topo maps religiously. He knew that a single dotted line represented a trail that might or might not be passable in his four-wheel-drive truck, that little tufts of grass meant a marsh or swamp, that a black square represented a dwelling or a cellar hole where a dwelling had once stood. Thin blue lines were brooks or streams. A swath of pale green meant a woodland. You could estimate the steepness of a hill by how close together the contour lines were drawn.

Lyle collected stories about that fire and loved to share them with Calhoun.

Most of the old-timers who'd been burnt out in '47, the stoic old Yankee farmers, had shrugged, cleaned away the ashes of their homes, and set to work rebuilding. But many hadn't. The woods west and south of Sebago Lake were dotted with old cellar holes filled with charred timbers and rusted bedsprings and old crockery. The dirt roads that led into them—single-dotted lines on the topographic maps— were now growing thick with alder and poplar.

Lyle's legends were scattered across Map 4, hillsides and ridges and swamps and ponds that he'd circled in black felt-tip pen, many of them labeled in Lyle's neat printing—"Big Buck," "Hot Corner," "Bear Shit" —names that not only stood for places, but were for Lyle McMahan also the titles of memorable stories.

Calhoun closed his eyes, squeezed them tight, and brought up his memory-picture of Lyle and Fred Green bent over the open gazetteer on the hood of the Power Wagon. Green was pointing with his forefinger. Lyle had been holding a pencil in his hand.

When he'd come back inside, Lyle had told Calhoun that they were heading for Green's secret pond.

He opened his eyes, fished his fly-tying glasses from his shirt pocket, and bent to the map. He focused on South Riley and worked his way systematically outward in ever-widening circles, until, about two and a half inches—five miles—south and west of the elementary school where Lyle's Power Wagon sat, in the town of Keatsboro in York County snug against the New Hampshire border, Calhoun spotted a faint X made with a pencil.

He translated from the map—a single dotted line ran off a double dotted line and curved over widely spaced contour lines to a marshy area with a thin blue line running through it. The dotted line passed over the blue line and twisted over several more contour lines to a little black square on the top of the hill—a dwelling of some sort, or perhaps a former dwelling, a burned-out or abandoned farm-house, now a cellar hole.

Lyle had drawn his X where the dotted line intersected with the blue line. The blue line thickened a bit there, indicating that the stream widened into a large pool, or perhaps even a skinny pond. This was Fred Green's secret trout place.

Calhoun guessed that somebody—probably the farmer who had lived on the hilltop, if he was a farmer—had built himself a milldam on the stream that ran through the marshy area, creating a little pond—perhaps for power, perhaps to collect water for his livestock, or maybe both. He'd built a bridge over the dam, so that he could drive his tractors and trucks all the way in from the dirt road to his place on the hilltop.

Most farmers built close to the road for the obvious practicality of it. But this one had chosen to locate himself as deep into the woods as he could get. Taking into account all of its twists and turns, the trail from the dirt road to the top of the hill would be about a mile long, Calhoun estimated—half a mile to the stream, and another half mile to the dwelling. It was a lot of road to keep open in the wintertime and in mud season, a lot of work for a notoriously pragmatic Yankee farmer. In fact, another town road ran along behind the hillside where the house had been built. A driveway out to this road would've been just a couple hundred yards long. But there was no indication of any old driveway on the map.

Calhoun took off his glasses and rubbed his eyes. He was not par-ticularly interested in the man who lived—or used to live—on the hilltop a mile from the road. He was interested in the whereabouts of Lyle McMahan.

He shut the gazetteer. Ralph, who had been lying by the door, lifted his head and looked at him.

"Sorry, pal," said Calhoun. "I'm leaving, and don't know where I'll end up or how long I'll be gone. You stay here and answer the phone."

Ralph dropped his chin back onto his paws, sighed, and closed his eyes.

Calhoun snagged a Coke and a couple of apples from the refrigerator. He considered bringing a fly rod. If nothing else, he could give Fred Green's secret trout pond a try.

But he had no heart for fishing. Not this time. This was a hunting trip.

If he were headed for the big woods up north, he'd bring his compass and waterproof matches and maps and a sidearm. But there were no big woods around Keatsboro. It was all old farmland, intersected with roads, some paved and some dirt, studded with apple orchards and cornfields and farmhouses and pretty New England village greens, more or less like Dublin. Even a flatlander from New Jersey or Connecticut would have trouble getting seriously lost in the woods of southwestern Maine.

So Calhoun gave Ralph a rawhide bone for companionship, tucked Lyle's gazetteer under his arm, carried his Coke and apples out to his truck, and headed for Keatsboro.

CHAPTER EIGHT

THEY'D RELEASED Calhoun from the VA hospital five years earlier, on a bright Thursday morning in late March—spring in Virginia already. He'd headed instinctively north on Interstate 81 in his new secondhand Ford pickup, drawn by the Maine images that ricocheted around in his brain. The grass along the highway in Pennsylvania was so green it hurt his eyes. Shrubs were flowering and dandelions bloomed and woodchucks sat up on their haunches in the fields, and he was so eager to get there that he stopped only twice—first outside of Scranton and then again somewhere in Connecticut, for gas and coffee and a couple of Hershey bars.

He'd taken the first exit off the Interstate as soon as he crossed the bridge over the Piscataqua River and entered Eliot, Maine. It wasn't as if he'd planned to take that exit or had any conscious reason to. Nothing in his brain actually told him to click on his directional signal, slow down, turn the steering wheel. He'd had no specific destination in his mind—just Maine.

He'd followed secondary highways and then back roads, meandering through the countryside in a more-or-less northwesterly direction.

The Maine meadows were still winter-flattened and brown. Patches of old snow huddled in the woods and along the stone walls, and the ice in the ponds had not yet melted.

In the late afternoon he drove through Berwick and Sanford and Alfred and Shapleigh, sometimes not even knowing what town he was in, and then he came to a stop sign at a crossroads. A white Congregational church in need of paint hunkered on one corner. In front of it stood a big glass-faced bulletin board with the message: CHRIST THE LORD IS RIS'N TODAY. ALLELUIA. EASTER SERVICES, 10:00 SUNDAY.

Beside the church sat a ramshackle mom-and-pop store with gas pumps out front and an old Coca-Cola sign over the door. A big square fieldstone building stood diagonally across from the church. A sign over the door read DUBLIN TOWN HALL.

Calhoun knew, although he didn't know how he knew, that he'd come to the end of his journey and the beginning of his own resurrection. This town felt like home.

He'd pumped himself a tankful of gas at the mom-and-pop store, then went inside to pay. A bell dinged when he opened the door. Coming out of the brilliant afternoon sunshine, it took his eyes a minute to adjust to the dimness inside. It smelled oddly familiar, a nostalgic combination of vinegar and sharp cheddar cheese and propane, and he flashed on a kitchen, a white-haired woman in a flowered apron standing at the stove, children seated around a bare wooden table . . .

"Help you, son?"

Calhoun blinked. Behind the counter a bald man in a blue flannel shirt and red suspenders was perched on a stool eating a donut. He was old—somewhere in his late seventies, Calhoun guessed—but he had alert, intelligent eyes.

Calhoun went over, took out his wallet, and gave the man a twenty-dollar bill. He'd paid for the pickup with the bank check and arranged to take his change in cash. Now he had a wad of bills worth fifteen thousand dollars in his pants pocket and nine hundred more in his wallet. "I filled it up," he said to the man. "Eighteen dollars' worth."

The old man cocked his head and peered at Calhoun through his steel-rimmed glasses. "You ain't from around here, are you?"

"No, sir," Calhoun said. "My name's Calhoun. They call me Stoney."

"I'm Jacob Barnes." Barnes opened his cash register, put Calhoun's twenty in, and removed two ones, which he slapped down on the counter. "They was some Calhouns had a farm up on the county road," he said. "Got burnt out in the fire, never come back. That was before your time, I reckon." He laid his forearms on the counter and leaned forward.

"When was the fire?" Calhoun said.

"October of forty-seven."

"That was before my time, all right. Different Calhouns, I guess."

Barnes shrugged. "I expect so. It warn't much of a farm to start with. They raised chickens and pigs and kids, all of 'em running around up there in the mud so's you couldn't tell which was which."

Calhoun smiled. "That does sound like my family," he said, although in fact, he had no particular reason to think so. "Can you direct me to a real estate agent?"

Barnes jerked his head in a northerly direction. "Talk to Millie Dobson. She's the only realtor in town. You lookin' to buy?"

"Yes," he said, although until he'd said it, he hadn't known that it was the truth.

Calhoun had followed Jacob Barnes's directions and found Millie Dobson's gray-shingled bungalow squatting close to the roadside. The sign out front read M. DOBSON: REAL ESTATE, TOWN CLERK, NOTARY PUBLIC, FAX. A green Jeep Cherokee sat in a small pea-stone parking area, and he pulled his truck in beside it.

He climbed the front steps and rang the bell. Some kind of loud rock music was playing inside, and he waited several minutes before the music abruptly stopped and the door opened, revealing a woman with short black hair, dark eyes, a lean, angular body, and a towel around her neck. She was wearing sweatpants and a powder-blue T-shirt that bore the message DUBLIN FAIR 1997—THE WORLD'S BIGGEST PUMPKIN. She was, Calhoun guessed, around forty.

"Exercising," she said. "I'm Millie Dobson. What can I do for you?"

"My name's Calhoun," he said. "I'd like to buy some land."

She pulled open the door. "You came to the right place, Mr. Calhoun." She laughed. "Hell, you came to the only place. Come on in."

Her living room doubled as her office and exercise studio. Against the front wall stood a big oak desk with a computer and fax machine. It was flanked by a pair of shoulder-high file cabinets. A bookcase in the corner held a CD player and a television with a VCR, and beside it was a treadmill and a rowing machine.

She brought them coffee and fetched a thick photo album from her desk drawer, and they sat side by side on her sofa.

Calhoun told her he'd come from Virginia with all his savings in his pocket, hoping to buy a secluded piece of property to build on. He made it up as he went along, since he wasn't sure what he really wanted, but trusted that what came out of his mouth would be true.

"Why here?" she said. "If you don't mind me asking."

He shrugged. "I like this part of the world. Small towns. Maine. Away from the seacoast. Always have."

"You're from away," she said. "I hear it in your voice. I'm from Madrid originally." She pronounced it with the accent on the first syllable. *MAD-rid.* She smiled. "That's the town in Maine, not Spain. How about you?"

"South Carolina," he said.

She nodded as if she knew he was hiding something and it was all right with her. "Can you describe what you have in mind?"

"Something in the woods. With water. It's got to have water."

"Pond or stream?"

"Either one's fine with me."

She frowned. "Lemme think for a minute . . ." Then she snapped her fingers. "There's a piece of land few miles north of here, been sittin' there for ages. Nice little brook runs through it. The folks who had it got burned out, and no one ever rebuilt on it."

Calhoun remembered what Jacob Barnes had said about a family of Calhouns being burned out in a fire and abandoning their place. "This place wouldn't be on the county road, would it?" he said.

Millie Dobson gave him a little frown, then said, "Yes, as a matter of fact, it is."

"Can I see it?"

"Well," she said, "people from New Jersey own that piece now. Don't know as it's even available. But I could check. Who knows? The right offer . . ." She shrugged. "Let me change my clothes, we'll go have a look at it."

Fifteen minutes later they had parked Millie's Jeep at the end of an old overgrown tote road and begun walking. The roadway wound through several hundred yards of second-growth hardwood forest and ended at an old cellar hole. The fieldstone chimney was still standing, and the granite foundation looked solid. A pair of ruts led down the slope beyond the cellar hole to a pretty spring-fed brook, stopped at a burned-out bridge, then continued into the forest on the other side.

Millie said you wouldn't find it on any map, but the local folks called the brook Bitch Creek. The story was, someone had named it after a trout fly, Millie said, though she personally figured it was just some man naming it after his wife.

From somewhere in the recesses of his chaotic memory, Calhoun remembered a fly called the Bitch Creek Nymph.

If that were true, it probably meant there were trout living there. He liked that the little brook had a name. That seemed to give it a history. Calhoun was interested in history.

In fact, he liked everything about the place. He wanted to buy it. He felt like he'd come home.

He told Millie he'd tear down the old chimney and put it back together with the same stones. He'd build his house over the old foundation. He'd do the work himself, he said.

She asked if he was handy, and he said, "Yes," and after he said it, he believed it was true.

Millie dickered with the people from New Jersey, and three weeks after leaving the hospital in Arlington, Virginia, Stoney Calhoun owned forty acres of overgrown farmland in Dublin, Maine, along with several hundred yards of Bitch Creek, a good fieldstone foundation, an almost-passable tote road, and what felt like a future.

For the first few months, he'd lived in a tent on the site of his new house. He woke with the birds every morning and worked until sunset. He cleared the tote road with a chain saw so delivery trucks could bring in lumber, and he opened up the hillside where his house would sit so the morning sun could stream in through the front windows and he'd be able to glimpse the silvery ribbon of Bitch Creek at the foot of the hill. Its gurgle was loud enough for even a one-eared man to hear, and it kept him company while he worked.

Gradually his hospital-softened body grew hard and lean. His thoughts became sharp and decisive, and now and then a piece of memory would fall into place.

He was burning slash on a misty afternoon late in May, leaning on his garden rake close to the smoke where the blackflies couldn't get at him, when an old Dodge Power Wagon came rumbling into the clearing.

The Power Wagon pulled up beside Calhoun's pickup, and a long-legged kid stepped out, lifted his hand in greeting, and sauntered over to where Calhoun was standing.

"Good day for burnin'," the boy said.

Calhoun had nodded, squinting at his fire.

"Guess you're Mr. Calhoun," the boy persisted. "I'm Lyle. Lyle McMahan." He held out his hand.

Calhoun glanced at it, then grasped it. "Didn't ask for any company that I recall," he said.

Lyle McMahan had a ponytail and an earring, and he towered over Calhoun. "I used to catch trout from there," he said, jerking his head toward Bitch Creek.

"Well, you can't anymore."

The kid shrugged. "I've got plenty of other places. You're planning to build here, I understand."

"That's right."

"Lot of work for one man."

"I've got a lot of time," said Calhoun.

"If I owned that water," said Lyle, "I wouldn't let anyone fish in it, either. Tell you the truth, I wouldn't fish in it myself. I'd just keep it, appreciate it, take care of it. I never kept any of those trout. I'd catch a couple, put 'em back, then quit. Native brookies. Pretty special. They've been here since the glaciers moved out, or at least their ancestors have. You aren't a fisherman, then."

Calhoun had turned and smiled at him. "No, I'm a fisherman, all right. And I go fishing every day in that little creek. I don't bring my rod, though. I just sit on a rock and watch 'em. Try to figure out what they're eating, or why they aren't eating, or just generally ponder it. I appreciate a good mystery, and trout always give a man something to think about."

Lyle had moved to the slash pile, dragged some branches over, and thrown them onto the fire. Then he'd picked up a hoe and shoved at the dirt around the edges.

And by the end of the afternoon, Calhoun had hired Lyle McMahan to help him build his house in the woods.

~~~
~~~

Calhoun and Lyle took down the old chimney stone by stone, and they patched up the granite foundation and made it plumb. Calhoun figured he must have built a house before, although he couldn't remember where or when, because he found that he knew how to erect beams and sills and joists and bearing walls. He and Lyle fit stones, laid pipe, and strung electrical wire, and by the middle of July they had the place framed in and Calhoun was sleeping on the floor in what would be his kitchen.

The two of them found a natural rhythm working together. Calhoun didn't need to tell Lyle what to do. The boy always had the right tool in his hand, and he'd lug over the right piece of lumber just at the moment when Calhoun needed it. Hours would pass when neither of them would speak. Calhoun had power lines strung in to run the tools, and he kept a radio tuned to the classical station out of Portland. Lyle seemed to like that music as much as Calhoun did.

When they talked, it was usually about fishing. And sometimes Calhoun called it quits early and the two of them piled some gear into Lyle's old Power Wagon and followed back roads to bass ponds and trout streams deep in the woods, or headed for the coast to try for striped bass in the estuaries and along the rock-strewn coastline.

That first summer, Lyle was between his sophomore and junior years at a small college in Vermont, which he'd chosen, he said, because it was near some nice trout streams and grouse covers. He'd grown up in Fryeburg, up to the north and west of Sebago Lake, and had spent most of his life in the woods. He was majoring in history. He wanted to teach high school. He said he'd learned a lot of history by wandering around the woods. He liked to read stories off toppled, hand-etched gravestones in overgrown family plots. He could reconstruct several generations of family history by the stone walls and tote roads and caved-in cellar holes and well stones he found while hunting deer or tracking down a new trout pond.

Lyle always made a point of talking with local old-timers, collecting their stories. He was writing them down, he told Calhoun that first summer when they worked together, and one day he might try to put them into a book. Lyle believed that this generation of old-timers—the men and women who'd scraped a living from the stingy Maine soil, who'd raised pigs and cows and chickens and had poached deer and ducks to feed their families, who'd survived the Second World War and the Great Fire of '47 and whose sons and grandsons had died in Korea and Vietnam—they represented the end of something. "It's got to be preserved, Stoney," Lyle had said more than once. "If it isn't written down, it'll be gone forever."

But as interested as Lyle was in history and stories, he never inquired about Calhoun's personal history, which saved him the trouble of telling the boy that he didn't know much about it anyway.

After Calhoun began working for Kate Balaban and she'd decided to start offering guide trips, it was natural enough that he'd suggest they hire Lyle McMahan.

He was good at it—enthusiastic, knowledgeable, and easy with people. Lyle was a natural teacher. He could identify every species of bird and wildflower and insect native to Maine, and he liked to share his knowledge of local history with his clients. He could spot the flaws in anybody's fly-casting technique, and he knew how to offer suggestions without giving offense. He was especially good with kids.

Lyle liked everybody, and he had no trouble winning over even the crustiest client who might be inclined to mistrust a gangly college kid wearing a ponytail and an earring.

Calhoun was proud of Lyle McMahan, proud that he'd "discovered" him, and proud to have him for a friend.

These were the thoughts that bounced through Calhoun's head as he drove to Keatsboro, heading for the **X** on Lyle's topographic map, the secret trout pond that Fred Green—or whatever his name really was—had wanted to fish.

Calhoun absolutely believed that he, Calhoun, Lyle's best friend, was solely responsible for whatever had happened to Lyle.

CHAPTER NINE

An APPLE ORCHARD AND A COUPLE of dairy farms, widely separated by dense pine forest, were the only signs of human activity along the dirt road, which twisted through the rolling countryside to the single dotted line that led to the penciled X on Lyle's topographic map. Calhoun drove slowly, studying the old tumbledown stone wall that kept appearing and disappearing in the woods along the right-hand side of the road, and when he came to a wooden bridge spanning a brook he knew he'd gone too far.

So he turned around and headed back, and this time he spotted the break in the wall where an old tote road had once cut into the woods. He pulled to the side, got out, and looked around.

Tire tracks in the hardened mud led off the road to the opening in the wall. Someone had recently turned in here. Crushed weeds showed where the vehicle had parked behind some trees, hidden from the sight of anyone passing by.

Lyle always tried to hide his truck. Lyle believed—and Calhoun agreed with him—that there was no sense spending a lifetime collecting secret trout streams and bass ponds and grouse covers and then giving them away to some passing out-of-stater by leaving your vehicle in plain sight.

Only a big old truck with four-wheel drive—such as Lyle's Power Wagon—could have made it through the mud and over the rocky ruts to the hiding place behind the screen of pines. Calhoun doubted a rented Taurus could've negotiated the deep ruts that far off the dirt road without ripping away its undercarriage.

He took a final look at Lyle's map. If this break in the stone wall did indeed mark the place where the single dotted line on the map led down a long slope to the brook, then all he had to do was follow the ancient ruts and he'd come to Fred Green's secret trout hole.

He started walking. Another, smaller stone wall perpendicular to the one along the dirt road paralleled the old tote road into the woods. The ancient ruts were still distinct, although what had once been a road where a tractor could pass was now thickly grown with alder saplings and briars and milkweed and goldenrod.

Calhoun tried to imagine Lyle lugging two float tubes, two fly rods, two pairs of waders, and a lunch basket over this trail while Fred Green puffed along behind. Calhoun had made many similar treks himself. Usually the clients carried their share of the gear. Somehow he doubted that Mr. Green would have offered. Clients like Mr. Green believed that guides were paid to do all the work, and Lyle was too sweet-tempered to ask for help.

After a few hundred yards, the ruts angled off to the left and began descending down a long gradual slope. Here and there Calhoun noticed old gnarled apple trees mingled with the oak and birch and juniper, and in a couple of places other stone walls marked the boundaries of old fields and orchards and pastures.

Lyle could reconstruct elaborate stories from this old handiwork. He would know which stone-bounded areas had been for cattle to graze and which had been cornfields and hayfields and vegetable gardens, which stone walls had been designed to fence cows in, and which had simply served as a convenient way for the farmer to dispose of the rocks he'd dragged from his fields.

The ground began to level off, and then through the pines and saplings Calhoun saw the glint of sun on water and heard the musical gurgle of a small waterfall. The ruts were more distinct here, and he followed them to a sturdy old stone dam, which had survived half a century or more of spring floods and was still doing its job.

Off to the right, the stream twisted out of the woods and flattened into a long, skinny millpond. At the foot of the pond it poured over the top of the dam and then became a stream again. Above and below the pond, where the stream was a stream, it wasn't much bigger than Bitch Creek. But the pond itself held quite a bit of water. Cattails and reeds grew along its rim. It looked shallow and muddy along the edges, but Calhoun assumed that a deep channel, the original stream-bed, cut through the middle. The water was clear but stained a coppery color, tannin from the decades of leaves and bark that had settled on the pond's peaty bottom.

Calhoun kneeled and dipped his hand into the water above the dam. It was sixty degrees, maybe—certainly a good temperature for brook trout. Undoubtedly trout had always lived in the stream itself. Big ones would likely lurk in the deeper water of the millpond. Maybe Fred Green had been on to something.

He stood up, made a visor of his hand, and looked around. Now that he was here, he didn't know what he expected to find. The tire tracks in the mud by the dirt road convinced him that Lyle and Fred Green had been here. But now Lyle's Power Wagon was sitting behind the elementary school in South Riley.

On the other side of the dam, the old ruts continued over a long stretch of flat marshy land before climbing up a hill and disappearing into the woods. According to Lyle's map, a house perched on top of that hill—or, more likely, a cellar hole where a house had once stood. A lot of nineteenth-century farms had been abandoned by discouraged farmers whose sons had fled for factory work in the city. Many others had been leveled by the fire of '47. The Maine woods told stories of tragedy and failure and plain old loss of will.

Calhoun wondered if Lyle and Fred Green had caught anything. Gazing over the little millpond, he saw no evidence of trout—no rings of surface-feeders, no swirls or darting shadows in the shallows.

But neon-colored damselflies and tan caddisflies skittered over the water, and Calhoun found himself slapping the blackflies that were eating the back of his neck and clouding around his head. The pond would breed plenty of insects and other trout food—big ugly nymphs, small baitfish, maybe crayfish and freshwater shrimp, leeches and scuds.

As he gazed over the pond, something in the reeds along the opposite bank caught his eye—a rounded, olive-brown hump in the water. A mossy rock, maybe. But to Calhoun's eye, it looked anomalous, not quite like something in nature. He stepped up onto the dam, raised himself on tiptoes, squinted at the shape, and from that angle something alongside the hump reflected in the sun.

He forced himself to look away. He shut his eyes, hoping that when he opened them again the hump in the water would not be there, or if it was, that it wouldn't look like a human body—that this was just his brain playing another dirty trick on his consciousness.

But when he looked again, the hump was still there, and it still looked like a dead man.

He crossed the dam, looked again, muttered, "Oh, shit," and started running. The ground was mucky and studded with grassy hummocks and potholes, and he fell down twice before he got to the edge of the pond.

He stopped there, ankle-deep in the water, dripping mud, breathing heavily, his feet sinking into the soft bottom. The hump he had seen was what he'd thought it was—a man's rear end dressed in waders. The glint had been the reflection of sunlight off the varnished surface of a bamboo fly rod that angled out of the water beside that

Lyle had liked to sing. He knew all the Beatles songs, and whenever they went out on a boat, he'd wail "Rocky Raccoon" or "A Day in the Life" over the roar of the outboard. "I'd love to turn you on," he'd bellow, grinning as if he knew he was about to get laid.

Calhoun remembered the time they'd met at four in the morning to catch a striper tide down toward the mouth of the Kennebec. About the time they'd launched the boat it had started raining, and then the wind turned so that the hard raindrops came at an angle, pelting their faces like birdshot. Lyle had smiled grandly, loving it. "Here comes the sun," he'd bellowed, "and it's all right."

A leech had attached itself to the side of Lyle's neck. Calhoun plucked it off and flicked it away. Lyle's skin felt like a trout's body, cold and rubbery, about the temperature of the pond water. It was, in fact, about the color of a trout's belly.

Calhoun pushed himself to his feet. "Be right back," he told Lyle. He sloshed back to where he'd found Lyle, picked up the Thomas & Thomas rod, and reeled in the line. There was no fly on the end of the tippet. Calhoun wondered if Lyle had been fighting a big fish when whatever happened to him had happened. Maybe some great brook trout had tangled in the reeds along shore and broken off.

And then Lyle had died.

It made no sense.

Calhoun disjointed the two-piece rod, carried it back to where he'd left Lyle, laid it gently on the ground, and then knelt beside him. "I fetched your rod," he told him.

He took off Lyle's vest, which bulged with fly boxes and all the other junk a fly-fishing guide had to carry. A big wool patch over the left breast of the vest was studded with a variety of flies, stuck there to dry after they'd been used. You could read the stories of dozens of fishing trips from the flies that were hooked in that wool patch. There were lifelike crayfish imitations for smallmouths and fancy Atlantic salmon flies that resembled nothing in nature, big flashy pickerel flies and tiny drab trout flies. Some of them were bedraggled from being chewed by fish. Some had been tried briefly, without success, then retired.

Calhoun shook his head, remembering all the fishing trips he'd shared with Lyle, the stories that hid in that random assortment of flies stuck into that wool patch.

He slipped the fins off Lyle's feet, pulled the deflated float tube down off his legs, then peeled off his waders, which were half-full of pond water.

He wrestled Lyle's body up onto his shoulders in a fireman's carry and headed back to the road.

Lyle was tall and skinny—all bone and sinew. Calhoun was nearly six inches shorter, but he weighed more, and it was all wood-splitting, canoe-paddling muscle; the first couple hundred yards went easy. But then he began to climb the brushy old tote road, and about halfway up the long slope he ran out of adrenaline and began to stumble. "Gotta take a break, bud," he mumbled to Lyle as he went down on his knees and rolled the body onto the ground.

He sat beside Lyle, taking deep breaths and looking at his friend's swollen face.

He hadn't done much thinking since he'd seen Lyle's ass sticking up in the reeds. He hadn't tried to imagine what could have happened, how Lyle could have drowned in a shallow little millpond, how his float tube could deflate so quickly that he couldn't get to shore.

Maybe he'd been playing a big trout, trying to follow it around the little pond, and his feet had sunk into the bottom and slowly sucked him down. Those peaty bottoms were like quicksand. You often encountered it in beaver ponds, and the harder you fought it, the quicker you sank. If you panicked, you went down fast, even wearing swim fins on your feet.

But Calhoun had never seen Lyle panic. The boy had certainly played plenty of big fish, and he was cool in any crisis. One frigid December morning when they'd been hunting sea ducks out on Casco

Bay before daybreak, a sudden squall had blown in off the ocean. In the darkness, and in the heavy driving snow, they couldn't see each other from one end of the duck boat to the other. The tide was running hard and the seas were heavy in the wind, and it was so cold that the snow and the salt spray froze instantly on their hats and jackets. If Calhoun had been navigating, they'd have ended up in Africa, if they didn't freeze to death or capsize first.

Lyle had calmly brought them directly to the dock, singing the entire *Revolver* album over the roar of the wind and the throb of the outboard.

Lyle had found himself stuck in peaty pond bottoms before. He'd been in tighter situations than that. It was hard to imagine that he'd ever panic.

Anyway, Lyle hadn't been stuck in the mud when Calhoun found him.

What the hell had Fred Green been doing when Lyle got in trouble?

Calhoun knew he wasn't thinking clearly. He tried to slow down his brain, sort out the facts, make some kind of sense out of it.

Lyle and Green had driven here in the Power Wagon. They'd parked near where Calhoun's pickup was now parked, unloaded their gear, and trekked into the pond together. Lyle had finned out onto the pond in his float tube. Maybe Green had, too. Or maybe the old man had started casting from the dam. Then Lyle's tube suddenly deflated. Lyle had struggled toward shore, begun to sink. His waders started filling with water.

He'd yelled for help.

He hadn't received it.

Reconstruct it, Calhoun told himself. Okay. So Green had been unable—or unwilling to try—to help Lyle. When he realized what was happening, he panicked. He walked out of the woods, got into Lyle's truck, and drove to the place where they'd left the rented Taurus— behind the elementary school, apparently, although it was a damned strange place for Lyle to leave a car.

Then Green had swapped cars, leaving the keys in the Power Wagon's ignition, and driven off in his Taurus. He did not go for help or report what had happened. He just . . . drove off.

Well, as far as Calhoun had been able to determine, Fred Green was not the man's name. That single fact raised questions about everything.

It was too much to think about just then. He hoisted Lyle back up on his shoulders and resumed his trek out of the woods.

He was about to take another break when he saw the glint of sunlight off the windshield of his truck. So he staggered the last thirty yards and collapsed in the weeds beside the road. He lay on his back gasping for breath with Lyle on his stomach beside him. Even after his heartbeat had slowed to normal, Calhoun continued lying there with his eyes closed, thinking about Lyle . . . the Beatles songs he bellowed in the rain . . . the stories he created from the gravestone legends in old family plots deep in the woods . . . the way he blushed whenever Calhoun asked him about living in a big old house with a flock of pretty young female roommates running around in their underwear . . . the July afternoon Lyle had appeared at his door lugging a cardboard box that turned out to have an eight-week-old Brittany puppy in it . . . the stormy March night they'd been tying flies and listening to Beethoven's *Pastoral Symphony* at Calhoun's house, when Lyle had talked Calhoun into smoking marijuana—said you could really dig Beethoven when you were stoned—and an hour later, when they'd turned up the volume as high as it would go and Calhoun was using the tip section of a fly rod to conduct the grand choral finale, Kate had showed up wearing a little black skirt and fishnet stockings . . .

"Hey, mister? You okay?"

Calhoun's eyes snapped open. A lanky, gray-haired woman was standing there with her hands on her hips, frowning down at him. She was wearing sneakers and baggy jeans and a flannel shirt with the tails flapping. A blue bandanna held her hair in place.

"My friend," said Calhoun. "He's—"

"Dear Lord," she said, peering down at Lyle's body. "He's dead, ain't he?"

Calhoun nodded.

"Don't mind me sayin' so," the woman said, "you look half dead yourself."

"I just lugged him out."

She shook her head and blew out a long breath. "What happened?"

"I guess he drowned."

"Ayuh, I'd say he did, by the looks of him." She arched her eyebrows, inviting him to elaborate.

"It's a long story, ma'am," he said.

"Well, you best save it for the sheriff. You sit tight, I'll go call. I live just down the road a piece."

"Trust me," said Calhoun. "I'm not going anywhere."

CHAPTER TEN

CALHOUN PROPPED HIMSELF UP ON HIS ELBOWS and watched the woman stride back to a ragtop Jeep Wrangler. From behind she looked like a man, raw-boned and narrow-hipped. She climbed in, glanced back at him, held up one finger, then drove off.

He lay back and closed his eyes again. Fred Green's face popped into his head. Calhoun held it there so he could study it. Nice even teeth—capped, probably, or maybe expensive dentures—face deeply tanned, pale eyes with deep squint wrinkles at the corners, wire-rimmed glasses hooked around big, protruding ears, white hair to match his teeth. He scanned the rest of the man's picture—green polo shirt buttoned to the throat, creased chino Dockers, shiny oxblood loafers, manicured nails, tanned and liver-spotted hands, no wedding ring on his finger, gold Rolex on his left wrist.

From Key Largo, Green had said.

He'd been fishing all over the world, he'd bragged, and Calhoun was inclined to believe that. Yet Green claimed he'd never caught a native brook trout. Looking back on it, that seemed like a stretch. Native brookies weren't as plentiful as they'd been a hundred years ago, for sure, but they weren't exactly an endangered species. Any serious world-traveling fly fisherman would surely try for the monster brookies that still ate big mayflies and small rodents off the surfaces of wilderness lakes in Labrador and brawling rivers in Quebec, never mind the little survivors that still reproduced in the headwaters of the legendary Catskill trout streams like the Beaverkill and the Willowemoc and the Neversink.

If you were a big-time angler like Fred Green claimed to be, you probably wouldn't choose a little rag-tag fly shop in Portland, Maine, to fix you up with a guide for the first native brook trout of your life.

Well, the man had apparently lied about his name. Who knew what else he had lied about.

Calhoun heard the Wrangler chugging back down the road, recognized its distinctive engine noises.

A minute later the woman was crouching beside him. "Called the sheriff," she said. "He said to sit tight, wait for him, don't touch anything. Here. I brought you a beer."

Calhoun shielded his eyes with his hand. She was holding a can of Coors.

"Appreciate it," he said. "I can't take alcohol."

She rolled her eyes, then nodded. "Stupid me," she said. "I should've asked. I know plenty of folks got that problem."

I'm not an alcoholic, he wanted to say. It's a physical thing. Because my brain chemistry got messed up. "One day at a time," was what he actually said, because it was easier. "Thanks anyway, though."

"I've got a jug of water in the car."

"That would be terrific."

She came back with a dewy plastic one-gallon milk container of water, and Calhoun drank nearly half of it before he lowered it. He wiped his mouth with his wrist. "That hit the spot."

"Hard work," the woman said, "lugging a big fella like that one out of the woods. Where'd you find him?"

"He was fishing in the pond back there. When he didn't come home, I went looking for him."

She made a hard line with her lips. "Damn shame," she muttered. Then she cocked her head. "Listen, I'm Anna Ross. My husband and I, we've got that property across the road." She jerked her chin over her shoulder, and through the trees Calhoun saw a white farmhouse up on a knoll perhaps fifty yards down the road on the opposite side.

She held out her hand, and he grasped it. "Calhoun," he said. "Stoney Calhoun. I've got a place in Dublin. This is Lyle McMahan. Friend of mine. My best friend, I guess you could say."

She nodded. "How the hell did he drown in that little millpond?"

"I don't know."

She sat on the ground beside him, hugged her knees, and squinted up at the sky.

"I appreciate all your help," said Calhoun after a minute. "I'm okay. You probably have things to do."

She laughed quickly. "Nossuh. Nothin' at all. Figure I'll hang around, if it don't bother you. Maybe I can help when the sheriff gets here."

"It doesn't bother me," said Calhoun. "Glad for the company."

Anna Ross told him how David—her husband—had grown up on the old farm where they now lived. She was from Kittery originally. Met David at Old Orchard Beach in the summer of 1953 when she was eighteen and he was twenty, got married a year later. They had two kids, one of each, all grown up now, the girl living in Oregon, the boy in Michigan. Four grandchildren who they hardly ever saw.

David was the local jack-of-all-trades, she said with what Calhoun took to be great pride. Every small town in Maine had a David Ross—a man with a barn full of tools and vehicles and spare parts, always on call to plow your driveway, get your balky well pumps working, patch your leaky roofs, jump-start your tractors and trucks, shut down your vacation homes in the fall and open 'em up in the spring. Still at it, Anna said, though the old goat was over seventy.

Couldn't seem to stop. Nobody else to do it, and too many people depended on him.

She didn't seem curious about Calhoun's life story, and since he had no interest in volunteering it, Anna Ross chattered on. A family named Potter had lived up there—she jerked her chin back toward the woods in the direction of the millpond where he'd found Lyle. Mr. Potter had died in the fire of '47. David had been a teenager on that day in October. Stayed home from school to protect his family's farm. It was just David and his mother. He'd lost his father a year or so before. They'd wondered if the Potters were okay. But David and his mum had their hands full, hosing down the house and making sure the livestock were safe, and it wasn't until a few days after the fire had burned its way east, leaving a big swath of blackened forest and empty cellar holes in its wake, that anybody bothered to check the Potter place.

They'd found Mr. Sam Potter lying on the ground next to what was left of his house, a charred body just resting there as if he'd been laid out.

Sam Potter was the only person from these parts who didn't survive the fire, Anna Ross said. Odd thing was, he'd opened all the gates and let their horses and pigs and chickens loose so they wouldn't get caught in the fire. Sam, he knew it was coming right at him, but he still couldn't get away. It came that fast.

David still talked about that day, she said, and it had happened over fifty years ago. All the old folks who'd been alive in '47 talked about that fire. Anna herself was going to school down in Kittery at the time. The fire didn't get that far south, but she'd heard about it on the radio. Of course, she didn't know David in '47, so she didn't have anyone to worry about. Even so, it was a scary time.

She tapped Calhoun's arm. "Appears to me that place is spooked," she said. "I mean, the ghost of that poor dead man flyin' around the woods, and now your friend drowning in that little millpond." She frowned at him. "You believe in ghosts, Mr. Calhoun?"

"Maybe." He thought of the people he'd known before the hospital. They were ghosts to him now, flitting presences that appeared and disappeared in his thoughts, too elusive to pin down and identify, but real, nevertheless. And there were the visions that appeared unannounced, like the naked body with the flowing hair in Bitch Creek. Not to mention the real ghosts, like Lyle.

Anna Ross plucked a blade of grass from the ground beside her and clamped it between her front teeth. She peered up at the sky. "I've seen 'em," she said quietly.

A minute later a green Explorer skidded to a stop in the dusty road and Sheriff Dickman stepped out. He left the door open and the engine running and strode over to where Calhoun and Anna Ross were sitting. He took off his Stetson, tapped it against his leg, and nodded at them. "Stoney," he said. "Miz Ross." He shifted his gaze to Lyle McMahan's body lying prone beside them and shook his head. "Goddam," he muttered. He scootched down beside them. "You better tell me about it."

Calhoun told Dickman how he'd figured out where Lyle had taken Fred Green fishing by studying the map in the gazetteer that Lyle kept under the front seat of his Power Wagon, how he'd found his body facedown in the millpond wearing his deflated float tube, how he'd lugged Lyle out, and how Mrs. Ross had happened along and made the phone call.

"That's it?" said Dickman.

Calhoun nodded.

"So how do you figure it?"

"The bottom of that pond is all peaty," said Calhoun, "and you know how that stuff sucks you down so that the harder you try to pull loose, the stucker you get."

"Except he wasn't stuck in the mud when you found him."

Calhoun shrugged. "Nope.

"You said he had a client with him."

"Yes," said Calhoun. "That Fred Green."

"Well . . ."

Calhoun nodded. "I know. Where the hell was he?"

"You should've left the body right where you found it, you know," said Dickman.

"Not likely," said Calhoun. "Not Lyle."

The sheriff held Calhoun's eyes for a moment, then nodded. He went over and knelt beside Lyle. He laid the back of his hand on the dead boy's cheek, put his forefinger in Lyle's mouth, moved his fingers through Lyle's hair, pushed on his chest. Then he looked up and narrowed his eyes at Calhoun. "Well, I'd say he drowned, all right. But it's not up to me. We'll have a proper post mortem done on him."

"What're you thinking?" said Calhoun.

Dickman shrugged. "I'm thinking that this is a big strapping young man who knew his way around woods and water. I'm thinking, that he wasn't alone when this happened."

Calhoun nodded. "Mr. Green must've driven Lyle's Power Wagon to South Riley."

Dickman nodded. "It's curious, all right." He cocked his head, then stood up, and a minute later an ambulance pulled up behind the Explorer.

Two EMTs jumped out. Dickman went over to speak to them. One of them came over, knelt beside Lyle for a couple of minutes, then looked up at Calhoun and Anna Ross. "Well, he's been dead for some time, looks like." He stood up. "Bring the bag, Will," he called to his partner.

The two of them zipped Lyle into a black plastic bag, loaded him onto a gurney, and wheeled him to the ambulance with the casual efficiency of men who'd done it many times. After the two of them climbed back into the ambulance, Sheriff Dickman talked with the driver through the window.

The ambulance pulled away and Dickman came back. "They're taking him to Maine Medical in Portland," he said to Calhoun. He wedged his Stetson back onto his bald head, touched the brim, and made a small bow at Anna Ross. "Ma'am. Thank you for your help."

"Any time," she said.

Dickman put his arm around Calhoun's shoulders and steered him toward his wagon. "Stoney," he said quietly, "I want to talk to that Mr. Green."

"So do I. I called all the motels and inns, and nobody heard of him."

"You did that?"

"I did."

"He was driving a rented Ford Taurus, you said."

Calhoun nodded. "White sedan. I tried all the car rental places, too."

"Well, we'll keep an eye out for it." Dickman slid into his wagon and closed the door. "I'll be in touch," he said. Then he pulled away.

Calhoun stood there, watching the Explorer disappear around the bend in the road.

When he turned, Anna Ross was standing beside him. "Wish I could do something," she said.

"I'd be grateful if I could use your phone," said Calhoun. "I need to call Portland."

"Sure thing," she said. "Follow me."

He got into his truck, followed Anna's Wrangler up a curving gravel driveway to the pretty white farmhouse he'd seen from the road, and pulled to a stop next to a big barn.

When he got out of his truck and slammed the door, a man stepped out of the barn. He wore scuffed work boots and baggy overalls over a sleeveless undershirt. He held a big Stilson wrench in his left hand and the stub of a cigar in his teeth. He was short and wiry almost to the point of being scrawny, with a deeply creased face that made him look at least as old as he was. Tufts of yellowish-white hair poked out from under his John Deere cap. White stubble on his chin and cheeks, a couple of missing teeth, friendly brown eyes.

Anna slid out of her Wrangler. "Mr. Calhoun," she said, "this here is my husband, David."

David Ross came over, wiped his hand on his leg, and held it out. "You're the fella who found that body, huh?"

Calhoun shook his hand. "I did. He was my friend."

"Damned sorry to hear it," said Ross. He kept flexing his arm, holding the heavy wrench in his hand, as if he were exercising his skinny bicep. "Over to the Potter place, was it?"

Calhoun nodded. "He drowned in the millpond. Fishing."

"Fishin'," Ross repeated. "Never heard of anyone fishin' there."

"Lyle was a guide. A damned good one."

"And he drowned, huh?"

"Looks like it."

"Fishin' guide ought to know better than to drown himself."

Calhoun shrugged. "Your wife said I could use your telephone."

"I don't mind," said Ross. "You help yourself. Tell Anna to give you a beer."

"She already offered. Thank you."

Ross nodded, then turned and went back into the barn.

Anna took Calhoun's arm and led him to the back door of the farmhouse. "Don't mind David," she said. "He likes to act crabby by way of makin' up for the fact that he's really a kind and gentle old poop."

Calhoun smiled. "He seemed fine to me."

Anna's kitchen smelled of rosemary. She pointed to the wall phone, then left the room.

Calhoun dialed the shop, and when Kate picked up, he said, "I found Lyle. There's no easy way to say this. He's dead."

She was silent for so long that Calhoun said, "You there, honey?"

"I'm here," she said. "What happened?"

"He drowned, looks like."

"What about Fred Green?"

"Good question. Mr. Green has gone missing, and it doesn't make sense for Lyle to drown." He let out a long breath. "I lugged Lyle out, Kate, and the sheriff came and they loaded him into an ambulance."

"Jesus, Stoney."

"Kate, listen," he said. "I need to be with you. I've never asked you before, because we agreed I wouldn't, but I'm asking you now. I really need to see you tonight."

"You didn't need to ask, Stoney. I would've come anyway."

"I guess I figured you would. But I needed to know it. It'll keep me going, knowing you'll be there. Not hoping, but knowing. You understand?"

"Of course I do. Where are you now?"

"Just down the road from where I found Lyle. These nice folks let me use their phone. Listen, honey. Can you find that number for Lyle's girlfriend, that Penny Moulton? I copied it on the calendar on your desk."

"I'm out front right now. Hang on."

She came back a minute later and read the number to him. "What're you going to do?" she said.

"Somebody's got to tell Lyle's friends and kin what happened. I guess it might as well be me."

Penny Moulton's number in Standish rang about a dozen times, and Calhoun was ready to hang up when she picked up and said breathlessly, "Yes? Hello?"

"It's Stoney Calhoun again, Miz Moulton. I talked to you yesterday?"

"Oh, yes. Lyle's friend. What—?"

"I'm in the neighborhood," he said. "Wonder if you'd mind if I dropped by."

She was silent for a moment. Then she said, "Something's happened, hasn't it?"

"I'm afraid so."

"Is he . . .?"

"Lyle's dead. I'm sorry."

"He's . . ." She blew out a long breath. "Well, Mr. Calhoun, you don't beat around the bush, do you?" She hesitated. "I knew it was something terrible. Lyle always shows up when he says he will. I knew it all the time. . . . I *knew* it." She was silent for a moment. "What happened?" she said.

"Maybe it'd be better if we talked in person," he said.

"Sure. Okay." Calhoun heard her sob. Then she cleared her throat. "Where are you coming from?"

"From Dublin. Tell me how to find you."

She lived on the first floor of a rented house in the village of Standish. Calhoun didn't even need to write down her directions. When she gave them, he sketched a picture of her place in his head. He'd been to Standish before.

"I'll be there in about half an hour," he said, "if that's okay."

"I'll be right here, Mr. Calhoun."

CHAPTER ELEVEN

ANNA ROSS GAVE HIM A COKE and walked him out to the truck. He opened the door, then turned to her. "Thank you, ma'am. I appreciate everything."

She smiled and patted his shoulder. "If there's anything else, don't you hesitate."

"Tell your husband good-bye for me."

"I'll do that."

He climbed in behind the wheel, started it up, drove down the curving driveway, and headed for home. He found a rock station on the radio and played it loud, trying to concentrate on the lyrics, trying not to think about Lyle, but he didn't have much luck at it.

When he pulled into the yard, Ralph came bounding down off the deck and jumped against the door. Calhoun opened it, and the dog scrambled in over his lap and sat on the seat beside him. Calhoun put an arm around his neck and pulled him over, and Ralph licked his face.

"Lyle's dead, bud," Calhoun told him.

Ralph looked into Calhoun's eyes, gave his cheek one final lick, then curled up on the seat with his chin resting on Calhoun's leg. There were times when he knew damn well that the dog understood what he was saying and even what he was thinking.

It took about twenty minutes to find Penny Moulton's little white clapboard bungalow on the outskirts of the village of Standish. Her mailbox was decorated with a fancy painting of a wood duck, and a newish red Saab sat in the driveway—an unusual car for rural Maine, with its endless winters and prolonged mud seasons, where most folks, regardless of their taste in automobiles, bowed to the necessity of four-wheel drive.

He pulled in behind the Saab, shut off the ignition, and turned to Ralph. "You sit tight," he said. "I shouldn't be too long."

He climbed the front steps and rang the bell.

A minute later the door opened. "You're Mr. Calhoun?" she said.

She was cute in a short, chubby sort of way, with a helmet of tight blond curls, a round face, a stubby little nose, and a small, pouty mouth. Behind her glasses, her grayish eyes were red and swollen.

"Yes, ma'am," said Calhoun.

She pushed open the screen door. "Well, come on in, then. I've got some coffee on." She was wearing tight-fitting blue jeans, a green flannel shirt knotted over her belly, and her feet were bare. She led him into a living room of glass and chrome and pale oak furniture. It was dominated by an incongruous six-point whitetail's head, which gazed balefully down from the wall above the brick fireplace. "Have a seat," she said. "How do you take it?"

"Huh?"

"Your coffee. Black, I bet."

"Milk, no sugar, actually," he said. "I got used to having milk in it because my dog prefers it that way."

She gave him a quick puzzled smile, then left the room.

Calhoun sat on the sofa. Current issues of *Field & Stream*, *Shooting Sportsman*, and *American Angler* were scattered on the glass-topped coffee table, and in the corner bookcase he noticed titles by

Jack O'Connor, Robert Ruark, Ray Bergman, Nick Lyons, Sparse Grey Hackle, Roderick Haig-Brown—

"Here you go." Penny Moulton, in her bare feet, had padded up behind his deaf left side. She handed a mug to Calhoun. "Hope I got the milk right."

"I'm not fussy," said Calhoun.

She sat on the sofa beside him. "I've been crying ever since you called. Tell me what happened, please."

He sipped his coffee, then put the mug down and recounted his discovery of Lyle's body in the millpond. "I guess Lyle drowned," he said. "It appears that his float tube sprang a leak and he got stuck in the peaty bottom, couldn't get out."

She shook her head. "That makes no sense, Mr. Calhoun. I've been fishing and hunting with Lyle. He wouldn't drown in some little millpond. If he got stuck in the mud, he'd just slip out of his waders and swim away."

Up close, Penny Moulton looked older—thirty, minimum, a few years older than Lyle. She had the beginnings of crow's feet at the corners of her eyes, as if she'd spent a lot of time squinting into sunrises.

"I thought of that," said Calhoun. "And he wasn't stuck in the mud when I found him. But I can't figure anything else."

"He was with a client, wasn't he?"

"Yes."

"Did you talk to him?"

"The client? Not yet."

"Why not?"

"We can't find him."

She frowned. "I don't get it. You mean Lyle was fishing with a client, and he drowned, and that client didn't stick around?"

"That's how it looks, miss."

"And you don't find that peculiar?"

"I find it very peculiar," he said. "Didn't you tell me Lyle called you before . . ."

"Before he died," she finished. "Yes, he did. Twice, as a matter of fact. Once to tell me he had a guide trip over in this neck of the woods, would I like to make dinner for him when he was done. Which, of course, I said I would, because I could never say no to Lyle McMahan regardless of how long it might've been since I'd heard from him. Then he called again a couple hours later when I was at work, just saying he wouldn't be late, that we could plan to eat around eight and he figured he'd be over in time to have a beer or two beforehand. Lyle was considerate that way. Making sure the food would be ready when he was ready to eat it, you know?"

Calhoun smiled. "Where was he calling from, did he say?"

"First time he said he was home. Second time he and his client were dropping off one of the cars and there was a pay phone right there." She hesitated, gave Calhoun a sad smile, then shook her head. "So Lyle, being all sweet the way he could be, decided to get me to thinking about him. Which, of course, I did." She took off her glasses and rubbed her eyes. "I scarcely believe this, Mr. Calhoun. I've got to tell you. Lyle McMahan had a lot of girlfriends, I always knew that. I was just one of them, and I might've wished I was the only one, but I knew I wasn't. I could live with that. There aren't that many sweet, cute guys in this part of the world who are also smart and funny like Lyle. Know what I mean?"

Calhoun nodded. "Did Lyle mention anything about where he was headed, or anything about his client, when he talked to you?"

She cleaned her glasses on her shirt. Then she fitted them back on her face and poked them up onto the bridge of her nose with her forefinger. "He sounded pretty enthusiastic," she said. "I mean, Lyle was an enthusiastic man. He could get all bubbly, start dancing around if he spotted an osprey or a mink or something, and I loved that about him. His client was interested in local history, he said, and you know how

Lyle grooved on that stuff. Probably talked the poor man's ear off. They were setting out on what he liked to call an *ex*-plore. They were looking for some trout pond that Lyle had never been to, but it was almost as if the fishing wasn't even important."

"How so?" said Calhoun.

She shrugged. "Just the way he mentioned this client's interest in history, I guess. Nothing really specific."

Calhoun nodded and took a sip of his coffee. "How did you meet Lyle?"

"A mutual friend introduced us. A lady who knows I like to hunt and fish, said she knew a guy who'd appreciate a woman who could shoot a rifle and cast a fly." She shook her head. "Funny thing is, we hardly ever went hunting or fishing. The truth is, Lyle loved screwing even more than shooting and fly casting." She cocked her head and looked at him. "Oh, sorry. Did I shock you, Mr. Calhoun?"

He shrugged. "A little. Not about Lyle. But you saying it that way."

She folded her hands in her lap. "Sorry."

"So did you shoot that buck?" He pointed up at the mounted deer head over the fireplace.

"I sure did. Neck shot from about seventy yards. Dropped him in his tracks. Helluva shot, if I do say so. That was two seasons ago, up near Greenville, which is where I grew up. Lyle and I had that in common. Growing up in the woods around here, prowling around with rods and guns as soon as we could walk." She blinked away the tears that had welled up in her eyes. "Damn. I did love him, Mr. Calhoun."

"So did I." Calhoun pushed himself up from the sofa. "Well, I just wanted to tell you about it in person. Thought maybe you'd know how I could get ahold of his family."

She stood up. "Far as I know, he doesn't have any. What he told me, his folks both died, and he was an only child. He might have cousins or something, but I don't know about that."

Calhoun nodded and turned for the door. She followed him, and when he opened it she put her hand on his arm. "You don't really think he just panicked, got stuck in the mud and drowned, do you?"

"Knowing Lyle, it doesn't make much sense," he said. "But that's sure how it looks."

"It doesn't make any sense at all," she said.

She walked barefoot to the truck with him, and when she saw Ralph sitting there on the front seat, she said, "Oh, a Brittany. I love Brittanies. What's his name?"

"Ralph Waldo. I call him Ralph."

"An independent critter, I bet."

"A regular transcendentalist."

She poked her hand in through the cracked-open window, and Ralph obligingly licked it.

Calhoun slid in behind the wheel and rolled his window down. Penny Moulton came around to his side. She reached in and touched his arm. "Thank you," she said. "It was very kind of you to come talk to me."

He nodded. "Sure." He turned the key in the ignition and she stepped back from the truck. He threw it into reverse, then hesitated. "Ah, Penny?"

"Yes, Mr. Calhoun?"

"When Lyle called you? That second time? He was at a pay phone, you said."

She nodded.

"Said it was right there where they were leaving one of their vehicles?"

"Un-huh." She frowned. "Yes. That's right. Why?"

He shrugged. "Probably nothing. Look—you take care of yourself." He lifted his hand, then backed out of her driveway.

As he pulled away, he glanced back. Penny Moulton was standing there in the driveway, hugging herself as if she were cold, although in fact it was coming to the end of a long, hot, muggy June day in Maine.

Back in the village of Standish, he pulled to the side at the crossroads. A left turn would take him to Portland, where he might drop into the shop and see Kate. He needed to see Kate badly. She was coming over tonight, she'd promised him that. But he wasn't sure he could wait. The left would also take him to Lyle's house in South Portland, where he would have to break the news to the housemates sooner or later.

Straight across the crossroads hooked him onto the road back to Dublin. He wouldn't mind spending an hour sitting on the slab of granite beside Bitch Creek with Ralph beside him peering at the trout, which should start rising as soon as the sun was off the water. Drink a cold Coke, watch the mayflies, calculate how he might catch those trout if he ever wanted to actually try it, and do some thinking.

It didn't make any sense, Penny Moulton had said. She was right. Lyle was too damned resourceful to drown in a little millpond, no matter how peaty the bottom was.

He shut his eyes and conjured up the picture of the parking lot behind the South Riley Elementary School. He didn't understand how it worked—hell, there were big chunks of his life he couldn't remember at all, and most of the rest of it was all blurry—but he'd found that he could re-create mind-pictures of events since the hospital as sharp and detailed as photographs, and he was able to hold them there in his mind's eye so he could study them. Now he saw each of the cars parked behind the school, remembered their colors and makes and models, the new ones and the older ones, with Lyle's big old Dodge Power Wagon off to the side, nosed up to the playground. He saw the swing sets and the seesaws and the jungle bars, the earth under them worn bare from years of elementary-school sneakers. He saw the back of the school, many of the windows hung with penmanship samples and big colorful fingerpaintings.

He scanned the vivid mental picture, moving his eyes slowly over the details. He saw no pay phone anywhere.

He took the right at the crossroads and headed for South Riley.

The parking lot was almost empty. Lyle's truck was still there. An old Toyota pickup and a newish Ford Bronco were the only other vehicles. School was out and all the teachers had left for the day.

He got out and held the door for Ralph, who sauntered over to the Bronco and lifted his leg against the right rear tire.

Calhoun turned around slowly, comparing the actual place with his mental snapshot of it.

No pay phone.

Ralph had wandered over to the swing set, another prime leg-lifting spot. Calhoun whistled, and Ralph swiveled his head around, shrugged in that I'm-only-obeying-because-I-feel-like-it way of his, and trotted over.

Calhoun turned back to his truck.

"You come for that vehicle, mister?"

He turned and saw Miss Russo, the janitor, standing there with her hands on her hips.

"No," he said. "The sheriff will be coming for it. Actually, I was wondering if there's a pay phone nearby?"

"You gotta go back to town," she said, jerking her head in a souther-ly direction. "Couple miles down the road on the left-hand side, you'll come to Harry Bogan's garage. They got one inside, though they're probably closed by now, come to think of it."

"I meant here," he said. "Maybe inside the school building."

"If it's an emergency, I can let you use the phone in the office."

"But no pay phone?"

"No, but it's no problem, mister, provided it's a local call. I can't let you make a toll call. You understand."

He smiled. "That's all right. Thanks anyway. I guess no one's come around looking at the Power Wagon, huh?"

"Just you," she said.

"Well, it'll be gone soon." He whistled again to Ralph, who was snuffling along the edge of the woods beyond the parking lot. Ralph came trotting over, and Calhoun opened the truck door so he could hop in.

He turned to Miss Russo. "Thanks again, ma'am," he said. Then he got in beside Ralph, started up the engine, and headed back to Dublin.

"Okay," he said to Ralph as he drove. "Help me out here. If Lyle called Penny Moulton from a pay phone, and if the phone was right there where he was leaving that rented Taurus so he and Mr. Fred Green could take the Power Wagon over the back roads, then if I'm not completely crazy, which is certainly subject to debate, it means they did *not* leave the Taurus behind the school, since there's no pay phone there. Which confuses the hell out of me, Ralph, because I can't figure how Mr. Green managed to get Lyle's truck behind the school if his Taurus was somewhere else. You see my problem?"

Ralph just sat there with his nose pressed up to the windshield, offering no help at all.

CHAPTER TWELVE

AFTER HE GOT HOME, Calhoun fed Ralph and then they went out to sit on the deck. He listened to Bitch Creek burble over the pebbly streambottom and around the rocks. The breeze sighed in the pines. A barred owl hooted from somewhere in the distance as darkness descended.

He rocked and drank Coke and gazed up at the night sky and thought about Lyle and tried not to think about Kate.

She'd get there when she got there, and thinking about it wouldn't bring her there any faster.

When he checked the time, it was almost midnight.

If something had come up and she couldn't make it, she'd call.

But if something happened to her, nobody would know enough to call him.

She was right. It was better when he didn't know she was coming, when she surprised him. He couldn't worry about her that way.

Lyle was dead, and it made Calhoun realize that you couldn't depend on anything. If Lyle could die, anything could happen to anybody.

He had about decided to go inside and call Walter, find out what time Kate had left, when he saw the flash of headlights bobbing and jiggling down the driveway through the trees. Then he heard the grumble of her busted tailpipe.

He climbed down off the deck and stood beside his truck, and when the headlights appeared in front of him he stepped aside so she could pull in.

He went around to the door of her Blazer and opened it. She stepped out, clamped her arms around his neck, and pressed herself against him. She tucked her face into the crook of his neck, and he felt her shuddering. He held her, stroking her back and shoulders, smoothing her hair against the back of her head, touching her face, feeling the tears well up in his own eyes.

After a minute she stepped away from him and looked into his face. "Please, Stoney," she said. "I don't want to talk."

He knuckled the tears off her cheeks. "Suits me," he said.

She tried a smile, touched his face, moved her fingertips over his eyes, his nose, his lips. Then she moved against him again and brushed his mouth with hers. He held her face in both of his hands and kissed her softly.

They held it for a long moment. Then she broke it off. "Come on," she whispered, and she took his hand and led him directly to the bedroom.

The night after they'd talked to Walter five years ago, when they'd asked his permission to become lovers and he gave them his blessing, Calhoun had waited for Kate to come to him. But she didn't. He'd wanted to talk with her about it the next day at the shop, try to clarify their situation, but her body language told him not to say anything. This is separate, she was saying without words. At the shop, it's business. We don't mix the two things.

She hadn't come the next night, or the night after that, either. He'd kept expecting her, and she'd kept not showing up and then not saying anything about it at the shop the next day.

After a few miserable evenings of waiting and anticipating, he'd stopped expecting her.

Then, close to midnight almost two weeks later, he heard her Blazer pull into the yard. He'd wanted to run outside. But he didn't. He went over to his comfortable chair, sat down, and opened his anthology on his lap. When she came in, he looked up, said, "Oh, hi, Kate," marked his place in the book, and put it on the table beside him.

She'd stood there smiling at him, and he knew by that smile that she knew how he'd been expecting her and then gradually had decided it was better not to expect her, and that she'd intended it that way.

She went over, sat on his lap, snuggled there with a little satisfied sigh, and he'd held her for the first time ever. He cupped her face in both his hands and moved his fingertips over the planes of her forehead, the curves of her cheekbones, the edges of her ears, the outline of her lips, memorizing her face with his fingers. He traced her eyebrows with the balls of his thumbs as he looked into her eyes. They were solemn, gazing evenly back into his.

When she tucked her face into the hollow of his throat, he began to move his hands over her body, learning her bones and muscles through her soft cotton dress, running his hand over her hip, up along her side, brushing her breast, down over the back of her leg, then easing up the hem of her dress, stroking the soft secret skin along the back of her knee and over her thigh, and she kept her arms locked tight around his neck.

Finally she'd lifted her mouth to him, brushed his lips with hers, touched them with the tip of her tongue, and then a little "Oh!" came from deep in her throat and she'd pressed her mouth hard onto his, her butt wiggling in his lap, her arms tight around him, her tongue prodding and probing, her lips and teeth trying to consume him. It was the first time they'd kissed. Calhoun felt as if it was the first time he'd ever been kissed by a woman.

Then Kate had slipped off his lap. "Come on, Stoney." She held both hands to him.

He stood up and let her lead him into the bedroom. They'd undressed each other slowly, taking their time, laying aside the articles of clothing carefully, seeing each other's bodies for the first time. When they finally slithered under the covers, they just held onto each other, touching and caressing, not saying much, getting used to the feel of their bodies together.

When she touched the puckered skin of the scar on the back of his left shoulder, she said, "What's this?"

"Long story, honey."

"We got all night."

He'd rolled onto his back and stared up at the ceiling. "Thing is," he said slowly, "I don't know the whole story. That scar is where I got hit by lightning."

She was quiet for a moment. "You got hit by lightning?"

"Yes."

"That's so—so random."

"Actually," he said, "it's not that uncommon. They told me that about a thousand people in the United States get hit by lightning every year."

"Do they—I mean, are they all . . . like you?"

He laughed. "Like me? No, honey. Everybody's different. Depends on where they get hit, I guess. Some people end up chronically depressed, or have panic attacks. Some are paralyzed or have heart problems. Some lose their short-term memory. Some can't remember how to spell or multiply. Me, I guess I was lucky. I've just got these holes in my memory, can't hear anything out of my left ear, can't drink alcohol. That's why I spent eighteen damn months in a hospital. Because they needed to get my head working right again. It's still not working that well, as you know."

"I like the way it works," she said. She rolled him onto his side facing away from her, traced with her fingertips the jagged edges of the scar that ran from the top of his shoulder blade halfway down his back. Then she bent to him and touched his scar with her lips and her tongue. "I didn't know people could get hit by lightning and survive," she said.

"Actually, about ninety percent of them don't die. The guy I was with got me breathing and my heart beating again, carried me off the mountain."

"What was it like, Stoney?"

"I don't know. I don't remember anything about it. Oh, I get these little flashes in my head, especially when I hear thunder or smell the rain, but they come and go so quick I can't pin them down. I don't know what I was doing up there on a mountain, and I don't know who it was that saved my life. I kept asking at the hospital, but either they didn't know or they wouldn't tell me. There's a man out there somewhere, and I owe him, big-time."

When she'd asked him what he did remember, he tried to explain about the big holes in his mind, the odd clarities that came to him sometimes, the characters that flitted like ghosts into and out of his consciousness, people he'd once known whom he'd forgotten except when they dropped unexpectedly into his mind and who refused to stay around long enough to get reacquainted. He told her about his dreams, and how he knew they came out of what he thought of as his Life Before Memory, before ten thousand volts of electricity had zapped him on a mountain somewhere. He didn't mention the phantoms that came to him when he was awake, the naked bodies that appeared in rivers and in the woods when his eyes were open, how they seemed real even after they'd disappeared. He wasn't ready to tell her about them yet.

"You know Frankenstein," he'd said to Kate that first night in bed. "Well, that's how I feel. Like some kind of monster that got killed and then brought back to life with a big jolt of electricity."

"I don't think you're a monster," she said. "What about your family? Didn't they help you remember?"

"I guess I don't have a family," he said. "The folks at the hospital tried to fill me in. Told me some facts, which feel to me like they might as well've been about somebody else. Like somebody else's biography. My parents aren't alive. I know I grew up in Beaufort, South Carolina. I get flash-pictures of Beaufort sometimes. My mother's name was Libby—Elizabeth—and my father was Daniel. I had a wife, they told me, but she divorced me some time before I got zapped. Nobody came to see me at the hospital except doctors and shrinks, who were all pretty interested in my case, but not necessarily interested in me, if you know what I'm saying. I guess if I'd had any close family, they would've come to see me in eighteen months."

She had pushed him onto his back, slid a leg over his, and laid her cheek on his chest. "I feel bad for you, Stoney," she said.

"Don't feel sorry for me, honey. It's not so bad. The way I look at it, I've probably forgotten more bad stuff than good. Anyway, things keep coming back to me, and I'm getting some of it sorted out."

"Sure," she said. "I guess one day you'll probably wake up and suddenly remember there's a woman somewhere who you love."

He'd stroked her hair and urged her mouth down to his. They held a long kiss, and then he peered into her eyes in the darkness of the bedroom. "I'm awake right now," he'd said, "and I know exactly who that woman is and where she is and what she tastes like. And I know I'll never forget any of that."

And in the five years since that first night, he'd never doubted that Kate Balaban was the first true love of his life.

Shortly after sunrise, after a night when he didn't sleep much, thinking about Lyle, Calhoun was sitting on the rocks beside Bitch Creek with Kate and Ralph, drinking coffee and watching three nice trout sipping March Brown spinners in the pool below the washed-out bridge. The biggest of the three—Calhoun guessed he'd go close to fourteen inches—had set up in a tricky eddy against the opposite bank. "You watch close," he said to Kate. "See how he seems to be facing downstream? That's because the current's twisted around, bringing the food up to him. You try to stand downstream to cast to him, he'll see you. Problem is, if you stand upstream and cast down into that eddy, the main current'll drag your fly away from him. You need to make a quick mend in your line while it's still in the air, throw a lot of slack into your tippet, and lay that fly about a foot from his nose . . ."

He glanced at her. She was grinning at him.

"What?" he said. "What's so funny?"

"You love that, don't you?"

"Love what?"

"Problems. The harder they are, the better you like 'em. You'd ignore those two other trout there along the seam of the main current, because they'd be easy to catch. You'd just go for that tricky one."

"The point of fishing isn't catching 'em, honey."

She hooked her arm through his and leaned her head against his shoulder. "What is it, then?"

He shrugged. "Trying something you don't know if you can succeed at. Working at it till you get it."

"And suppose you don't get it?"

"That's good. That's what keeps you coming back."

"You're a strange man, Stonewall Jackson Calhoun," she said. She tilted up her face, and he kissed her softly.

Suddenly Ralph, who had been sitting there watching the fish, jerked himself to his feet, perked up his ears, looked back toward the house, and growled.

"Shut up," Calhoun said. He turned, shielded his eyes, and followed Ralph's gaze.

"I heard a car pulling in," said Kate.

Calhoun heard a door slam, and a moment later Sheriff Dickman appeared at the top of the slope. He waved and came down to them. "How they bitin'?" he said.

"They're pretty fussy this morning," said Calhoun. "You just dropping in for coffee?"

Dickman squatted down beside them. "Wish I was," he said. He looked at Kate, then back at Calhoun. "Afraid I've got some news."

"Lyle?" said Calhoun.

Dickman nodded. "Somebody shot him, Stoney."

"Oh, Jesus," said Kate. She groped for Calhoun's hand and gripped it hard.

"What happened?" said Calhoun.

"Well, of course, what happened is what we got to figure out, and I'm going to need some help with that." He took off his hat and ran his hand over his bald head, smoothing back his imaginary hair. "I convinced Doc Pritchard to come in last night, give us a quick autopsy. It didn't fit, drowning there in that little pond, big strong young man like that." Dickman poked himself in the solar plexus with his forefinger. "Had a hole in him right here. Perfect center shot. Doc dug a twenty-two long-rifle slug out of him."

"So he didn't drown," said Calhoun.

"Actually," said the sheriff, "he did drown. That little slug tumbled around in there, tore him up some, and there was a good deal of bleeding. It accounts for why he didn't get to shore. Poor bugger had to 've been in a lot of misery. But what killed him was drowning, all right."

"I carried him out of there," said Calhoun. "I didn't see any bullet hole."

Dickman shrugged. "A twenty-two makes a little hole less than a quarter of an inch in diameter. Not a hole you'd notice in a man's fishing shirt. I guess any blood would've been washed away in the pond."

Calhoun nodded. "Fred Green," he said.

"Guess so," said the sheriff. "We've got to find him, Stoney. The quicker the better. You're the only one who saw that man."

Calhoun stood up and helped Kate to her feet. "Let's go up to the house," he said.

The three of them sat at the kitchen table sipping coffee. "I need a good description of Mr. Green," said the sheriff.

Calhoun closed his eyes. "I can see him perfectly." He looked up at Kate. "Honey, reach behind you, hand me that pad of paper and a pencil."

She did, and Calhoun frowned for a minute, then began sketching. As he did, he talked. "Five foot nine or ten," he said. "I'd say about one-forty-five, one-fifty. Blue eyes. Pale, kinda washed-out, more gray than blue, actually. Wire-rimmed glasses. Big ears that stick straight out. Howdy-Doody ears. Like this." He drew Fred Green's ears, cocked his head, and nodded. "Little scar beside his left eyebrow, crescent-shaped, maybe half an inch long. Soft hands, liver spots. Tanned face, thinning white hair, widow's peak. Wrinkles here"—he was sketching Fred Green's face, filling in the details, watching it magically appear as the pencil moved over the paper—"and here, alongside his mouth. Perfect teeth. Capped, probably. If they're dentures, they're expensive ones. He was wearing casual clothes—short-sleeved cotton shirt, buttoned to the throat, chino pants with pleats in front, braided leather belt, shiny oxblood loafers—all new, clean, top-of-the-line. Gold Rolex on his left wrist. Manicured fingernails. Nicest fingernails I've ever seen on a man." He put down the pencil, cocked his head at the sketch he'd just drawn, then shrugged and turned it around for the sheriff. "That's him. That's how he looks."

Dickman glanced at it, then frowned at Calhoun. "Where'd you learn to do that?"

"Huh?"

"I didn't know you were a damn artist, Stoney."

Calhoun shrugged. "I'm not. This is just what I see in my head, that's all."

"I think that's what artists do," said the sheriff. "They make pictures of what they see in their heads. It's a gift."

"Well, I can't say anything about that. I wasn't thinking about it, Sheriff. I just did it. Saw it in my head and put it down there on the paper."

"This is a professional piece of work," said Dickman. "And all that detail you remembered. You've been trained for this, haven't you?"

"I don't know," Calhoun said. And as he said it, he had one of those quick memory-flickers—a dark classroom, others in the room, sitting in rows, a desk that was a little too small for him, a projection screen, photographs flashing on it one after the other, changing every few seconds, a dozen of them, maybe more, squinting at them, concentrating, forcing himself to remember them, to line them up in his head, to *see* those photographs . . .

Then the memory was gone. Calhoun shook his head. "I don't know how I did that, Sheriff. But that's him, all right. That's Mr. Fred Green who says he's from Key Largo, Florida, who was with Lyle when he got shot. That's exactly what he looks like."

The sheriff picked up the paper, then stood up. "I've got to fax this back to the office right away. Stoney, if you don't mind, I'd like you to come with me."

Calhoun nodded, then looked at Kate. "Can you handle the shop this morning, honey?"

She nodded. "We've got no guide trips booked. I'll be fine. You just keep me posted, okay?"

CHAPTER THIRTEEN

CALHOUN RODE SHOTGUN AND THE SHERIFF drove to Millie Dobson's house. He pulled into her driveway, parked beside her green Cherokee, and glanced at his watch. "It's not even eight yet. I need to use her fax. Suppose she's open for business?"

"Millie's always open for business," said Calhoun.

They climbed out of Dickman's Explorer, and Calhoun followed him up onto Millie Dobson's front porch. The sheriff rang the bell, and a minute later the door opened.

Millie was wearing a silky white blouse with several of the top buttons undone, a string of pearls around her neck, a narrow black skirt that stopped several inches above her knees, and stockinged feet with no shoes. She was trying to hook a big dangly earring into her left ear. "Uh-oh," she said when she saw the sheriff. "What'd I do now?"

"I don't know, Millie," he said. "Something, I'm damn sure of that. I could arrest you just for the way you're looking right now. But the fact is, it's that fax machine of yours I'm after today."

She glanced over Dickman's shoulder and caught Calhoun's eye. "You're keeping bad company, Stoney. Folks're gonna start talking."

"I expect they already are," he said.

She pushed open the screen door. "Well, come on in, then. Make it snappy. I've got people who want to buy a house coming by any minute, and I sure don't want a pair of derelicts like you two hanging around here scaring them off."

Dickman tipped his cap as he entered. "We'll be out from under your feet in no time, ma'am."

"Coffee's plugged in," she said. "Help yourself. I've got to finish dressing. Think you can work the machine by yourself?"

"I've done it once or twice before," said the sheriff.

She left the room, and Dickman found a piece of blank paper. "Now, Stoney," he said, "you tell me all those descriptors of Fred Green again, so I can write 'em down and send 'em to the office along with this portrait you drew for me."

Calhoun shut his eyes, conjured up his mind-picture of Green, and told the sheriff everything he saw, right down to the man's approximate shoe size.

"Okay," said the sheriff. "Now what about that car he was driving?"

"White Ford Taurus," he said. "Four doors. Maine plates. This year's model. A rental, I'd say."

"Why would you say that?"

Calhoun shrugged. "He was from away. Said Key Largo. Maybe, maybe not—but definitely not a Mainer. So that wouldn't be his car. Seems like all rental cars are new and white."

The sheriff smiled and shook his head. "You've got a cop's mind, Stoney."

"I've got a weird mind, is what I've got."

"Same difference, I guess."

Dickman ran the papers through the fax machine. Then he pulled out his wallet and laid a ten-dollar bill on Millie's desk. "We're done, Millie," he called in the direction of where she had disappeared to. "Thank you."

"Any time," came her reply. "You boys clear out quick, now. I don't want those nice people thinking I've got trouble with the law."

Back in the sheriff's Explorer, Calhoun said, "Now what?"

"Let's drop in on Jacob Barnes. Then I want to take a look at the place where you found Lyle."

As they drove, Dickman said, "Millie's an attractive lady, isn't she?"

Calhoun said, "You're not tempted, are you, Sheriff?"

Dickman laughed. "Not hardly. Jane and I've been married thirty-two years, and I can honestly say I haven't regretted a minute of it. No, I'm just saying it's kind of odd someone hasn't won her heart. She's got about everything a man could want—including plenty of money." He chuckled. "If Dublin had a mayor, no doubt she'd be it. Nobody'd dare vote against her. She knows everything about everybody, going back to their ancestors. Bet she gave you the entire history of that piece of land of yours."

Calhoun shrugged. "It used to belong to a family named Calhoun who got burned out in forty-seven, is all I know."

"Kinfolk of yours?"

Calhoun shrugged. "Guess not. I'm not from around here."

"Ask Millie sometime," said the sheriff. "She'll give you the whole story."

Five minutes later the sheriff pulled up beside the little mom-and-pop store across from the church at the crossroads. Calhoun followed him inside.

They found Jacob Barnes pouring water into the coffee machine in the back corner of the store. The old man either hadn't heard them come in or else had decided to ignore them, and he didn't turn until the sheriff said, "Morning, Jacob."

"Oh, mornin', there, Sheriff. Stoney, how you doin'?"

Calhoun nodded. "Not bad."

Barnes got the machine switched on, then gestured to the chairs that were gathered in a semicircle. "You boys come to make a purchase,

Calhoun loved to study topographic maps, to translate their legends into mental pictures and to read the stories they told, and like Lyle, he'd discovered a few secret ponds and trout streams in the middle of the winter by reading a topo map at his kitchen table.

Of course, he knew that there really wasn't a single truly secret pond or stream left in the entire state of Maine. After nearly four centuries of lumbering and farming and deer hunting and trout fishing, not a square foot of topography had been left unexplored, even in this state where thousands of acres that were owned by lumber companies still did not have names.

But there were some streams and ponds that were too small and inaccessible and unpromising for most people to bother with, even in the more populated southern part of the state. Calhoun assumed that Fred Green's secret pond was one of these.

The western shore of Sebago Lake jutted into the upper-right edge of Map 4, which covered the western half of the skinny southern part of Maine over to the New Hampshire border. South Riley sat west of Sebago, only about six crow-flying miles from New Hampshire, in Oxford County just north of the York County line. Most of this country west of Sebago featured large unbroken patches of green and a lot of irregular blue lines and shapes, representing streams and lakes and ponds. It was crisscrossed with roadways, most of which were double dotted lines—dirt roads that were, in theory, passable by any sort of vehicle.

It was rural country, and Calhoun knew that all the towns—like Dublin, where he lived—were small, and that most of it was rolling old farmland, much of it now in the advanced stages of reverting to mature forest.

The Great Fire in October of 1947 had roared through here on its way to the sea, destroying houses and barns and woods and bridges and forests and a few entire villages, leaving several people and hundreds of head of livestock and uncounted numbers of wildlife dead in its wake.

hump. Calhoun recognized the body and the rod at the same time. The rod was the sweet little seven-and-a-half-foot Tonkin cane Thomas & Thomas that Calhoun had refinished and given to Lyle for his twenty-sixth birthday the previous winter.

The body, of course, was Lyle's.

Calhoun waded in. The spongy peat bottom sucked at his feet when he lifted them up.

Lyle seemed to be kneeling in the water like a praying Muslim bowing to the east. His arms and shoulders and head were on the bottom under about three feet of water. His knees had sunk a ways into the mud. The air in the waders had gathered in the seat, lifting that part to the surface.

Calhoun saw Lyle's long ponytail waving gently in the coppery water, and he flashed on the phantom body he'd seen drifting in his spring creek with its hair undulating underwater.

Lyle was wearing his fishing vest. His completely deflated float tube had slipped down around his knees. He had lost his cap, but he still had fins strapped onto his feet. His Thomas & Thomas rod lay beside him, the butt end in the water, the tip caught in the reeds. The line trailed out into the pond.

Calhoun put his arms around Lyle's chest, hauled him out of the mud, and dragged him through the marsh and bog along the edge of the pond. He kept falling down in the mud with Lyle's dead weight on top of him.

Finally he managed to haul Lyle up onto the dry land beside the dam. He collapsed on the ground beside the body, gasping for breath, and waited for the hammering in his chest to slow down and the fire in his brain to subside.

After a few minutes, Calhoun got up on his hands and knees and looked at the dead boy. Lyle's face was puffy and bloated. His pale blue eyes were staring up at the sky and his mouth gaped open as if he had been singing when he died.

or to set?" As if to express his own preference, he slouched into one of the chairs.

"Neither," said the sheriff. He handed Calhoun's sketch of Fred Green to Barnes. "Wondered if you might've seen this man. He was driving a new white Taurus."

Barnes squinted at it, then looked up at the sheriff and shrugged. "Can't say that I have. Who is he?"

"A young man drowned up in Keatsboro the other day," said the sheriff. "We think this man might know something about it."

Barnes nodded. "I heard about that. Up to the Potter place. Damn shame. What's this fella got to do with it?"

"We're not sure."

"Well," he shrugged, "afraid I can't help you. Maybe Marcus knows something. Hey," he yelled toward the door that opened from the back of the store. "Hey, Marcus. Come on in here, boy."

A minute later the door opened and Marcus Dillman, Jacob's grandson, his daughter's fatherless son, came in. Marcus was a hulking young man in his early twenties. He wore a bushy blond beard, overalls over a black T-shirt, a faded New York Mets baseball cap with the visor tugged down low over his eyes, and a perpetually good-natured grin.

Jacob had once confided to Calhoun: "Marcus ain't too swift. Truth to tell, he's numb as a hake. But he's a good boy, strong as an ox, and he'll work his ass off, so long as it don't require spelling or multiplying."

Marcus looked at Calhoun and the sheriff and nodded. "Mornin', gentlemen," he said. Then he touched Jacob on the shoulder. "What's up, Grampa?"

"You ever seen this fella?" Jacob handed the sketch to Marcus.

Marcus frowned at it, then shook his head. "Nossuh." He looked up at Calhoun and grinned. "Funny ears, huh?"

Calhoun smiled.

Dickman took the sketch from Marcus. "Supposing I use that machine of yours," he said to Jacob, "and leave a copy of this man's face with you. Tack it up there beside the door."

Barnes shrugged. "Nickel a copy."

The sheriff went over to the photocopy machine, and Jacob said, "Help yourself to coffee, Stoney."

"I'm all set," said Calhoun.

"That was your friend, Lyle McMahan, wasn't it? Who drowned himself up there at Potter's?"

"Yes."

"You found him, I hear?"

Calhoun smiled. "Do you hear everything, Jacob?"

Barnes nodded. "Suppose I do."

"Well, if you hear anything else—you, too, Marcus—you be sure to let the sheriff know."

Barnes squinted at him. "Sounds to me like this wasn't no accident."

"I guess you'll have to ask the sheriff about that," said Calhoun.

Dickman came back and handed a copy of Calhoun's sketch to Jacob. "I wrote my number on the bottom," he said. "You might point it out to folks who come in, ask them to take a look and feel free to call."

"Guess I can do that," said Barnes.

They left the store and climbed into Dickman's truck. "Now," said the sheriff, "I want you to take me to the crime scene." He glanced sideways at Calhoun. "Which, I've got to mention, Stoney, you have already corrupted."

"Because I lugged Lyle out of there?"

Dickman nodded.

"Be damned if I was gonna leave him in the water."

"No, I suppose you wouldn't do that."

"Nobody would do that." Calhoun turned to Dickman. "You're checking out Lyle's Power Wagon, I assume."

The sheriff nodded. "I called the state police, suggested they get their forensic boys onto it. Of course," he said, "you've corrupted that piece of evidence, too."

"If I hadn't gone into it for that map," said Calhoun, "we wouldn't've found Lyle in the first place."

"Valid point," said Dickman.

It took about fifteen minutes to drive from Jacob Barnes's store in Dublin to the barway beside the dirt road in Keatsboro, where the overgrown cart path led through the woods and down the long slope to the milldam where Calhoun had found Lyle. The sheriff pulled his Explorer off the road. They both got out.

"Lead on, Macduff," said Dickman.

They pushed through the saplings that overgrew the old ruts through the woods, and after a while Dickman said, "How far we got to go, Stoney?"

"I figure it's about a half mile in, altogether. We're getting there."

"And you lugged that big fella all the way up this hill and through the woods?"

It didn't seem to be a question that needed an answer, so Calhoun said nothing.

Lyle's deflated float tube, vest, fins, waders, and fly rod were piled on the other side of the milldam where Calhoun had left them. Dickman went over and scootched down beside them.

Calhoun stood there, looking around. It was actually a pretty spot in the little valley, with the forest rising from scrubby hardwoods to tall pines on both sides. Red-winged blackbirds chittered in the reeds along the rim of the pond, and down toward the far end he spotted a great blue heron, poised in the shallow water as still as a stump, his head drawn back and his neck arched like a bow at full draw. A pair of red-tailed hawks cruised on the thermals high overhead. A quiet, peaceful place, the kind of place Lyle loved. Not the kind of place where someone would shoot a man.

"Hey, Stoney," said the sheriff. "Look here."

Calhoun squatted beside Dickman.

The sheriff was holding Lyle's waders on his lap. He poked his little finger against a hole in the bib—right about where they would cover a man's solar plexus. "Doc Pritchard said the entry wound was just about straight on. If Lyle was floating on the pond, the shooter must've been kneeling or lying on the ground, because in one of those float tubes, his chest is only a foot or so out of the water."

Calhoun glanced around. "About the only dry land around here where someone could set up to shoot is right here, around the dam."

"Assuming he was out there in his tube when he was shot," said Dickman.

Calhoun nodded. "They could've moved him, you're thinking. Shot him first, then stuck him in his tube and pushed him out, let him drown on his own. Or maybe shot him, held his head under water till he died, then stuck him in his tube."

Dickman shrugged. "I'm not complaining, Stoney. But it would've been a helluva lot easier to figure out if you hadn't . . ." He waved his hand. "The hell with it." He gazed up at the sky. "Are those red-tails?"

"Yup."

"Thought so." The sheriff looked at Calhoun. "Wonder if your Mr. Fred Green was packing a twenty-two handgun."

"Not when I saw him," said Calhoun. "I don't know what he might've had in that rented Taurus of his. You got a scenario in mind?"

Dickman shrugged. "Just the obvious one. What I'm missing here, of course, is a motive."

"The fact that we don't know it doesn't mean there isn't one."

The sheriff was poking through the pile of stuff that Calhoun had taken off Lyle's body. Calhoun was watching the heron when Dickman said, "Aha!"

Calhoun turned to him. "Aha?"

Dickman was peering at the flaccid float tube. "Look at this, Stoney."

His fingertip lay beside a round hole in the tube. He moved the tube around and pointed out another hole on the opposite side.

"So he shot a hole in the tube," said Calhoun. "That's how he deflated it. So what?"

Dickman shrugged. "Not sure."

"Look," said Calhoun. "Lyle was out there in his tube when he got shot. Shot in the belly like that, he must've been looking square at the guy. I think the man plugged him, then shot a hole in the tube so Lyle would go down and drown."

"How do you figure?"

"Well, there's current in this pond. It comes in up there, slows down considerably, then picks up a bit down here by the dam. It looks like a pond, but it's still a stream. You toss a stick into the water up by the far end, eventually it'll come down here and pass over the dam."

"So," said the sheriff, "if Green shot Lyle here, say, then pushed him in the water—"

"He wouldn't've ended up back there in the reeds," said Calhoun, pointing. "Which is where he was when I found him. Green is pushing seventy, and he's not a big man to start with. No way he's going to shoot Lyle then lug him up through all that marshy muck to the head of the pond. Nope. Lyle was out there on the water when he got shot."

The sheriff squinted out over the pond. "Where'd you find him?"

Calhoun pointed. "Up there, near those reeds. I just saw his butt sticking up."

"And he must've been even farther up when he was shot, to drift down to there." Dickman nodded. "Which means he was shot with a rifle, not a pistol. Nobody could center him from this distance with a handgun." He looked at Calhoun and grinned. "See what you can learn, even from a corrupted crime scene?"

"Maybe we ought to check the edge of the pond for footprints before we jump to conclusions," said Calhoun.

Dickman shook his head. "You've had some kind of training, son."

Calhoun shrugged. "I wouldn't know about any of that."

They started slogging through the boggy ground that rimmed the pond. There were no prints in the mud leading around the near side, and they followed it all the way up to where the stream came in. Then they retraced their steps back to the dam, crossed over, and started around the far side. Here there were two distinct sets of bootprints in the mucky ground.

"Assume these belong to you," said the sheriff.

Calhoun nodded. "You can see how those coming back are deeper and closer together than the ones going in. See how the reeds are all broken over? That's where I dragged Lyle out."

They finished their examination of that side of the pond and found no prints in the mud except those that Calhoun had made the previous day.

When they got to the dam, the sheriff said, "Okay, now let's look around."

"What're we looking for?"

"Cartridge cases. Size twenty-two."

The sheriff went down on hands and knees, and Calhoun imitated him. They crept around, poking through the dead leaves and weeds, and about ten minutes passed before Calhoun spotted two little brass cartridge cases glittering in the grass. "We got 'em," he said.

"Don't touch," said Dickman. He came over, squatted down, and picked up one of the empty cartridges on the end of a twig. "Long-rifle," said Dickman. "Looks like he was lying on his belly right here"—he pointed to a place where the weeds were matted down—"nice solid prone position. With a decent rifle and a scope, you could put a man's eye out anywhere on the pond from here. Two shots. One to the belly, one through the tube."

"You figure these were shot out of a rifle," said Calhoun, pointing at the cartridges, "not a handgun?"

"Makes sense, that's all." Dickman shook his head. "Can't tell by looking at them. Give me the gun, we can tell if it was the one that shot them. You can tell by the ejector marks and the imprint of the firing pin here along the rim. That's the best we can do."

He fished a plastic bag from his pants pocket and dropped the two empty cartridges into it. Then he stood up. "Let's get out of here, Stoney."

"You got it figured out, Sheriff?"

"Enough to know that the sooner we catch up with Mr. Green, the better off we'll be."

They picked up Lyle's gear and started back up the slope toward the road. Halfway out, Dickman said, "Time out, Stoney. I'm winded. Damned if I know how you carried that big young man out. A deflated float tube has got me tuckered."

They squatted on the ground. "Something's bothering me," said Calhoun.

"What's that?"

"If you've got the scenario right, it means Green carried a twenty-two rifle in there with him for the purpose of shooting Lyle."

Dickman shrugged. "That's how it looks, all right."

"Well, how do you suppose he explained that to Lyle?"

"I don't know, Stoney. Guns are pretty much standard equipment around here. Wouldn't've bothered Lyle, I don't think. Maybe it was taken apart. Little twenty-two, you could fit the pieces in a gear bag and Lyle wouldn't have even known he had it." Dickman shrugged. "I guess that's another question we've got to ask the man when we find him."

CHAPTER FOURTEEN

WHEN THEY GOT BACK to the road, they loaded Lyle's gear into the back of the sheriff's Explorer. Dickman slammed the tailgate shut, then paused and gazed across the road. "Anna and Dave Ross live up there," he said.

He pointed at the white farmhouse that stood on the knoll about fifty yards down the road on the opposite side.

Calhoun nodded. "She's the one who called you yesterday."

"From up there, if you happened to be looking, you could see people coming and going down here."

"She saw me bring Lyle out. Came down in that little Wrangler of hers to help out."

Dickman frowned. "Wonder if either of them saw anything else."

"You mean the day Lyle got shot?"

He nodded.

"I've got a pretty wild idea, Sheriff."

"And what's that?"

"Why don't we go ask 'em?"

Dickman smiled. "That's brilliant, Stoney. Never would've thought of that."

They climbed into the Explorer and drove down the road and up the curving driveway to the Rosses' farmhouse. Dickman parked in front of the barn beside a pickup truck with a plow hitch on the front and a light bar on the roof. Beside the barn were two tractors, a backhoe, and a flatbed truck. Anna's Wrangler was not there.

When Calhoun stepped out, he heard loud rock 'n' roll music coming from inside the barn. The music was punctuated by the rhythmic clanging of metal crashing against metal.

He went to the doorway and looked in. David Ross was lying on his back on the barn's plank floor with his head under the rear end of an old John Deere tractor. He was holding a chisel and pounding up on it with a steel mallet, working at the underside of a mechanism attached to the back of the tractor.

The sheriff went over and squatted down beside Ross. "What's the problem, Dave?" he shouted.

Ross took one more whack at the chisel, then rolled his head to the side and looked up. He jerked his chin toward the radio, which sat on a workbench along the wall. "Whyn't you shut that damn thing off."

Dickman went over and turned off the radio.

Ross continued to peer up at the underside of the tractor. "This here piece of shit belongs to Obie Hoyt. Hitch is rusted up so bad he can't hook up his harrow. I gotta bust it off and rig a new one for him." Ross narrowed his eyes, gritted his teeth, set the chisel, then slammed it again.

He was wearing overalls with no shirt underneath. The stub of a dead cigar was clamped between his teeth, and his forehead and thinning yellow-white hair were damp with sweat. "So," he grunted between blows on the chisel, "what's on your mind, Sheriff?"

"Wondering if we could talk for a minute?"

Ross nodded. "I guess so."

He slid out from under the tractor, laid down his tools, stood up, and wiped his hands on his overalls. "Mr. Calhoun," he said with a nod. "Didn't see you there. Suppose we go fetch us some iced tea?"

Calhoun and Dickman followed David Ross across the yard to the farmhouse. In the kitchen, Ross took a plastic jug of iced tea from the refrigerator and three glasses from the dish rack beside the sink, and they sat around the table.

"So, how can I help you?" said Ross.

"You know that a young man drowned in the pond across the way the other day," said the sheriff.

"Over to Potter's," said Ross.

Dickman nodded. "We think another man might've been with him. Wondered if you saw anything."

"What day was this?"

Dickman glanced at Calhoun. "Tuesday?"

Calhoun nodded.

Ross shook his head. "I saw you yesterday," he said, looking at Calhoun. "Told Anna to take a run over. It appeared you could use some help."

"I appreciate it," said Calhoun.

"I was hoping you or Anna might've noticed this other man we think was with the fella who drowned," said Dickman. He reached into his shirt pocket and took out the sketch Calhoun had made of Fred Green. He unfolded it on the table and turned it so Ross could see it.

Ross dragged it in front of him and peered at it for a long moment. Then he looked up at the sheriff. "Sorry."

"You ever notice anyone who looked like they might be going fishing in there?" said Dickman.

"Over to Potter's little pond?" Ross shook his head. "Nobody that I ever seen."

"It looked like it ought to hold trout," said Calhoun.

Ross turned to Calhoun. "You're a guide, ain't you?"

Calhoun nodded.

"Well," said Ross, "I wouldn't waste my time in there. Ain't been trout in that little pond or upstream of it for a long time."

Calhoun nodded. "Your wife said Mr. Potter died in the fire."

Ross took a long gulp of iced tea, then put down his glass and wiped his mouth on the back of his wrist. "It was over fifty years ago," he said. "We knew it was comin' a whole day before it got here. Smoke so thick you couldn't see the sun. Made your eyes water, burned your throat." Ross shook his head. "Me and my mother, we kept hosin' down our house here, but it had been such a dry summer that our well was near empty, and all we got was a little trickle. If that fire had decided to come sweepin' over this hill it would've leveled us. But it jumped the road less than a mile from us, burned out the bridge, and went aboilin' down the valley over on the Potter's side. I guess Sam figured he was safe up there on his hill. Hell, everyone knows a fire burns uphill faster'n it burns down." He shook his head. "Lucky his wife and kids wasn't there. October the twenty-second, nineteen forty-seven. A Wednesday."

Dickman nodded, drained his glass, and stood up. "Well, Dave, you'd be doing me a favor if you mentioned this to Anna. Perhaps she saw something that might be of help. Have her give me a call."

"I'll do that," said Ross.

He followed Dickman and Calhoun out to the Explorer and stood there in front of the barn as they turned around and headed down the driveway.

"Guess I better drop you off, Stoney," said the sheriff as he turned onto the dirt road. "I've got to get back to the office, organize a hunt for Mr. Fred Green, not to mention all the other problems that've probably piled up on my desk by now."

"So what've we learned?" said Calhoun.

Dickman shrugged. "Can't tell yet. Sometimes you hear something, it doesn't mean anything at the time, but later on, after you've heard two or three other things, it all of a sudden makes some sense, fits in somewhere. It might've helped if Dave Ross had seen Mr. Green coming out of there."

They drove in silence for a while, heading back to Dublin. As they turned into Calhoun's long driveway through the woods, he said, "Do you know everybody in York County, Sheriff?"

Dickman grinned. "Nope. Not everybody. But the folks who've been around a little while—Millie, Jacob and Marcus, Dave and Anna Ross, folks like you and Kate—I guess I do. They're good people to know. Whatever's going on, they know it—who's driving around drunk, who's breaking into gas stations, who's shooting their thirty-thirties at road signs—and if they trust you, they'll tell you. Folks around here don't like crime, Stoney. They're pretty old-fashioned that way. They actually appreciate sheriffs and deputies and police in general. Dave'll remember to ask Anna if she saw anything, and if she did, she'll jump on the phone. So one of the main things I do in this job is, I get out and talk to people, tell 'em what's going on, what I need. Word gets around. When we catch up to Mr. Green, I expect it'll be because somebody's seen him and lets us know about it."

The sheriff pulled into Calhoun's dooryard. Kate's Blazer was gone.

When Calhoun got out, Ralph came sauntering down off the deck with his entire back end wagging. Calhoun squatted down so that Ralph could lick his face. Then he stood and went to the back of the sheriff's Explorer where they'd stored Lyle's gear.

"Leave that stuff," said Dickman. "Those bullet holes are evidence."

"If you don't mind," said Calhoun, "I want to keep Lyle's rod. That's not evidence, is it?"

"Guess not," said Dickman. "Sentimental reasons, huh?"

Calhoun shrugged. "It's a damn good rod."

He took out the Thomas & Thomas bamboo fly rod, then went around to the driver's side of the sheriff's Explorer. They shook hands. "You'll keep me posted," Calhoun said.

Dickman nodded. "You too, Stoney. Where'll you be today?"

"At the shop. I'm thinking I should drop by Lyle's house on the way, tell his housemates what happened."

"Sad business." The sheriff shifted into reverse, started to turn around, then stopped. "Appreciate everything, Stoney. Real sorry about Lyle. You know that." He lifted his hand, and Calhoun watched him drive away.

He and Ralph went inside. Kate had cleaned up the kitchen. She'd left a note on the table. "Call me first chance," it read. She'd signed it with a big "K" and several Xs and Os.

He sat at the table and dialed the shop. Kate picked up on the third ring. "Kate's Bait and Buggers."

"It's me, honey."

"I want to hear all about it," she said. "But I've got people here now."

"I'm coming in." He glanced at his watch. It was a few minutes after noontime. "Give me a couple hours. I've got to stop by Lyle's house first."

"Okay. That's fine." She dropped her voice. "Just tell me—did you learn anything?"

"Not really. Looks like Green shot him, all right. I'll fill you in when I get there."

Calhoun showered, shaved, and climbed into a clean pair of jeans. He filled Ralph's water dish, gave him a rawhide bone, then got into his truck and drove to Portland.

Lyle and his commune of housemates rented a sprawling old Victorian south of the airport in the Pleasantdale section of South Portland. The Fore River, which was really a long skinny tidal cove opening into Casco Bay, ran along the foot of the hill behind the house. Lyle had loved that place, because he could keep a fly rod set up on the back porch and stroll down the path to the river and catch stripers on the outgoing tide and sometimes bluefish on the incoming.

Calhoun parked between a yellow Volkswagen Rabbit and a rusty Dodge pickup in the gravel turnaround out front. An aluminum canoe leaned against the side of the house, and several trash barrels stood by the corner. The paint was peeling and cracking and the shrubs needed trimming. Calhoun remembered Lyle complaining about their landlord, who seemed to expect the tenants to be responsible for the upkeep of the place. "I don't mind cutting the grass," Lyle had once told him. "But damned if we're gonna paint the house or replace those rotten sills or patch all the leaks in the roof. This old heap can collapse, far as I'm concerned. We'll just move somewhere else."

It hadn't collapsed yet, but it looked like it was seriously considering it.

Calhoun climbed onto the porch and rang the doorbell. A minute later the inside door opened and a small blond woman blinked out at him through the screen. She was wearing a pink terrycloth bathrobe and her feet were bare. Her short hair was tousled. She knuckled her eyes, then smiled. "Hey, Stoney," she said. "Lyle's not here."

Calhoun had met all of Lyle's housemates at one time or another, but he couldn't keep them sorted out. "Julia?" he said.

She nodded. He noticed that her toenails were painted pink to match her robe.

"Actually," he said, "I came over to see you."

"Me?"

"You and your housemates."

"What's up?"

"You going to invite me in?"

She shrugged and pushed open the screen door. "Sure. Come on in. I got coffee on."

Julia was about Lyle's age—twenty-five or twenty-six—and Calhoun thought he remembered that she was taking courses over at the University and waitressing at night.

He followed her into the kitchen, where a skinny young man in a sleeveless T-shirt and blue jeans was hunched over a cereal bowl at the table. A radio on the counter was playing rock music. A Rolling Stones tune.

"Danny, you remember Mr. Calhoun?" said Julia.

Danny looked up, nodded to Calhoun with his mouth full, then returned his attention to his cereal. He had pale eyes and long, thin, hairy arms.

"Sit down, Stoney," she said. "I'll pour us some coffee. You want coffee, Danny?"

Danny shook his head without looking up.

Calhoun sat down across from Danny. Julia went to the counter, turned off the radio, and a moment later she was back with two mugs. She sat down beside Danny, who was spooning up the milk from the bottom of his bowl.

"Okay, Stoney," she said. "What's up?"

Danny stood up, took his bowl to the sink, mumbled something, and started to leave the room.

"Hang on a minute," Calhoun said to him.

Danny turned. "Me?"

"Yes, please. I wanted to talk to both of you."

Danny shrugged and sat down. "What's up, man? I gotta get to work."

Calhoun shook his head. "It's not good news, I'm afraid."

Danny frowned. "Huh?"

Julia was staring at Calhoun. Her mouth opened, then closed, and then she shook her head. "Lyle? Don't tell me . . ."

Calhoun nodded.

CHAPTER FIFTEEN

"Lyle's dead," said Calhoun, watching first Julia's face, then Danny's.

Julia shook her head. "What? You mean, like . . .?" She was clutching the folds of her robe together at her throat, frowning at him.

Calhoun shrugged. "I'm sorry. I don't know how to say it any different."

"He—Lyle died?"

Calhoun nodded.

She stared at him for a moment, then smiled quickly. "See, I thought you meant . . ."

Danny was sitting there frowning. "The man said he was dead, Jules. Jesus."

Calhoun nodded. "I dragged his body out of the woods yesterday."

She got up from the table and went over to the sink. She gazed out the window with her back to him, hugging herself. "What happened?" she said in a small voice.

"He got shot."

"Shot, huh?" She made a little snorting laugh. "Sure. That figures."

"Christ," said Danny. "What the hell is that supposed to mean?"

She snapped her head around. "It means what it means. Like you don't know?"

Calhoun remained seated at the kitchen table, watching the two of them, wondering if they were trying to put on some kind of act for him. If they were, he didn't know what he was supposed to get out of it. "What *do* you mean?" he said.

She turned around and leaned back against the edge of the sink with her arms folded across her chest. "By what?"

"You said 'it figures.'"

"Some girl plugged him."

"Oh, come off it," said Danny. "That's plain stupid."

Calhoun smiled. "A girl?"

"Like that Penny Moulton. That new one. She's been calling here for Lyle ever since he started seeing her. Always asking where he was, telling us to make sure he called her, then calling back an hour later accusing us of not giving him the message. Hell, Stoney. She's not the only one. There's a zillion girls pissed at Lyle."

"That's the truth, Mr. Calhoun," Danny said. "Doubt if any of them'd plug him, though."

"He was guiding a man that day," said Calhoun. "We figure he's the one who did it."

"What man?" said Julia.

Calhoun sighed. "Out-of-stater. Older guy. Came into the shop, wanted to go fishing. It was—I should've taken him. It was my turn. But I didn't like the man, so I gave him to Lyle."

Julia came back to the table and sat down. "You're saying that some stranger showed up, asked for a guide, and then went out in the woods with him and shot him? Why would anybody do that?"

Calhoun shook his head. "Damned if I know."

"If you ask me," she said, "it was some girl. Lyle broke more damn hearts . . ."

"Oh, right," said Danny. "Some broken-hearted chick, loved him so bad she shot him. Jesus!"

Then Calhoun saw Julia's eyes brim and overflow, and she sat there across from him with a little half-smile, looking at him with her blurry wet eyes, crying silently.

"You?" he said.

"Her and everybody else," said Danny. "Lyle's got that magic. Chicks see Lyle, they just lay down and spread their legs."

"Will you shut up?" Julia turned to Calhoun and nodded. "Sure. Me. Danny's right. Lyle feels like he's got to screw every girl he sees. I guess he about does, too. He's a wicked sexy guy. I can't exactly explain it. He's so—arrogant, you know? I mean, quiet, very polite, doesn't say much. Like he knows he doesn't have to. He never hits on a girl, and that makes you wonder what's wrong with yourself, so you feel like you've got to try to seduce him. It's like he knows you want him, and he's just waiting. But afterwards, he loses interest. Like he did what he set out to do. Oh, he'll keep you going for a while. He wants you to be interested in him even when he doesn't care anymore." She glanced at Danny. "I don't guess any girl would shoot him, though. You just keep loving Lyle McMahan, is what you do. He makes you feel like one day he'll see the light and be back. That's how Lyle is."

Calhoun noticed Julia's use of the present tense and figured it hadn't sunk in for her yet. "That doesn't sound like the Lyle McMahan I knew," he said.

She said, "You're not a girl."

"Listen, both of you," he said, shifting his eyes from Julia to Danny. "Did Lyle ever mention anybody named Green?"

Danny looked up at the ceiling for a moment, then shrugged. "Nope. Don't think so."

"Julia?" said Calhoun.

"Not that I recall."

"His client that day might've been named Green," said Calhoun.

"Might've?" said Danny.

"I'm not sure he gave me his right name. Said he was from Florida. Any of Lyle's girls from Florida that you know?"

Danny nodded. "I get it. You think Lyle screwed this man's wife or girlfriend or daughter or something. He would've, too. Wouldn't've bothered Lyle if someone was married or something." He stopped. "But wait. Didn't you say you were supposed to take the man out? Did he ask for Lyle?"

Calhoun shut his eyes, scrolling back, re-creating the scene in the shop that morning. "Someone who really knows the back roads and woods," Fred Green had said. "A native. A real Mainer." Those had been his words. They described Lyle better than they described Calhoun. Maybe he *had* come specifically for Lyle. Calhoun had made it easy by turning him over to Lyle. Perhaps if he hadn't, the man would have gone out with Calhoun. Then maybe it would've been Calhoun who got shot.

Or maybe not. Maybe the man had come to the shop because he intended to murder Lyle.

"No," said Calhoun. "He didn't ask for Lyle. Not by name, anyway. He just asked for a guide."

"I don't know any Green girl, offhand," said Julia. "Nobody from Florida, either, for that matter."

"Me, neither," said Danny.

Julia shook her head. "I can't believe this."

Calhoun glanced at Danny. He was staring at Julia without expression.

Julia turned to Calhoun. "Guess you're feeling kinda guilty, huh?"

Calhoun looked at her. "Why?"

"You're thinking you should've taken that man out, not Lyle. Then Lyle wouldn't've gotten shot."

He nodded. "Yes. Tell you the truth, I'm feeling real bad. I dragged Lyle out of bed so he'd come take Mr. Green off my hands. If I hadn't . . ." He shrugged.

"I'm awful sorry," she said softly. "I know you were real good friends. He thought the world of you, you know. Talked about you all the time. You were like a brother to Lyle."

Calhoun found himself nodding, reluctant to speak. His throat felt tight and his eyes burned.

Danny shoved back his chair and stood up. "I've got to get going, Mr. Calhoun. What can I do?"

"Tell the rest of your housemates what happened to Lyle. Tell them he was murdered. If any of them thinks of anything, have them call me over at the shop where I work. Here. I'll leave a number." Calhoun fumbled one of Kate's business cards from his wallet.

Danny took the card and stuck it on the refrigerator door with a sunflower magnet. "Okay," he said. He held his hand out to Calhoun. The young man's grip was firm. "I guess I haven't quite digested what you've said. Lyle is—was—a buddy. This don't seem real."

After Danny left the room, Calhoun stood up. "I've got get over to the shop," he said to Julia. "I just wanted you folks to know what happened. Be sure to tell the rest of your housemates."

She nodded.

"And you might mention the name Green, see if it rings any bells with anybody."

"Sure," she said. "I'll do that. I'll call you if I hear anything."

He started for the front door.

She followed him, and when he put his hand on the knob, she touched his arm. "Hey, Stoney," she said softly.

He turned, and she came against him, hugging him around the waist with her face pushed against his chest. He held her for a moment, then kissed the top of her head. "I'm real sorry, Julia," he said.

"Me, too," she said.

During the ten-minute drive from Lyle's house to the shop, he thought about what Julia and Danny had said. Lyle had left behind a lot of broken hearts. Jealousy or disappointment didn't strike Calhoun

as much of a motive for murder. But he couldn't come up with anything better.

Several unfamiliar cars were parked in the lot in front of the shop.
Sure. Friday afternoon. Everybody was gearing up for a weekend of
striper fishing.

Inside, he found Kate at the counter in deep conversation with two
men wearing business suits. She glanced up when the bell over the door
dinged, lifted her chin at Calhoun, then resumed her conversation.
"Okay," she was saying, drawing on a piece of paper. "Tide's about half
out around six, so you should find 'em at the estuary, here, along this
channel, waiting for the bait to wash out of the creek. They come in
along this dropoff, and you can wade out onto this sandbar . . ."

Calhoun wandered over to three guys—they looked like a father
and two late-teen sons—who were studying the rack of rods. "Need any
help?" he said.

One of the younger ones turned to him. "You work here?"

"Ayuh."

"What do you think about stripping baskets?"

"Wade fishin' for stripers, you sure need one," said Calhoun, shifting into full Downeast twang. "Keep your line from gettin' tangled in
the weeds or sloshin' around in the surf, all twisted around your legs."

The boy turned to the other two. "See?"

"You can make one for yourself," said Calhoun. "Just get yourself
a plastic dish tub and a bungee cord. Punch holes in two of the corners,
hook your bungee cord into 'em, snug her around your waist, and
you're in business."

"Don't you sell them here?" asked the older man, the father.

"Oh, sure," said Calhoun. "Store-bought ones work, too."

For the next several hours, a steady stream of customers wandered
into and out of the shop, and Calhoun barely had the chance to nod
and smile at Kate as the two of them gave away advice and recommen-
dations. Most of the customers had the courtesy to buy a few flies or

spools of tippet material, and Calhoun did sell an Orvis eight-weight outfit—he even nail-knotted a leader and backing to the ends of the line and then spooled it onto the reel for the guy—but considering the volume of customers, Calhoun figured they hadn't made much money.

It was after six o'clock when he realized that he and Kate were alone. He went out back and fished two Cokes from the cooler. He took them to the front counter, where Kate was bent over the ledger in which they kept track of everything they sold. He put the can of Coke beside her elbow.

She glanced up. "Oh, thanks, Stoney."

"Figured you could use it."

"It's been a damn zoo," she said, still peering at her entries in the ledger. "Last two days, I've been running around like a trout foul-hooked in the tail. Without you and Lyle around to help out . . ."

"I'm sorry, honey."

She glanced up at him. "Don't call me that here."

"Somethin' bothering you, Kate?"

She shook her head.

"What is it?" he persisted.

"Nothing, Stoney. Just leave me be."

"Somethin's eating at you. You ought to let me in on it."

She said nothing.

"Kate," he said. He touched her shoulder. "What's going on? If it's about Lyle, I—"

"I just wish it was more businesslike around here."

"Meaning what?"

She put down her pencil and looked up at him. "Look," she said, "I'm trying not to go broke here. You don't have to worry about it. But I do. I've got to worry about it. If I don't, nobody does. We've got folks asking for guide trips, and I don't feel like I've got any guides except myself. And what'm I going to do, close up the shop so I can take people fishing?"

"You've got me."

"I got you when you feel like it," she said. "When you don't feel like running around with the sheriff playing detective. Dammit, Stoney. The last two days've been . . ." She waved her hand in the air. "Forget it," she said. "Not your problem."

"Lyle was killed," he said. "Murdered."

"Well, hell," she said. "I know that. And I feel bad about it. You know I do. And I know how you feel about it, how much Lyle meant to you."

"He was shot, Kate. Someone shot him while he was out in his float tube. I can't just—"

"You can't just let Sheriff Dickman handle it? That what you mean?"

He looked up at the ceiling for a minute. Then he said, "Kate, listen. It was you who said for me to go, help out the sheriff, do whatever I needed to do."

"Since when have you been indispensable to the sheriff?"

"Since I found Lyle lying there in the mud with a bullet in his belly, I reckon." He shook his head. "No. Since I decided I didn't want to take Fred Green fishing and gave him to Lyle. I can't just let it go, honey."

She looked down at the ledger, shaking her head. "Right," she said. "It's all your fault."

He shrugged. "It feels like it is. I don't get why you don't understand that."

"Look, Stoney," she said. "I got to finish toting up these numbers. Then I'm going to lock up and go home. Doesn't look like anyone else'll be in tonight, so you can leave if you want."

"I thought you wanted to hear about what we learned today."

"Sure. Next time you drop in, if it's not too busy, you can tell me all about it. Meanwhile, Lyle's dead and nothing's going to change that."

"I'll be in tomorrow to open up."

"You do what you want to do, like always."

He let out a long breath. "Well, goddammit, Kate, that's what I want to do. I'll be here at seven."

"You be sure to let me know if you change your mind."

"I'm not going to change my mind."

Calhoun swept the floor and emptied the wastebaskets into the Dumpster out back. Then he straightened out the displays, moving items that customers had been looking at back to where they belonged, glancing through the boxes of flies to be sure that they were all in the right compartments.

By the time he finished, Kate had hung the GONE FISHIN' sign on the door and had moved to the back office, where she was talking on the phone. Calhoun stood in the doorway, and after a moment she glanced up, gave him a quick smile that her eyes did not participate in, then looked down at her desktop and resumed her conversation.

He shrugged, walked out, and got into his truck, and all the way home he tried to figure out what had happened. He didn't even pretend to understand women, never mind one as complicated as Kate Balaban. He knew their minds worked different, and that was about it. Men, he'd learned, tended to say what they were thinking and ask for what they wanted. Women expected you to know what they were thinking and wanting, and when you didn't, they thought you didn't love them.

On the other hand, if Kate wasn't so damn complicated, she wouldn't be so interesting. And if she wasn't so interesting, Calhoun figured he wouldn't love her so much.

She was all upset about Lyle. That was probably it.

Sometimes, he knew, Kate was thinking about Walter, feeling guilty. She told him that Walter had never mentioned anything about it, not once since the night when they'd talked to him. But she said that sometimes she could feel Walter's eyes on her, even when she was at Calhoun's house and Walter was back in Portland. Calhoun tried to talk to her about it, but she told him to forget it, it was her situation and she'd handle it herself.

He didn't know if he could do what Kate was doing, living with somebody who loved her—and who, he knew, she loved, too—and being with somebody else who she also loved. Calhoun didn't blame her for second-guessing herself, for growing distant sometimes, for taking it out on him.

Maybe she'd come tonight. She'd feel bad about being snippy with him. She'd appear, maybe wearing the peasant blouse with the scooped neck and the full skirt that swirled around her legs when she walked and all that jangly silver and turquoise jewelry that made her look like a gypsy. She'd give him a big hug, whisper that she was sorry she'd been bitchy . . . and everything would be all right.

He shook his head. It had taken him a long time to learn not to expect her, to understand that she came when she could and when she wanted to, and that she would never come to him unless she felt right about it. He supposed that most nights she didn't feel right about it, and that was why she didn't come more often.

Yesterday he'd asked her to come, and she had. But that was an exception. Yesterday he'd found Lyle's body.

Maybe that was it. Maybe she was upset that she'd broken her own rule, or that he'd asked when they'd agreed that he never would.

She would not come tonight. He was certain of that.

Dusk was falling as he turned into his driveway. Well, Ralph would be glad to see him. Ralph was always glad to see him. No matter what he did or where he'd been, Ralph was the same.

Dogs were a helluva lot more predictable than women.

When he topped the last hill to his place, he saw the dark green Audi sedan parked where he always left his truck.

The man in the suit had returned.

CHAPTER SIXTEEN

THAT WAS HOW CALHOUN THOUGHT OF HIM: The Man in the Suit. He appeared to be a few years older than Calhoun, and his sandy hair was turning gray. It looked washed-out, sort of colorless, like his eyes. Pretty much like the entire man. He was tall and skinny and stooped-over, with a long nose and a narrow face and a small mouth that barely moved when he talked. He'd never given Calhoun his name. He always wore a gray suit, and he showed up at unexpected times, more or less every couple of months.

Calhoun got out of his truck and saw the Man in the Suit sitting in a rocker up on the deck. He was smoking a cigarette, absolutely relaxed, as if he had all the time in the world to sit there waiting for Calhoun to come home.

Ralph was lying beside the man, and when he saw Calhoun he lifted his head and wagged his stubby little tail but did not bother getting up.

Calhoun went in the front door, took the Remington autoloader off its hooks, and carried it out through the kitchen, through the sliding glass doors, and onto the deck.

The Man in the Suit looked up and smiled. He opened his hand and showed Calhoun the three shotgun shells he was holding. "Come on, Stoney," he said. "Have a seat. Catch me up."

Calhoun had been putting up drywall in the living room on a rainy afternoon in July of his first summer in Maine. It had been four months since he'd left the hospital, and he'd almost stopped thinking about it. Lyle had left after lunch to go bass fishing, and Calhoun was thinking that if Lyle brought back a good report, maybe tomorrow he'd take a break from his house building and try it himself, when he'd heard a voice call, "Mr. Calhoun?"

The front door was open and a man was standing on the porch with rainwater dripping off the roof onto his trench coat. A green Audi sedan was parked out front beside Calhoun's truck. Under his open coat the man wore a gray suit and striped necktie. Calhoun didn't remember ever seeing him before.

"Come on in," he said. "It's raining out there." He figured the man was an insurance salesman. The folks who handed out religious pamphlets generally traveled in pairs.

The stranger stepped inside and stood there. "I was just passing by, thought I'd drop in and see how you were doing."

He was not from Maine. He had one of those vague, homogenized accents. Someone who moved around a lot, who had a talent for blending in, a man who people would have trouble remembering.

"I don't believe I know you, sir," Calhoun said.

The man had stepped into what would eventually be the kitchen, but which then had a bare plywood floor. "You never used to talk like that," he said, shaking the water out of his hair.

"Like what?"

"That accent."

Calhoun had shrugged. "It's how I talk. So what do you want?"

"Well, to tell you the truth, they asked me to look in on you, make sure everything was going okay."

"They?"

He flapped his hands and smiled.

"From the hospital, you mean?"

"Right," he said, and Calhoun knew by the way he said it that it wasn't exactly the truth.

"Tell them I'm fine," said Calhoun. "Thank them very much for their concern. Tell them they don't need to check up on me. I don't want to be checked up on. In fact, tell them that in the future I intend to shoot trespassers. Okay? Will you tell them that?"

He gave Calhoun a patient smile, the sort of smile a priest might give a sinner. "They care about you, Mr. Calhoun. That's all."

"And they want to know what I'm remembering."

"Well, yes. That. And just, in general, if—"

"Nothing. Tell them I remember nothing. I'm starting over. Okay?"

The Man in the Suit had stood there with his eyebrows arched, as if he'd expected Calhoun to elaborate. After a minute, he shrugged. "Okay, Mr. Calhoun." He turned to leave, hesitated, then said, "They will keep checking on you, you know."

"From now on," Calhoun had said, "I'll be shooting trespassers. Be sure you tell 'em that."

The next time the Man in the Suit appeared at the door, Calhoun had greeted him with the Remington on his shoulder.

"You're not going to shoot me, Stoney," the man said, and when Calhoun looked down, he saw that the man was holding a little automatic pistol in his hand and was pointing it in the direction of Calhoun's balls.

"I just want you to go away and not come back."

"Can't do that," the man said. "I'd lose my job, and they'd just send somebody else."

"Am I that important?" said Calhoun.

The Man in the Suit smiled. "Got a beer or something?"

"No," said Calhoun. "You want a Coke?"

"Oh, right," said the Man in the Suit. "No alcohol."

Calhoun hung the Remington back on the wall, took a couple of Cokes from the refrigerator, and he and the man sat in the rockers on the deck.

"You've done a nice job here," the man said, tucking his automatic into a holster under his left armpit.

"Why don't you loosen your tie," said Calhoun. "Relax, listen to the birds sing."

"I don't like this any more than you do," the man said. "If it was me, I'd just leave you alone. But that's not going to happen."

"They're afraid I'll remember something," said Calhoun.

The Man in the Suit shrugged.

"I don't," said Calhoun. "I don't remember anything."

"Good," said the man. "Best all around."

"What if I do remember something?"

"Best if you don't tell anybody."

"You don't want me to tell you?"

"Don't tell anybody, Stoney. Especially me."

"How do I know what it is they don't want me to remember?"

"You'll know." The man shifted in the rocker so that he was peering into Calhoun's face. "But you've got to give me something now and then. That way, I drop in occasionally, you update me, and I leave. If you don't, if you get hard-assed with me . . ." He waved his hand in the air and slumped back into the rocker.

"I told you I was going to shoot trespassers," said Calhoun.

"Good," the Man in the Suit had said. "Paranoia is good. Okay. What else've you got for me?"

Calhoun went out onto the deck. The Man in the Suit was sipping a Coke that he'd helped himself to from the refrigerator. He put the shotgun shells on the table and arched his eyebrows. "Well?"

"I was some kind of cop, wasn't I?" said Calhoun. He noticed the bulge of the shoulder harness under the man's jacket.

"I'm not at liberty to say."

They'd done this dance before, but Calhoun wanted to reaffirm it. "But you are at liberty to say if I'm wrong."

The Man in the Suit smiled. "Sure."

"You aren't saying I'm wrong."

"No, I'm not saying that."

"But if I was wrong, you'd say so."

"Yes. We've already established that. Now tell me. What makes you think you were some kind of cop?"

"Nothing specific," Calhoun said carefully. "We've got a murder up here, and it just feels . . . I don't know. Familiar."

"Familiar? How so?"

Calhoun remembered a dark classroom, pictures of faces flashing on a screen, a feeling of intense concentration, of being tested and challenged, of wanting something very badly. There were other images . . .

Better not to share too much of this with the Man in the Suit.

He shrugged. "Just that old déjà vu shit. Like I might've investigated murders before. Nothing I could pin down."

"What have you remembered since last time?"

Calhoun shook his head. "Those quick memory flashes. They come and go before I can store them away. They don't stick."

"You've got to give me something, Stoney."

"What've you got for me?"

"You've got to be patient."

Calhoun said, "I'm finding that I don't forget a damn thing since . . . since the hospital. Everything's like a movie in my head, and I can rewind it and replay it, slow it down and stop it and study every frame. We've had this murder—"

"I know about the murder," said the Man in the Suit.

"What do you know?"

"You found Lyle McMahan's body. They're looking for a man named Fred Green." He shrugged.

Calhoun reached over and gripped the man's wrist. "What else do you know?"

"Nothing, Stoney. Really. It's got nothing to do with us."

Calhoun stared at him for a minute, then slumped back in his chair. "I still get those—those ghosts," he said. "The day before I found Lyle, I saw a naked body drifting down my creek." He shook his head. "I think it was Lyle."

"A ghost, huh?"

"Yes. An apparition. When I found Lyle, I thought I was seeing another one."

"You believe Fred Green killed him?"

"What do you know about Fred Green?" said Calhoun. "God-dammit, if—"

"It's unrelated," said the Man in the Suit. "We don't know any more about Fred Green than you do. I know about the murder because it's my job to know about you."

"I came up here because I didn't like you people snooping around inside my head."

"I know that, Stoney," he said. "We've been through all that. We've got an understanding, you and I." He lifted his Coke and took a sip. "And I'm sorry about Lyle."

Calhoun nodded. "Only other thing I can tell you is that I've found I've got a talent for sketching. I drew a picture of Fred Green for Sheriff Dickman, and damned if it didn't come out looking exactly like the man. I guess I was taught how to do that, huh?"

The Man in the Suit smiled. "I'm not at liberty to say."

"Tell them that I don't remember anything about the man who saved my life or what I was doing with him or where we were. Nothing. Tell them they've got nothing to worry about."

"Good."

"I want to know about my parents," said Calhoun.

"I understand. Maybe another time."

They sat there on the deck, both of them staring off into the woods, and the silence between them was not uncomfortable. After a couple of minutes, Calhoun said, "You're from the government, not the hospital." He continued to gaze into the distance. "Right?"

The Man in the Suit did not turn his head. "I'm not at liberty to say."

After the Man in the Suit left, Calhoun went inside. He reloaded the Remington—two shells in the magazine and one in the chamber—and made sure the safety was on. He fed Ralph and heated a can of spaghetti for himself.

Then he put on some music and sat with his anthology. He began reading Faulkner's "The Bear," a helluva good story, and one he knew he'd read before.

But his mind kept wandering. What if Fred Green had come up here from Calhoun's previous life, the one he couldn't remember? What if Lyle was dead because of something Calhoun had done before the hospital?

The Man in the Suit had denied it. But Calhoun knew he lied. They lied to each other. That was part of their understanding. They mingled lies in with some truth and left it up to each other to figure out which was which.

If it turned out that Fred Green had any connection whatsoever to his unremembered life, Calhoun swore to himself that he would shoot two people dead. First, Mr. Fred Green. Second, the Man in the Suit.

Around midnight he went outside to keep Ralph company while the dog sniffed around for good places to lift his leg, and as he was standing there enjoying the aroma of the piney woods and listening to the creek and watching clouds skid across the face of the moon, he suddenly saw Kate with her telephone wedged against her neck. She was gazing up at the ceiling. There was a smile on her pretty face, and he knew that everything was okay with her again.

He smiled, called Ralph, and went inside. He picked up the telephone, hesitated, and put it back on its cradle. No sense spoiling a good thing.

CHAPTER SEVENTEEN

CALHOUN BROUGHT RALPH TO THE SHOP WITH HIM the next morning, as he often did. Kate liked having Ralph there. She said it gave the place a kind of homey atmosphere that put customers at ease and encouraged them to spend money. Besides, Kate liked Ralph.

It was a Saturday in June, the busiest day of the week in the best month of the year for all kinds of fishing in Maine, so he got there a little before six. He turned the sign around so that it read OPEN and filled a bowl of water for Ralph. He threw one of his old sweaters in the corner and told him to lie down and take it easy. The customers liked seeing Ralph lying there, looking bored, and Ralph liked watching the customers out of his half-lidded eyes. Calhoun thought every fishing shop should have a bored bird dog lying in the corner on a ratty old sweater.

He found the NPR station on the radio and sat at the fly-tying desk to make some more sand eel flies. Stripers crashed sand eels along the beaches at night in June, and the shop's supply of fly-rod imitations was running low. He'd been experimenting with a design that used flexible nylon tubing and synthetic hair and Krystal Flash.

Customers began wandering in almost immediately, and between selling flies and giving away the locations of hotspots and other hard-earned lore, he had barely managed to turn out a dozen flies in the couple of hours before Kate got there.

She came to the desk and picked up one of Calhoun's sand eels. "Looks pretty good," she said. "How's it behave in the water?"

"Lyle tried some last week," said Calhoun. "Did real good with 'em, he said."

"Busy so far?"

He shrugged. "Gave away a lot of wisdom. Didn't sell a helluva lot."

"I'm real sorry, Stoney."

He looked up.

"About how I behaved yesterday."

He nodded. "Lyle said they were gobbling sand eels on those mudflats along the inside of Swan Island about an hour into the incoming last week. Just at dusk. You know those mudflats I mean?"

"I get scared sometimes," she said.

Calhoun stroked the tail of the fly in his vise. "What do you think?" he said. "Maybe needs a bit more flash?"

"Some guys came in yesterday morning," she continued. "They wanted to go trout fishing on the Kennebec up around Bingham, below the Wyman Dam. They'd heard it's really hot. Hell, it *is* hot. Everybody knows that. It would've been a good trip for us. Three lawyers. Well-connected local lawyers. First thing I thought was, well, I'll give these boys to Lyle." She shook her head. "It would've been a great trip for Lyle. I can't believe it, Stoney."

Calhoun didn't look up. He didn't want to see Kate's face right then. "I would've taken them," he said.

"See, that's it. You weren't here. And—and neither was Lyle. Just me. I was the only one here. So what did I do? I called around, found a guide over to Santo's for those lawyers." She sighed. "I hate giving business away. We're not doing so hot, you know."

"I've been telling you," he said. "I've got money. Make me a partner."

"You're not going to bail me out, Stoney. I've got to make this work."

He took the finished sand eel from the vise. "It wouldn't be bailing you out, honey. It'd be an investment for me. A good investment." He clamped another hook in the vise. "They keep putting money into my account. You know that. It's just sitting there."

"Invest it in something good, then," she said. "Not some stupid business that's gonna go belly-up."

"We aren't going belly-up," said Calhoun.

"Walter fell out of his wheelchair yesterday," she said. "Speaking of going belly-up. When I got home, he'd been lying there all afternoon. Couldn't get up, couldn't even get to the phone. He looks up at me and says, 'Kate, I wet my goddam pants. Will you please for Christ's sake put me away.'"

Calhoun looked up at her. "Are you thinking of putting Walter in a nursing home or something?"

She shook her head. "That's not what he meant."

"Let me buy in, Kate," he said. "Then we can hire somebody to mind the shop once in a while. Do some advertising. Get a new sign for out front. Free you and me up so we can do more guiding. Maybe even take a day off occasionally. Actually go fishing. Hell, when was the last time you and I went fishing?" He shrugged. "Give you some time with Walter. If we pump some capital into the shop, you can pay more attention to Walter."

She shook her head, turned, and started for her office in the back. Then she stopped. "You don't get it, do you?"

He smiled. "I never pretended to get it, honey."

She stood there for a minute with her hands on her hips, frowning at him as if he was somebody she thought she'd seen somewhere but couldn't remember where. Then she went into her office.

A little after noon, Calhoun asked Kate if she wanted him to go get them some lunch. She was at the counter talking with a couple of young guys who Calhoun figured would just as soon stand there all afternoon flirting with her, making her smile, and she glanced up at him and said, "No," as if he'd asked if she wanted him to chop off her thumb.

Whenever he looked her way, she managed to have her head turned in another direction.

Actually, he *did* get it. It wasn't complicated. If Calhoun became her partner, she'd be tied to him, and Kate needed things to be on her own terms.

Well, Calhoun didn't mind that. He understood it. It wasn't the way he preferred it, but it was okay.

In the middle of the afternoon he glanced up and saw Sheriff Dickman standing in the doorway. The sheriff jerked his head toward the parking lot out front, then walked out.

A few minutes later Calhoun went outside. Dickman was leaning against the side of his Explorer tapping his Stetson against his leg.

"What's up?" said Calhoun.

Dickman nodded. "Thought you'd want to know. We found that rented Taurus. One of the deputies spotted it in the lot beside the general store in Standish."

"Standish," said Calhoun. "Was Fred Green in it?"

"Nope." Dickman shrugged. "The gal in the store said Lyle was in on Tuesday, asked if she'd mind if he left it there. She said she thought it was only for the day, but when he didn't come by she guessed she got it wrong and didn't think anything of it. I showed her your sketch of Fred Green. She never saw the man."

"Did she mention anything about Lyle making a phone call?"

Dickman nodded. "They've got an inside pay phone on the wall by the door. Lyle bought some cold drinks and used the change to make a call."

"Wait a minute," said Calhoun. "I'm trying to figure this out."

"Welcome to the club, Stoney. We traced the car. It was rented from an Avis place at the airport in Augusta by a man calling himself Fred Green. He paid with a credit card."

"So Green *is* his real name."

Dickman shook his head. "Turns out the Fred Green who belongs to that Visa card recently moved into a nursing home in St. Augustine, Florida. He's eighty-two, and he's going blind from diabetes."

"The card was stolen?"

Dickman nodded.

Calhoun frowned. "I figured Green—whatever his name is—shot Lyle, drove his old Power Wagon to the school in South Riley, picked up that Taurus, and . . ."

"He didn't pick up that Taurus," said Dickman. "It was sitting there in front of the general store in Standish the whole time."

"So," said Calhoun, "unless Mr. Green is living in South Riley, there was a third vehicle. Which means—"

"Which means," said Dickman, "he had an accomplice."

"And that means that the whole thing must've been premeditated."

"Frankly," said Dickman, "I don't know what any of it means. I've been trying to create scenarios, and I'm not getting very far. We know Green showed up here at the shop on Tuesday. We know he and Lyle drove off, each of them in their own car. Lyle had a date with that Moulton girl that evening, so they stopped in Standish and left the Taurus there. Lyle called his gal from there. Then Green climbed in with Lyle. We know they went to that millpond in Keatsboro, and we know Lyle got shot and was left there in the water. We know that Lyle's truck ended up behind the elementary school in South Riley. We know that the Taurus hasn't moved." He shrugged. "The state boys've towed both of those vehicles away. They'll do their forensics, maybe come up with something."

"What we don't know," said Calhoun, "is why this Mr. Green would want to kill Lyle in the first place."

Dickman shrugged. "Everybody's got enemies, Stoney. When we catch up to Green I guess we'll know the answer to that."

"*When?*"

"Okay. If. The man does seem to have disappeared himself pretty thoroughly. But we've got your sketch and we've faxed it to the state police and every sheriff's department in Maine, along with the message that the man is wanted for murder. We've got people talking to the folks in the airports and bus terminals, and we've notified the authorities in New Hampshire and Massachusetts, and by Jesus, Stoney, we'll get the sonofabitch."

"If he's got an accomplice . . ."

Dickman shook his head, then put his Stetson back on. "I gotta go. I just wanted to keep you up to speed." He narrowed his eyes. "You got a mind for this stuff, Stoney. Think on it for me. You're the only one who saw Green, who talked to him. Anything you can remember, you let me know."

"You can count on it," said Calhoun.

Dickman slid into his Explorer and drove away. Calhoun stood there in front of the shop, staring off in the direction that the sheriff had taken, trying to add it all up. After a couple of minutes, he turned and went back inside.

They closed up at five as they always did on Saturdays. Calhoun decided he wouldn't ask Kate if she wanted to hang around, relax after a busy day, put her feet up, have a Coke. He knew she'd say no.

After he finished cleaning up, he went to her office in the back. She was doing some paperwork.

"I hope Walter's okay," he said.

She looked up and smiled. "Thank you."

"If there's anything I can do . . ."

She nodded. "Thanks, Stoney. I don't think so."

"Why don't you take the day off tomorrow. I can handle the place."

"I can't ask you to do that."

"You didn't. I offered."

She looked at him through narrowed eyes for a minute, then nodded. "That'd be wonderful. You're sure?"

"I'll be here," he said.

He whistled to Ralph, went out to his truck, and they headed for home. Along the way he managed to avoid thinking about Kate and wondering if she was trying to tell him that she wouldn't be coming by anymore. Instead he tried to focus on what the sheriff had told him.

He drove past the turnoff for Dublin and kept going, heading for Keatsboro. He wanted to look around again. He had no idea what he was looking for, but he felt drawn to the millpond where Lyle had died.

He pulled to a stop by the break in the stone wall just down the road from Anna and David Ross's farmhouse. He got out and Ralph scooted out, too.

They started down the woods road. Ralph went hunting, quartering back and forth, his head held high, questing for bird scent. Lyle had said that Ralph had bird hunting in his blood. He'd offered to train him, but Calhoun wasn't particularly interested in bird hunting.

So far, Ralph had shown a good deal of interest in trout. When he was a puppy, he pointed moths and grasshoppers, and once Calhoun had to take him to the vet after a close encounter with a porcupine. Calhoun figured he should let Ralph hunt. It's what he lived to do, and pointing brook trout probably wasn't entirely fulfilling for a bird dog.

The sun had settled behind a cloudbank low in the western sky by the time Calhoun descended the long slope to the millpond. Already it was starting to get dark. He whistled in Ralph, sat beside the old dam, and closed his eyes. He tried to visualize it, what had happened here, tried to conjure up a mind-picture of Fred Green lying in the grass, squinting through the sights of his .22, holding steady on Lyle's chest, the muffled pop of the small-caliber rifle, Lyle slumping over, Green jacking another cartridge into the chamber, aiming again, and shooting a hole in the float tube.

And then Lyle adrift out there, the tube hissing out air, growing soft and flabby, Lyle sinking deeper in the water, his bowed head going under, his weight sinking the deflated float tube and his waders filling with water . . .

Ralph was lying beside him with his chin on his paws, staring at him as if he was trying to figure it out, too. Calhoun reached over and scratched his forehead.

Then Fred Green had walked out, climbed into Lyle's Power Wagon, driven to South Riley, and left the truck behind the elementary school.

Then what?

Then Fred Green—which wasn't his name—had disappeared. He had not used his rented Taurus.

Where the hell was the man?

Calhoun thought about Lyle, his interest in folk history, his fascination with the 1947 fire, his collection of reminiscences, those taped conversations with the local old-timers. "They won't be with us forever," Lyle used to say. "We've got to save their stories."

Up on the hill on the other side of the stream a farmer named Potter had died in that fire. Calhoun could make out the overgrown cart path on the other side of the stream, winding into the dark woods and up the hill. Lyle would surely have wanted to follow it up to the burned-out cellar hole where Potter had died trying to save his home from the inferno.

Calhoun pushed himself to his feet. "Come on," he said to Ralph. "Let's go take a look."

The rutted old road curved up the hill and among scrubby second-growth hardwoods, and Calhoun wondered again about the unusually impractical Yankee farmer who would build his place so far from the road—especially when, according to the topographic map, another road passed just a couple hundred yards behind it.

A tall, scraggly lilac grew at the corner of the granite foundation. Dried brown blossoms still clung to it. Briars and weeds and sumac grew out of the cellar hole, tangled among some charred timbers and a rusted woodstove. The old chimney had toppled and a pile of fieldstones lay scattered on the ground.

Potter had expected the fire to miss his place, but instead it had come racing up the hill at him. Calhoun closed his eyes, and he could see it and smell it and hear it . . . a wall of flame higher than the tops of the trees, crackling and roaring, suddenly upon him, the very heat of it singeing his hair and burning his eyes, pine trees exploding, blazing branches crashing to the ground. It surrounded him, sucked the oxygen from the air and from his lungs, devoured the house, not even slowing down, leaving a corpse and an empty, smoking cellar hole behind.

It had been tinder-dry in the woods that summer of '47, Lyle had told Calhoun. Dozens of small fires had exploded all over southern Maine in August and September. Firefighters had squelched them, but many of them continued to burn underground, feeding on roots and powdery soil, and later popping up somewhere else. The Great Fire of '47 was actually many fires, stoked by the dry west wind on the twentieth of October, then exploding, too many fires moving too fast for the disorganized—mostly volunteer—local firefighters to control, all those fires racing eastward, joining and then splitting off, leveling whole towns, missing others entirely, choosing this house, skirting around another one.

The Ross family across the road, where David was a young teenager living with his mother in 1947, had been lucky.

Mr. Potter up here on the hill had been unlucky.

It didn't make any sense. But Calhoun knew how hard it was to make sense of things. Lyle's getting shot didn't make sense. Getting hit by lightning, that didn't make any sense, either.

He looked around. Where the hell was Ralph?

He whistled, then listened.

The sun had set and it had grown dark in the woods. A pair of nighthawks were swooping around overhead chasing mosquitoes and moths, their long pointed wings flashing white underneath. A soft breeze was ruffling the leaves in the oaks.

"Ralph," he called. "Goddammit, get your ass in here."

From somewhere in the woods came a yip, then a whine.

"Ralph," yelled Calhoun. "Come here, you."

Ralph continued to whine, and Calhoun thought that he might've hurt himself, maybe got his foot caught in a trap. He headed in his direction, following the sound of Ralph's whining. Calhoun's directional system didn't work so well. You needed two ears to hone in on the direction of a sound. But when he headed down the back side of the hill, Ralph's yipping got louder. He hurried through a shadowy grove of pine trees and found himself in some bottomland where the ground was soft and blanketed with last fall's leaves.

Ralph was sitting there, whining.

Calhoun went over to him. "Ralph, for Christ's sake, what the hell—?"

In the fading evening light, Calhoun saw something pale in the bottom of the depression that Ralph had been excavating.

He sat back on his heels beside Ralph, looking at the object that the dog had found.

It was a human foot, sticking up out of the ground.

CHAPTER EIGHTEEN

CALHOUN CLOSED HIS EYES. When he opened them, the foot was still there.

He started to reach out to touch it, to verify it, but then stopped himself and pulled back his hand.

He and Ralph sat there on their haunches, looking at the foot sticking up out of the dirt. It was a medium-sized right foot, and it was wearing a dirty white cotton sock. It could've belonged to a man or a woman. Calhoun figured if he pulled off the muddy sock he might be able to tell. But he was damned if he was going to corrupt another crime scene. The foot was cocked slightly to the side so that the big toe pointed up at the sky.

Calhoun pushed himself to his feet. "C'mon," he said to Ralph. "You better heel."

Ralph heeled, and they trudged back up the hillside to the cellar hole, down the other side, across the dam at the millpond, and up the long sloping hill through the dark woods to where he'd left his truck.

By the time they got there, the moon had risen. He needed a phone and looked across the road in the direction of the Ross's farmhouse.

He saw no lights up there, but Calhoun and Ralph got into the truck, and he drove up to the Rosses' anyway. Anna's cloth-topped Wrangler was parked in front of the barn. The truck with the plow hitch on the front was gone. No lights glowed from the windows of the farmhouse, and the barn itself was dark.

Calhoun went to the back door of the house and rang the bell. He heard it chime inside, but there was no sign of life.

So he went back to the truck and headed out to the main road. He remembered seeing a gas station and a general store along the way. He doubted if either of them would be open at this time on a Saturday night. But maybe there'd be a pay phone out front.

He ended up driving all the way to Gallatin, the next town east of Keatsboro, where he found Juniper's, a little restaurant with its lights blazing and the side parking lot jammed.

He parked on the street, told Ralph to sit tight and growl fiercely at strangers, and went inside. The front door opened into a tiny lobby. To the right was a dining room. A couple of family groups were seated in there, talking back and forth between tables, but it looked as if the dinner hour had come and gone.

The big room to his left was a bar, and it was jammed with folks seated at tables and at the bar itself and standing against the walls, a mixture of young men and women and older couples. Jukebox rock music played at high volume, competing with a TV over the bar showing a baseball game.

Calhoun caught the arm of a dark-haired cocktail waitress in tight jeans and a white T-shirt, gave her his best lopsided grin, and said, "Excuse me, miss. I need a phone."

She jerked her head sideways. "Ask Kevin."

Kevin, the bartender, was a smooth-faced young man with a thin black mustache and high forehead. Calhoun wedged himself between a middle-aged woman and a boy who didn't look legal, spotted the phone on a shelf behind the bar, and said, "Hey, Kevin."

The bartender turned and looked blankly at Calhoun. "How ya doin'?"

"Good. Look," he said, pointing. "I need to use that phone."

"It ain't a public phone, mister."

"It's an emergency."

Kevin shrugged. "House rules."

Calhoun leaned over the bar and crooked his finger. Kevin frowned, then bent toward him. Calhoun grabbed the front of his shirt and pulled him close so that their faces were inches apart. "Listen," he said. "I said I got a goddam emergency. Maybe you didn't hear me."

Kevin nodded. "Hey, no big deal, man. Use the phone. I don't give a shit."

Calhoun smiled, let go of his shirt, and patted his shoulder. "Thank you kindly. Appreciate it."

He moved around to the side of the bar, reached over, and snagged the phone. He pressed it against his good right ear, got the number for the sheriff's office from information, and dialed it, holding his hand over his deaf left ear.

"York County Sheriff." A woman's voice.

"I need to talk to Sheriff Dickman."

"He ain't on duty now, sir. I can put you onto Deputy Langley."

Calhoun hesitated, then said, "No, I've got to speak to the sheriff. This is an emergency. I've found a dead body."

"Who is this?"

"My name's Calhoun. It's connected to the murder up in Keatsboro."

"You say you found a body?"

"That's right. Can you patch me through to the sheriff?"

"Where are you?"

Calhoun told her.

"Right," she said. "I know the place. What's the number there?"

Calhoun read it off the phone to her.

"Sit tight, Mr. Calhoun. The sheriff will call you there."

He disconnected. When he looked up, Kevin was staring at him.

"I'm waiting for a callback," said Calhoun.

Kevin nodded. "You want a beer or something?"

"Coke would be good."

Kevin slid a glass of Coke in front of him. Calhoun took out his wallet. "How much?"

Kevin waved his hand. "On the house, man."

Calhoun nodded and put a dollar bill on the bartop for a tip. He took a sip of Coke and glanced at his watch. It was nearly ten.

The phone rang twenty minutes later. Calhoun grabbed it and said, "Calhoun."

"Stoney," came the sheriff's voice, "what's this about a dead body?"

"Ralph found somebody's foot sticking out of the ground," said Calhoun. "I figure there's a body attached to it. It's buried in the woods out in back of that pond where I found Lyle."

"You sure about this, Stoney," said Dickman.

"It's wearing a sock," said Calhoun.

"A foot, huh?"

Calhoun heard the doubt in the sheriff's voice. "You think this is another one of those . . .?"

"Ghosts? How the hell do I know, Stoney. What do you want me to do."

"I want you to come take a look. This foot wasn't any ghost, Sheriff. It was a damn foot. Look—even if you doubt me, don't you think you better see for yourself?"

"I don't doubt you saw it," said the sheriff. "Whether it's real is something else." Calhoun heard him sigh. "Okay, Stoney. I guess you're right. You wait there. It may take a little while to get this organized."

Calhoun hung up, drained his glass of Coke, waved at Kevin, and went out front to his truck. When he climbed in, Ralph, who was curled on the passenger seat, opened his eyes and looked up without lifting his head. Calhoun scratched Ralph's muzzle. "You might as well snooze," he said. "We've got a little wait."

So he sat there in the truck in front of the little restaurant in Gallatin while the Saturday-night folks filtered out, got into their vehicles, and emptied the parking lot, and it was nearly midnight before a car pulled in behind Calhoun's truck and left its motor running and its headlights on.

Calhoun got out and went back to the sheriff's Explorer. Two other vehicles had pulled in behind him. One of them was a state police cruiser. The other was an emergency wagon.

Dickman looked up at him through the open window. "Why don't you climb in here with me," he said. "We can talk about it on the way over."

"Ralph comes with us."

"That's fine."

Ralph hopped into the back of the sheriff's vehicle. Calhoun got in front. "Head over to where we went into the pond," he said. "It's a long walk in through the woods. Hope you've got flashlights."

"We got flashlights," said Dickman. "Now talk to me."

As they drove, Calhoun recounted his decision to revisit the place where he'd found Lyle, how he'd been trying to make sense of the fact that Fred Green's rented Taurus was right where he and Lyle had left it, how he'd been hoping for some kind of insight and hadn't received one, how he'd gone up the hill to the burned-out cellar hole because he figured that's what Lyle would've done, and how Ralph had found the foot buried in the boggy low ground behind the cellar hole.

Dickman did not interrupt, and when Calhoun finished, the sheriff said, "So you're thinking Mr. Green killed two people, buried one of 'em, left the other in the water."

"Guess so," said Calhoun.

"No one else has been reported missing."

"Well, someone's missing, all right. I found him."

"Maybe it's Mr. Green himself," the sheriff said. "I guess when we dig him up we'll have some answers. Assuming you can find him in the dark."

"I can find him, goddammit."

The sheriff glanced at Calhoun. "You don't need to get mad." He hesitated. "Everything okay with Kate?"

"The shop isn't doing that well. Walter's getting worse. She's upset about Lyle."

"That's not exactly what I meant."

Calhoun said nothing.

They drove through the dark countryside for a couple of minutes in silence. Then the sheriff said, "It's none of my business, Stoney, but—"

"That's right."

"—but a fella dropped by my office yesterday. He was asking about you."

"What'd you tell him?"

"Nothing."

"Really?"

Dickman shrugged. "Really."

"This man," said Calhoun. "He was wearing a gray suit?"

"Yes." The sheriff hesitated. "Understand, Stoney. It doesn't matter to me what you might've done. Your past is your past. None of my business. I like you. Consider you my friend. But if there's something I should know, I'd sure appreciate it if you'd share it with me."

"What was he asking you? That man in the suit."

The sheriff said nothing.

"You're not at liberty to say, is that it?"

"Something like that."

"What exactly are you thinking, Sheriff?"

Dickman let out a long breath in the darkness of the car. "You show up in these parts five years ago. You got all the money you need, apparently. You hermit yourself up in the woods like you never wanted to see another human being for the rest of your life. Word gets around that you spent some time in a hospital, that you've got no memory of what landed you there. You're a man without a past, Stoney. It makes a person wonder, can you understand that?"

"Why don't you say it straight out for me."

"Fair enough." Dickman turned onto the road in Keatsboro that would take them to the woods road into the millpond. "Was that really a hospital you were in, Stoney?"

"I don't get you."

"Christ," muttered the sheriff. "I mean, were you in prison?"

"Is that what that man told you?"

"No. He said nothing like that."

"But his questions . . ."

"They made me wonder. That's all I'm saying."

"The answer is," said Calhoun, "it was a hospital, not a prison. I got hit by lightning. It messed up my head."

"Lightning, huh?"

"Yes. I got a big scar down my back."

"What was it like, getting hit by lightning?"

"I don't remember."

In the lights from the dashboard, Calhoun saw the sheriff frown. "You've told me about your ghosts, Stoney. You can understand my confusion."

"Sure can, Sheriff. And maybe you can understand mine."

"Like I said, it doesn't matter to me."

"Sounds to me like it does."

"I was just wondering if that man might've talked to Kate, too."

"If he did," said Calhoun, "I'm promising you right now, I'll kill him."

"Speaking officially," said the sheriff, "I've got to advise against it." He slowed down and tapped Calhoun's knee. "There's a flashlight under your seat. Why don't you shine it along the side there, make sure we stop at the right place."

Calhoun reached under the seat and found the flash. It was one of those long, heavy-duty models that held six batteries. He rolled down his window and shone the light along the stone wall that paralleled the road.

"What're you thinking, Sheriff?" said Calhoun.

"Nothing at all."

"Sounds to me like you're suspecting me of something. I want to know what you're thinking."

"Now don't go getting paranoid on me, Stoney. I don't suspect you of a damned thing."

In the beam of the flashlight Calhoun saw the break in the stone wall where the old woods road cut into the millpond. "Stop here," he said.

They pulled to the side, and the other two vehicles pulled in behind them. They all got out, and Dickman introduced Calhoun to a state police forensic expert named Weems, a tall guy with two cameras around his neck whose name Calhoun didn't get, a homicide detective named Bellotti, a doctor from the State Medical Examiner's office named Scolnik, and a young EMT who went by the name Woody. Calhoun shook hands with each of them.

The gang of them stood there beside the road, each with a flashlight. "Okay," said the sheriff. "Stoney here will lead the way. It's a long walk in. I hope you're all wearing comfortable shoes."

"What about Ralph?" said Calhoun.

"You better leave him in the car," said Dickman.

Calhoun went to the sheriff's Explorer and made sure the windows were open a crack all around and that the doors were locked. "You sit tight," he said to Ralph. "You've made enough trouble for one night. I'll be back."

Ralph was standing on the backseat with his nose pressed up against the crack in the side window. Calhoun poked his fingers in and let him lick them, then turned and headed into the woods.

It was a moonless night, and the woods outside the cones of the flashlights were black. When they got to the millpond, the sheriff halted the procession and shone his light against the reeds where Calhoun had found Lyle's body. "That's where Lyle McMahan was found," he told the others. He moved his light to the ground beside where he was standing. "And here's where we figure our shooter, Mr. Green, was lying." He pointed his light across the dam to the hillside. "Up there is where Mr. Calhoun spotted the other body. Lead on, Stoney."

They trooped across the dam single file, then up the hillside to the cellar hole. Calhoun stopped there and flashed his light through the undergrowth on the other side of the hill. "Down there," he said. "It might take me a minute to find it."

He moved down the hillside, stopping every few steps to play his flashlight around. "There was still some light in the sky when I was here," he said to the sheriff. "The shadows were different."

"Take your time."

He closed his eyes for a moment, re-creating the picture of it, a sharp memory photograph. Then he quickly led them down to the foot of the hill, moved the light in a half circle over the ground, and said, "Okay. Got it. Over there. Around behind that patch of alders."

Bellotti, the homicide cop, cleared his throat. "Step carefully," he said. "This is a crime scene."

Calhoun led them around the little island of alders to the place where Ralph had dug up the foot. Then he stopped.

There was no freshly dug-up dirt. Nor was there a foot sticking out of the ground.

There was only the woods, with old brown leaves blanketing the earth where they had fallen quietly eight months earlier.

CHAPTER NINETEEN

"IT WAS HERE," SAID CALHOUN. "Right here."

He knelt down and moved his flashlight over the blanket of dry leaves, then turned and looked up at the others, who had gathered in a semicircle around him. "Here," he repeated.

The sheriff squatted down beside him. "Must've been someplace that looked like this," he said quietly. "Let's look around some more."

Calhoun shook his head. He raked some leaves away from the ground with his fingers. Underneath was a layer of half-decomposed twigs and pine needles, and under that was moist black earth. He began digging in the dirt with both hands. He felt the sheriff touch his shoulder. He shook away his hand. "Shine your light here," he said.

"Come on, Stoney," said Dickman. "This isn't the place."

"The hell it's not," said Calhoun. "It was right here."

"You said a foot was sticking up."

"It was here," Calhoun repeated.

One of the other men grumbled, "Jesus," and another said, "Let's move around. See what we can find."

"You're not gonna find anything," said Calhoun. "This is the damn place."

The others wandered away. Their flashlights flickered through the bushes. The sheriff squatted down beside Calhoun and put his hand on his shoulder. "Stoney, listen—"

"I'm not crazy, if that's what you're thinking." He scooped away some more dirt, on his hands and knees, digging furiously now, throwing handfuls off to the side, his fingers scraping into the soft dark earth, gouging out a hole the way Ralph had done.

Dickman grabbed him by both arms and held him that way until Calhoun sank back onto his heels.

"I'm not saying you're crazy," said Dickman quietly. "You've mistaken the place, that's all. It's a big woods. It looked different in the twilight, you said so yourself."

Calhoun shook his head. "I've got this gift," he said. "I can remember things exactly. I have these pictures in my head. It's why I could draw Mr. Fred Green's face for you. I can see him. You want, I'll draw you another picture, and you'll see that it'll look exactly like that other one. I got a picture of this place in my head, too, and by Jesus, it's here, right where I'm digging, where Ralph found that foot."

"Tell you what," said Dickman. "Suppose you and I come back here tomorrow when the sun's out and we can see it better. Maybe that picture in your head will be clearer then. What do you say?"

Calhoun turned to look at him. In the darkness, the sheriff's face was a shadow. But Calhoun had heard the kindness in the man's voice, a gentle concern mingled with doubt. There was no anger in it, no frustration that he'd been dragged out of his house at midnight on a Saturday night, that he'd assembled a posse of skeptical homicide authorities and been led on a wild goose chase through the Maine woods.

Calhoun figured he knew the difference between one of his brain tricks—like a naked body drifting in a trout stream—and the real thing.

Maybe not. He knew his grip on reality was shaky. Sometimes all of it—Kate, Ralph, his house in the woods—seemed to exist only inside his own imagination. Sometimes he wondered if he'd never regained consciousness when that lightning bolt zapped him five years ago, and while all these things were happening, he was actually lying motionless in a hospital bed somewhere, with tubes and wires and machines keeping him alive and doctors looking at him, stroking their chins and mumbling to each other.

He let out a deep breath, shrugged, and said, "Okay. I guess we can come back tomorrow."

The sheriff stood up and held down his hand.

Calhoun took it and pulled himself to his feet. He wiped his hands on his pants. "I know how it looks," he said.

Dickman shook his head. "It doesn't look like anything except that we can't find the place. It'll look different in the daylight. We'll bring Ralph. He'll help. Now let's get the hell out of here."

"Why don't we try Ralph now?"

The sheriff shook his head. "We'll do it tomorrow."

Calhoun stood there while Sheriff Dickman moved away and spoke to the others. They gathered around him and grumbled and mumbled for a few minutes in voices too low for Calhoun to understand, then the sheriff said, "Come on, Stoney. You've got to show us how to get back. These city boys're all worried about bears."

No one said anything as they trekked out of the black woods. When they arrived at their vehicles, Calhoun climbed into the sheriff's Explorer. Ralph, who'd been sleeping in the back, stood up and dropped his chin on the back of Calhoun's seat. "Wish you could talk," Calhoun said to him. "You'd tell them that I'm not nuts. Hell, you could tell me, too."

The sheriff was outside, leaning against the state police cruiser, talking to the others. In the rear-view mirror, Calhoun could see him gesturing with his hands while the other men stood there shrugging and shaking their heads.

After a few minutes, the sheriff climbed in behind the wheel, switched on the ignition, and pulled away. The others followed along behind.

"Are you in some kind of trouble for this?" said Calhoun.

"Nope," he said. "They don't like it, but the hell with 'em."

"Can't blame them," said Calhoun. "You dragged them out here in the middle of the night for nothing. They think I'm some kind of whacko, I bet."

Dickman chuckled. "That they do, Stoney. I guess if you'd seen yourself on your hands and knees digging in the dirt like a wild dog, you probably would, too."

They drove in silence for a while, then Calhoun said, "What do *you* think?"

"About what?"

"You think I'm a whacko?"

The sheriff let out a long breath. "Tell you the truth, Stoney, I don't know what to make of it. It's peculiar, you've got to admit that. Those other fellas covered all that ground down there behind that hillside, and they didn't find a single foot sticking up. Folks who're buried hardly ever change their minds, undig themselves, crawl out of their holes, shovel the dirt back in, cover it all over with leaves, and walk away in the middle of the night. Unless we're dealing with some kind of ghoul or something here."

"You're a good man, Sheriff," said Calhoun, "and I appreciate your tolerance. But this isn't a joke."

"I know. I've got to admit it. You got me worried."

"Me, too," said Calhoun. "That foot . . ."

"That's not what I'm worried about," said the sheriff. "Finding Lyle like that, lugging him out of the woods—pretty damn upsetting for a man."

Calhoun said nothing.

"Stoney, don't get me wrong—"

"It's okay," said Calhoun. "I don't blame you. Sometimes I wonder about it myself."

They arrived back at the restaurant where Calhoun had left his truck. He slid out of the sheriff's vehicle, opened the back door for Ralph, then leaned in. "So now what?" he said.

"Now you go get yourself some sleep. That's what I'm going to do. I'll get ahold of you tomorrow. We'll take it from there. I'll call you."

Calhoun stood there looking in at the sheriff. Dickman met his eyes for a minute, then turned to look out the front window. "I'm beat, Stoney. Give that door a good slam. It doesn't latch right."

Calhoun closed the door and the Explorer pulled away. Calhoun watched its taillights disappear around the corner.

Then he whistled in Ralph, and they got into the truck and drove home.

It was almost three in the morning. Calhoun had promised Kate he'd open up, and since it was a Sunday, another busy weekend day at the shop—a day when folks tended to stop in on their way to the water to check the tides, pick up some extra leader material, buy a few flies, and ask for advice—he should have the OPEN sign hanging on the door by six.

Going to bed didn't make much sense.

So he and Ralph sat out on the deck, with the kitchen lights glowing from inside and Bitch Creek gurgling peacefully in the darkness down at the bottom of the hill, and he waited for the time to pass. Calhoun never needed much sleep. Some nights he hardly slept at all, and it didn't particularly affect him the next day. He figured it was just another thing that getting struck by lightning did to a man.

Anyway, on this night he feared sleep and the dreams it would likely bring. He'd seen a foot buried in the woods—except now he found himself questioning it. Maybe it *had* been another one of those mind-tricks, another phantom drifting down a trout stream.

The sheriff doubted him, doubted his sanity. Kate was generally pissed at him, and Lyle was dead, and the Man in the Suit was apparently setting about to alienate those who knew him. That left him with nobody, which put him back to where he'd started five years ago when he'd left the hospital—alone and rootless, a man with no past and no clear vision of the future, only some vague unanchored mind-flashes that seemed to connect him to the Maine woods.

When he'd seen it, Calhoun had believed it was a real foot sticking out of the ground. Ralph had been whining. He didn't whine for no reason.

But Calhoun had to confront the possibility that this was another apparition, another ghost. Or a ghost's body part, anyway. He knew he'd found the place where he'd seen it, and it was pretty clear that there was no foot.

When he'd seen that dead body floating in Bitch Creek, it meant that he was going to find Lyle's body in the water.

So what did this foot apparition—if an apparition it was—mean?

Out there on the deck, the diffuse light from the kitchen made the woods absolutely black around him. Calhoun reached down and gave Ralph a scratch on his ribs. Ralph *had* whined. He knew that.

The rain on his face awakened him. The woods were still dark, but the sky had begun to brighten. His watch read a little after four-thirty. He stood up, stretched, went inside, and took a long hot shower. Then he put the coffee together, slipped on his windbreaker, and went out onto the deck.

He checked the sky and the wind, as he did automatically every morning. Weather, wind, tide—crucial variables for the saltwater fisherman. Today a layer of gray clouds hung thick and heavy over the woods, and the damp easterly breeze riffled the leaves at the tops of the oaks. The air smelled salty and wet, and the rain was soft and misty.

He figured it was already raining hard along the coast.

Well, Calhoun knew exactly what he'd say to the fishermen who'd come stomping into the shop shaking the rain out of their hair and looking for advice. "Don't forget your foul-weather gear," he'd tell them, and the smart ones would nod solemnly and share his joke. Then he'd explain to them how the wind would stir up the bait and drive it against the shore, and how a gray, rainy day emboldened striped bass, how even the big ones, normally nocturnal predators, might hang around inshore on a day such as this one.

It promised to be a tough day for fly casting, a miserable day to be on the water—but a good day to catch some fish.

He went back into the kitchen, filled his travel mug with coffee, whistled up Ralph, climbed into the truck, and headed for Portland.

In the five years that he'd been in Maine, Calhoun had explored the coast from Casco Bay to Boothbay, sometimes with Lyle or Kate, sometimes on his own. On a Sunday in June, even a cool, rainy Sunday, dozens of fishermen would drop into the shop looking for guidance, and Calhoun had learned how to spread them out, point them in a direction where they might find some fish without bumping into too many other fishermen.

Put them onto fish, make them believe they'd been directed to a special, secret place, and they'd come back to the shop, and next time they'd buy something. Send them off on a wild goose chase and they'd never return. That, Kate had repeatedly told him, was the essence of the fishing-shop business.

Fishermen didn't spend a lot of money on weekends. They got geared up during the week, stopping in on lunch breaks and on their way home from work to study the merchandise, maybe pull the trigger on that expensive Billy Pate reel or the latest-generation graphite fly rod. A fishing shop such as Kate's donated goodwill on weekends and made money during the week.

So Calhoun gave away free advice all morning while the east wind skidded clouds across the sky and blew a steady soft rain against the windows of the shop and Ralph snoozed on the sweater in the corner, and he was too busy to think very much about Lyle's murder or a foot buried in the woods.

Kate came in around noon, which happened to coincide with the first time the shop had been empty of customers all morning. She was wearing sandals and jeans and a pale blue T-shirt under an ancient yellow oilskin poncho.

She shucked off the poncho in the doorway, ran her fingers through her long black hair, and smiled at Calhoun.

God, she was beautiful.

"Morning, Stoney," she said.

"That," he said, "is the first smile you've given me in a couple days."

She came over to him and kissed him quickly on the cheek. "I know," she said. "I'm sorry."

He touched the place on his cheek where he could still feel the hot imprint of her lips. "I thought about calling you last night," he said. "Then I figured, hell, if she's still pissed with me, I'd rather not know it."

She shook her head. "Don't start on me, Stoney."

He shrugged. "How's Walter?"

"Suicidal, I think, though he tells me he's fine, not to worry. This morning when I left, I made sure the bottles only had enough pills in them to get him through the day. Brought the rest with me." She let out a long breath. "I can't live this way, and neither can he."

"You didn't need to come in," he said. "I can take care of it."

"I had to come in, Stoney. I've got to live my life. Hell, you know the last time I went fishing?"

"You went out with Lyle a couple weeks ago."

She nodded. "And before that it was another couple of weeks. You and I, we've got to fish, Stoney. That's our business. We can't let ourselves turn into goddam merchants. We got a fishing shop here, not a grocery store. What about tomorrow morning?"

Monday was the slowest day in the shop. In the off-season, they didn't open at all on Mondays, and during the season they opened at noon.

"I'd love it," said Calhoun. "Tide's just right. Get out there five-thirty or six, we'll catch the last three hours of the outgoing, first three of the incoming. Should be good after this weather we're having."

Kate smiled. "It's a date, then." She touched his arm. "I hope you can bear with me for a while here. Things aren't easy. I know I've been taking it out on you. I've got nobody else."

He shrugged. "It's okay, honey. It's what friends are for. I've got stuff on my mind, too."

She nodded. "I know you do, Stoney."

He wanted to tell her about finding that foot sticking out of the ground in the woods near where Lyle died. But then he'd have to explain about going back and not finding it, and then wondering if he'd actually seen it in the first place. So he just said, "We'll work it out," and then three men in slickers came stomping into the shop.

Toward the middle of the afternoon, Sheriff Dickman showed up. He chatted with Kate for a minute, then caught Calhoun's eye.

They went out onto the porch.

"Nasty day," said Dickman.

"Good day for fishing," said Calhoun.

The sheriff nodded. "Got a little news."

"Yeah?"

"Yeah. We found the motel Mr. Green was staying at. Little place on Route 1 up in Craigville called The Lobster Pot."

"He's not staying there now, is he?" said Calhoun.

"He checked in Sunday night a week ago, checked out on Tuesday morning. That was the day he showed up here. His room had already been cleaned and rented out again, so there was nothing to be learned from it. He paid with that same stolen credit card. It's peculiar, Stoney."

"What is?"

"The forensics boys went over that rented Taurus and Lyle's Power Wagon. Not a damn thing in either of them. No suitcase, no briefcase, no airplane ticket, nothing. Not even a useful fingerprint. Nothing in the motel room. There isn't a trace of the man anywhere." The sheriff shook his head. "I want to find him."

"What'd the motel keeper have to say?"

"Not much. One of the Lincoln County deputies talked to the woman who was at the desk. She checked Mr. Green in and out, said only that he was an old fella with a southern accent who stiffed them with someone else's credit card." Dickman shook his head. "Got the feelin' that it wasn't a very thorough interrogation. Like to go on up there, talk to her myself. But Lincoln County's out of my jurisdiction."

"Do it anyway," said Calhoun. "The hell with jurisdiction."

"Can't," said the sheriff. "I got to get along with those fellas. We're all pretty protective of our territory. I don't care for it when someone from another county starts hornin' into ours. I mentioned it to Bellotti, that state cop who was with us last night. Got the feeling that he's kinda soured on our case here." Dickman shrugged. "Somebody ought to talk to that woman."

"Last night I had the feeling you were a little soured on *me*," said Calhoun. "So I want to be sure I'm understanding you."

Dickman smiled. "I'm just thinking, a fella like you doesn't need to concern himself about jurisdictions. If you had a mind to wander up towards Craigville, happened to drop in on The Lobster Pot Motel and found that woman at the desk—Mrs. Sousa's her name—well, it wouldn't bother anybody, I don't think."

"I can do that," said Calhoun.

"You feel like taking another walk in the woods?" said Dickman.

"If you don't mind getting wet."

The sheriff shrugged. "Get wet every time I take a shower. It hasn't killed me yet. Bring Ralph."

Calhoun went back inside. Kate was sitting behind the front counter with her chin in her hands, staring into the distance. She turned and smiled at him. "I know," she said. "You and the sheriff have got to do some investigating."

He nodded. "Probably be gone the rest of the afternoon."

"I can handle it. You go ahead. Appreciate your opening up today."

"Kate—?"

"See you tomorrow," she said. "We got a date. Gonna do some fishing."

CHAPTER TWENTY

RAINWATER DRIPPED from the pines, and except for a quarrel between a pair of blue jays, the woods were silent under the wet gray sky. Ralph snuffled around in the bushes, apparently finding all kinds of interesting scent. As they trudged down the old cart path to the millpond, Calhoun thought about ways to get it off his chest.

Finally, he decided to just blurt it out. "I've got to ask you something straight out," he said to the sheriff. "Do you think I killed Lyle?"

"Hell, no. I think Fred Green did."

"Well, good."

"But understand, that doesn't mean I think you didn't. There's a difference, you know."

"Why would I kill Lyle? Next to Kate, he was my best friend."

"Hell, if I could think of a reason, I might suspect you actually did it. I've got to admit, for a while there I had some doubts. I wondered— and you've got to excuse me here, it's just how a cynical old cop thinks—I wondered if maybe Lyle and Kate had something going, or maybe he was horning in on your business arrangement, or he owed you money. Or maybe you were fooling around with his girlfriend." He waved his hand. "It's the motive in this thing that's got me."

"His housemates, Danny and Julia, they told me that Lyle left a long trail of broken female hearts in his wake. Including Julia's. Probably some pissed-off boyfriends and husbands as well. Maybe Mr. Green . . ."

The sheriff nodded. "Okay, sure. Like that. Lyle might've been fooling around with Green's young wife, or maybe his daughter. Got her pregnant or something." He shrugged. "However you want to look at it, though, Stoney, we're still looking for Mr. Fred Green. And if he did it, that means you didn't."

The path through the woods had become as familiar to him as his own driveway. It seemed as if he'd walked in and out of here a hundred times, and every time he did it, it seemed to take less time to get there.

They descended the slope, crossed the pond at the dam, climbed the hill to the cellar hole, and went down the other side. Calhoun led them directly to the place where Ralph had dug up the foot and where Calhoun himself had dug all over again.

Ralph sniffed around, then wandered off into the woods.

Calhoun called him back, but Ralph showed no particular interest.

"This was the place," said Calhoun. "I was hoping it would look different in the daylight. But it doesn't. It was right here."

"Stoney, listen," said Dickman. "There is no body buried here. You were mistaken. If you saw a foot sticking up out of the ground, it was somewhere else. Now, I came here to look around, check it out. I got my doubts, but I don't mind doing it. But you've got to help me, here. Okay, you thought this was the place. But it isn't. You can see that."

Calhoun shook his head. "I guess it isn't. It's just so damn clear in my mind," he said. "Let's look around."

They moved in ever-widening circles, beginning at the dug-up area, Calhoun and the sheriff walking side by side, until they'd covered the entire area at the foot of the hill.

He didn't expect they'd find anything, and they didn't. Ralph sniffed around but showed no particular interest in anything, not even the place where he'd dug up the foot yesterday. The rain had washed away whatever scent might've been there, Calhoun guessed. There wasn't even any sign that a gang of men had been tromping around there last night. Calhoun was pretty good at picking up signs in the woods—freshly broken twigs and leaves, bent-over branches and saplings, depressions in the moss, crushed grass. But the rain had erased everything.

Finally, Calhoun said, "That's enough, Sheriff. I give up."

Dickman put a hand on his shoulder. "I'm sorry, Stoney. It must be scary."

"What?"

"Thinking you saw something and thinking you didn't, all at the same time."

Calhoun nodded. He didn't know what to think anymore.

They headed back up the hill to the old cellar hole.

"Lyle loved these old artifacts," Calhoun said.

"Lots of stories in these woods, all right," said the sheriff. "A hundred years ago, this whole part of Maine was settled. Covered with farms. It was all cleared fields and pastures, and every stone on every wall that runs through the woods today was lifted up and set there by somebody. Now it's woods again."

Calhoun was wandering among the rubble of the fallen-down chimney, thinking about Mr. Potter, how he died, wondering if his ghost haunted the place.

A ghoul, more likely. A body-snatcher.

It looked like some of the chimney fieldstones had been moved recently, leaving bare depressions in the ground. He started to call to the sheriff, who was squatting on the other side of the cellar hole catching his breath, when he noticed that an area about two feet in diameter appeared to have been dug up recently. It was right at the northwest corner of the cellar hole. Whoever did it had filled it in again and tamped down the earth and placed a fieldstone on top of it. But the stone didn't fit the bare patch of dirt, and when Calhoun poked at it with his finger, the ground was softer than it would have been if that stone had been resting there for fifty years.

He glanced over at the sheriff and saw that Ralph was sitting beside him. The sheriff was scratching Ralph's ears and talking with him, gazing off into the distance where a hawk was cruising on the thermals. Ralph was staring up at the gray sky with his ears perked up, which meant that he saw the hawk, too, and was wishing he could fly so he could chase it.

Calhoun rolled the fieldstone away from the patch of bare earth and began scooping it out. Under the top layer of dirt were three softball-sized rocks. Calhoun guessed that whoever had dug it up and filled it in again had removed something and had used those rocks to occupy the space. He pulled out the rocks and dug some more.

Then he saw something glittering in the bottom of the hole. He reached in, picked it up, and blew the dirt off it.

If he didn't know better, he'd have sworn it was a gold nugget. It was squarish but irregular in shape and rounded off on the corners, about the size of a half-worn pencil eraser. Without his fly-tying glasses, he couldn't examine it too closely. But it certainly looked like gold.

"What've you got there, Stoney?"

He turned. The sheriff was standing behind him, frowning.

Calhoun held out his palm, showing him the little nub of gold. "I struck gold, I think."

Dickman squatted down and looked at it. "Looks like gold, all right." He picked it up, squinted at it, shrugged, and dropped it back into Calhoun's hand. "Well, I guess all kinds of things—maybe even gold jewelry—would fall to the ground when an old farmhouse burns down."

Calhoun squinted at the little hunk of gold. "I bet it's been here since forty-seven. Looks like it melted in the fire."

The sheriff shrugged.

Calhoun dropped the nugget into his pocket. "It looks like somebody was digging here," he said. "The earth was freshly dug."

"Where you just dug, you mean?" said the sheriff.

Calhoun nodded. "Sorry. I should've showed it to you first."

"Yes, you should've." The sheriff was staring down at the place where Calhoun had been digging. "Wonder if Fred Green came up here after he plugged Lyle."

"I was wondering that myself," said Calhoun.

"Well, we're not going to figure that out by standing here and talking about it." The sheriff glanced at his watch. "We better head back, before you dig the whole place up."

Calhoun pushed himself to his feet. "Damn sorry about this," he said. "I swear I saw that foot. Don't know what to make of it, and that's the truth."

"Don't worry about it, Stoney. I'd rather stroll through the woods on a rainy afternoon than push papers around my desk any day."

When they got back to the Explorer, Dickman said, "Let's see if Anna and David saw anything last night."

He drove up the Rosses' driveway. When they got out and slammed the doors, Anna came out the back door, wiping her hands on a towel.

She nodded at them. "Afternoon, boys."

"Afternoon, Anna," said the sheriff.

"You fellas've been busy across the street."

"It's a crime scene, Anna," said the sheriff. "You know how that works."

"Just from TV." She shrugged. "Do you usually visit crime scenes at midnight?"

"Sometimes we do. Did we disturb you?"

"Car doors slammin' and bangin' in the middle of the night when normal folks're trying to sleep? 'Course you disturbed us."

"I stopped by earlier in the evening last night," said Calhoun. "Needed your phone. The house was dark."

She frowned. "What time might that've been?"

"Oh, nine, nine-thirty."

"David and I went to a movie."

"What time did you get home?" said the sheriff.

She cocked her head and narrowed her eyes at him. "Why are you asking?"

"I was just wondering if any vehicles might've stopped across the street before our cavalcade arrived last night."

"Well, we got back around eleven, and we didn't see nothin' then. What's goin' on, Sheriff?"

"Oh, nothing, really. David's not around?"

"Nope. Said he'd be back for supper. You boys want some coffee?"

The sheriff smiled. "Thanks, but no, Anna. Got to get back to the office." He turned to Calhoun. "You ready to hit the road?"

Calhoun nodded.

"Sorry to bother you, Anna," said the sheriff. "Anything you see going on down here, I sure do want to know about it."

"You can count on it," she said.

Calhoun and Dickman got back into the Explorer. They went down the Rosses' driveway and headed back toward Dublin.

"I'd like to know what you're thinking about all this," said Calhoun.

Dickman shrugged. "I think you think you saw something. I think you were wrong. You been through a lot, my friend. Hell, anybody's mind can play tricks on 'em once in a while. Look—don't you worry about what I think. What I think doesn't matter. We'll figure this out, and when we do, everything'll make sense." He reached over and gripped Calhoun's shoulder. "You've already done a helluva lot, and I appreciate it."

Calhoun nodded. "I hope you'll keep me informed."

"'Course I will." He was silent for a minute, then said, "What happened to Lyle isn't your fault, Stoney."

"The hell it's not," said Calhoun.

He thought of driving up to Craigville to talk with the lady at The Lobster Pot motel. But it was already close to suppertime, and he found he'd lost his spirit for sleuthing around. He was confused and a little frightened by what seemed to be happening to his mind. The sheriff, despite what he said, didn't quite trust him, and all he wanted was to be alone for a while.

So he took Ralph for a long walk through the wet woods, following Bitch Creek to its origin at the spring seeps on the hillside, and he took a different way back, bushwhacking where there were no paths except those made by deer, and not once did he spot any feet sticking out of the earth.

He spent the evening fiddling around with his fishing gear, deciding what to bring the next morning with Kate, cleaning his fly lines, lubricating his reels, reorganizing his fly boxes. After a month of guiding, everything was pretty scattered.

He kept glancing at his watch. Kate would have to call him so they could decide when and where to meet. He had a few thoughts. Kate probably did, too. She usually knew what she wanted. They'd have to discuss it.

When eleven o'clock came and went and she hadn't called, he considered calling her. But he didn't.

He went out onto the deck, leaving the sliding glass door open to the kitchen so he could hear the phone. He tilted back his head and gazed up at the sky. It was clearing. The rain had stopped falling around sunset and the wind had shifted, and now the clouds were breaking up and skidding across clear patches of sky where stars glittered, and the air tasted moist and fresh. He tried not to think about Kate or Lyle or seeing a phantom foot sticking out of the ground. But except for Kate and Lyle, there wasn't much of anything he cared about.

When he first heard the distant rumble of the Blazer's busted tailpipe, he figured it was his imagination. Wishful thinking. And even when she pulled in beside his Ford pickup and turned off the ignition, he didn't quite trust his eyes. He'd been seeing too many ghosts lately.

But he pushed himself to his feet, sauntered down off the deck, went to her truck, and opened the door for her.

She slid out and stood there beside her Blazer, not smiling, just looking at him, her dark eyes large and solemn. She was wearing a long, loose-hanging, pale-orange dress that seemed to flow over her body like a waterfall, just touching her here and there—at her breasts and hips, hinting at the mysterious womanly curves underneath without revealing them. It had buttons all the way up the front. Kate had left several undone at the throat and at the hem, and Calhoun had to swallow hard against the sudden tightness in his throat.

He held out his hand, not to touch her, just to meet her half way. "Jesus, Kate—"

She shook her head. "Don't say anything, Stoney." Her voice was so soft Calhoun could barely make out her words. "I don't want to talk," she said. "Please."

She stepped forward, moved against him, circled his chest with her arms, tilted up her head, kissed his jaw, buried her face in the hollow of his throat. He felt her shudder. He moved a hand up to her neck, cradled her head, stroked her hair. His other hand slid down over her hip and held her there tight against him.

They stood that way for a minute, pressing hard against each other, not moving. Then she stepped back from him, and he watched as she unbuttoned her dress, one button at a time, moving slowly, her eyes fixed on his, not smiling, teasing him, he knew, teasing herself, too. She let her dress slip off her shoulders and drop to the ground. She was completely naked underneath.

"Kate, honey . . ."

She touched his mouth with her fingertips. "Shh," she said.

They made love on the soft damp blanket of pine needles beside her truck, and afterward they lay there gazing up through the trees at the sky, not talking, just holding each other.

After a while they went inside. They showered together, scrubbing the dirt and pine pitch off each other's bodies, toweled each other dry, then crawled naked under the covers.

She snuggled backward against him, fitting her back into the curve of his front. He hugged her from behind with one arm around her hips to hold her tight against him and the other under her neck, and for the first time since he'd dragged Lyle out of the pond, he fell quickly and completely asleep.

Then she was shaking his shoulder. "Stoney," she whispered. "Something's out there."

He sat up. "What is it?"

"Ralph started whining. Then I heard it. There's something outside."

"Porcupine or coon, probably."

"I don't know . . ."

Calhoun slid out of bed and pulled on his pants. While they'd been sleeping, the sky had cleared, and now there was enough moonlight filtering into the house for him to see without turning on the lights. He went to the front. Ralph was standing there with his nose pressed against the door, making little whining noises in his throat.

"I'm not letting you out just so you can get your nose stuck by a fat old porcupine," he whispered. He tapped the top of Ralph's head. "You stay."

Ralph sat down but continued whining.

He took the Remington autoloader off its pegs, then eased the door open and peeked out. He saw nothing. He pushed open the screen door, stepped out onto the deck, and stood there, peering into the shadows, listening hard.

Whatever it was that made him drop onto his belly didn't register consciously. Maybe it was the sandpapery sound of a boot shifting on the leaves or the soft snick of a safety being pushed off or the click of a hammer being cocked, or maybe his subconscious had registered a glint of moonlight on metal or a shadowy movement in the bushes beyond the opening where the trucks were parked.

In that one instant as he threw himself to the porch floor, he heard the quick pop of a small-caliber rifle, then the mechanical click of a bolt being thrown, and then another pop, and simultaneous with each shot, he heard a bullet thunk into the side of the house above him, right where his chest had been.

CHAPTER TWENTY-ONE

HE SAW THE TWO QUICK MUZZLE FLASHES, and from his position sprawled on the porch floor, he touched off a shot in their direction. Then, while the boom of the Remington 12-gauge was still echoing in the woods, he scrambled off the porch and darted behind Kate's Blazer, keeping low, holding his shotgun in both hands, his finger curled around the trigger guard, ready to fire again.

He crouched there, listening. The woods were silent. He eased his head up and rested the Remington on the hood of the Blazer. He listened and looked hard. Even with one deaf ear, he knew he'd catch any out-of-place sound. His ears and eyes were those of a woodsman, conditioned to register anything unnatural. But there was nothing.

He waited. Several minutes passed.

Then in the distance, in the direction of the road at the end of his driveway, he heard an engine starting up and a vehicle pulling away.

He gave it a few more minutes, then eased around the side of the house and went in through the sliding door.

Kate appeared in the bedroom doorway. She had pulled on one of his T-shirts and a pair of his boxers. "You okay?" she said.

He nodded.

She came to him and hugged him hard. "I heard shots," she said. "I figured you were all right. You shot after he did. What happened?"

"Someone tried to plug me," he said. "Fred Green with his twenty-two, if I'm not mistaken. The one he shot Lyle with. Guess I scared him off."

"We've got to call the sheriff."

He nodded. "I will."

"Think you winged him?"

Calhoun shook his head. "I keep that gun loaded with number-eight birdshot. It's for scaring people away, not hurting them. Might've peppered him, but it wouldn't even draw blood at that distance."

She sat at the kitchen table. "Now what?"

"Unless you think you can go back to sleep, I guess we might as well put on some coffee."

Calhoun and Kate sipped coffee on the deck. When the sky lightened and the birds started singing, he pointed across the opening. "He was in those bushes. I saw the muzzle flashes by that big pine."

She turned to him and put her hand on his arm. "What's going on, Stoney? Why's he trying to kill you, too?"

Calhoun shrugged. He realized he hadn't told Kate about the foot in the woods, how it looked like Fred Green was killing more people than just Lyle. Right now he didn't want to get into it. It would take too much explaining. So all he said was, "Let's go take a look around. There should be two empty cartridges on the ground."

They moved across the opening into the woods where he'd seen the muzzle flashes. "Around here," said Calhoun. He got down on his hands and knees, and Kate did, too. They crept around, scanning the blanket of pine needles, and fifteen or twenty minutes later, Kate said, "Here's one."

Calhoun went over and picked it up with a twig the way Sheriff Dickman had by the pond. It was a .22-caliber long-rifle rimfire, just like those they'd found at the millpond. A few minutes later he spotted the other one.

He took the two cartridges, impaled on twigs, to the house and dropped them into a plastic bag. Then he went back outside and showed Kate where the two bullets had thudded into the door frame. The holes were chest-high on him.

By now the morning sun was angling through the trees. They got some more coffee and returned to the deck.

"You gonna call the sheriff?" said Kate.

"I will," said Calhoun. "Give him a chance to wake up first. Nothing's going to change here."

"Tell me what you're thinking," she said.

Calhoun put his heels up on the railing, tilted back in the rocker, and rested his coffee mug on his belly. "I don't have much wisdom on it, honey. Mr. Green is aiming to kill me, too, I guess. Don't ask me why."

"But why was he hiding out there in the bushes? Why didn't he just come in and do it?"

"He probably didn't expect to see your truck here, had to take a minute to think about that. Maybe he heard Ralph growl, figured we'd wake up." Calhoun shrugged. "Your guess is as good as mine."

Kate reached over and took his hand. They sat there for several minutes, not talking, just listening to the birds and the creek, and watching the woods fill up with sunlight.

"A man was in the shop the other day," she said.

Calhoun said nothing.

"He was—I think he was interested in you," she said.

"How so?"

"Said he wanted to go fishing, needed a guide. I told him I guided some, and I could tell that didn't interest him. So I mentioned you, said I had a good man. His ears perked right up. Asked your name, and I told him. Claimed he'd heard good things about you." She shook her head. "He asked clever questions, Stoney. Trying to get me to talk about you, your—your stability, I think was his word, except the way he used it, it didn't seem personal. Afterward, when I thought about it, it seemed as if he was checking you out. And it wasn't for fishing. That man didn't know much about fishing."

"This man," said Calhoun. "He was wearing a suit?"

"Well, yes." She frowned. "Lots of men come into the shop wearing suits."

"Tall, mournful, gray guy? No accent you could pin down? Washed-out look to him, a face you can't quite remember?"

She nodded. "You know him?"

"Yes."

"A friend?"

He shrugged. "He's from before. I don't know if he's a friend or not."

"So why's he coming around asking questions about you?"

"I don't know that, either."

They sat for a while longer, still holding hands and rocking. Then Kate said, "We were supposed to go fishing today."

"We should've been on the water an hour ago."

"I was really looking forward to it," she said.

"Me, too. Too late now."

"I got an idea," she said.

He turned to look at her.

She yawned. "I didn't get much sleep last night," she said. "You figure Mr. Green is likely to come back with his twenty-two in the daylight?"

Calhoun shook his head. "Doubt it."

"How about a nap, then?"

"I'm kinda wired, honey," he said. "Not sure I can sleep."

"I bet we can figure out a way to get ourselves unwired." She stood up, stretched, then held both hands to him.

~~~
~~~

After they made love, Kate dropped off to sleep. Calhoun lay there for a while, watching her face and feeling the warmth of her leg where it pressed against his. He knew he'd never get back to sleep himself, so as soon as her breathing slowed and deepened, he slipped out of bed, gathered up his clothes, and shut the bedroom door behind him.

He dressed in the kitchen and put on some more coffee, and when it was ready, he poured himself a mug and took the portable phone and his coffee out onto the deck.

A high-pressure front had moved in behind yesterday's storm. The morning sky was cloudless. The sun was so bright he had to squint, and the air was dry and cool, almost chilly for late June. A persistent north-westerly breeze ruffled the oak leaves and swayed the high branches of the pines. It would've been a poor day for fishing—which was no consolation. A poor day of fishing with Kate was always a damn good day.

He sat there with the phone on his lap, sipping his coffee and thinking about what he wanted to do, trying to order his thoughts, to make sense of things. But his mind refused to focus. Fred Green had shot Lyle, and maybe he'd shot somebody else and buried them in the woods, and now he had tried to shoot Calhoun. Calhoun believed he would try again.

He had no idea why Mr. Green was doing this.

He picked up the phone and dialed Millie Dobson's number.

She answered on the second ring. "Millie here."

"It's Stoney Calhoun."

"Well, hello, there, stranger. You looking to buy some more property?"

He considered lying to her, then changed his mind. "Nope. Calling to ask for a favor, Millie. Nothing in it for you."

"What kind of favor you got in mind, Stoney?"

"You can trace deeds, right?"

"Well, sure. Of course, it takes a lawyer to make it legal. But I can do it as well as they can. It's not hard."

"What if that parcel happened to be up in Keatsboro?"

"Not a problem. I've got listings all over York County. You want me to check some Keatsboro property for you?"

"There's a piece of land up there that used to belong to folks named Potter. They got burned out in forty-seven. Mr. Potter died in the fire. I don't know the name of the road it's on, but I can show it to you on a map."

"Stoney," said Millie, "I know damn well that you found Lyle McMahan's body on that property last week. You want to tell me what you think I might find if I traced that deed?"

"I don't know what I expect, to tell you the truth. I'm just thrashin' around here."

"If you'll excuse me," she said, "I'm wondering why it's you who's doing the thrashin'. Isn't that the sheriff's job?"

"Lyle was my best friend," he said. "It's kind of personal with me, Millie."

She was silent for a moment. Then she said, "I'm a businesswoman, you know. I don't work for free."

"I'm happy to pay you for your time, Millie."

"You can buy me dinner at Juniper's tonight. I'll tell you what I find out then. Deal?"

"You drive a hard bargain, ma'am. Seven o'clock sound about right?"

"See you then, Stoney."

He disconnected from Millie, and when he turned to put the phone on the table, he saw Kate standing in the doorway buttoning up the front of her orange dress.

"Jesus," he said. "You snuck right up on me. When I've got a phone covering my only good ear, I don't hear much of anything."

She came onto the deck and stood beside him. "What're you doing?"

He waved his hand. "Nothing, honey."

"Having dinner with Millie, huh?"

He grinned. "You jealous?"

She smiled and rolled her eyes. "Millie's a very attractive woman, all right. And I bet she's got her eye on you."

"Aw, Kate—"

"But no, Stoney, I'm not the least bit jealous. Curious, though."

"Like I told Millie," he said. "I'm just thrashin' around, trying to figure things out."

"Did you call the sheriff?"

"Not yet."

"You're going to, aren't you?" She narrowed her eyes. "Dammit, Stoney. You could've got yourself killed last night. Somebody came here to shoot you, remember?"

"I know what I'm doing, Kate."

She shook her head. "Like hell you do. We've got an attempted murder here. Who do you think you are?"

He gazed up at the sky for a moment. "I think I'm a trained investigator," he said.

She cocked her head. "What'd you say?"

"I've spent the last five years trying to figure out who I am. I haven't had much luck at it. But in the last few days, since Lyle got killed, things are starting to click for me. I haven't figured it all out by a long shot. But I'm observing how my mind's been working, and I'm collecting some new memories, and I don't think that man in the gray suit showed up by accident. I'm pretty sure I used to be a cop of some kind, and I want to do this my own way, see where it leads me, see what it teaches me about myself. Does that make any sense to you?"

"No," she said. "Frankly, it doesn't. I don't care what you were. You got zapped by lightning and you know as well as I do, it messed up your brain. You're gonna go thrashin' around until that Fred Green shoots you dead, and when that happens, Stoney, so help me . . ."

Tears had welled up in Kate's eyes. Calhoun reached over to touch her hand, but she yanked it away. "Don't," she said. "I don't want to lose you, too."

"You aren't going to lose me, honey. I promise you that."

"Don't make promises you can't keep," she said. "I should've known better than to give my heart to you." She shook her head, looked into his eyes for a long moment, then smiled. "But I guess I did, didn't I?"

Calhoun nodded. "That's what we both did," he said. He hesitated for a moment, then said, "I think it would be best if you steered clear of me for a while."

"You think I'm scared?"

He shook his head. "I just . . . need to take care of business."

She stood up, folded her arms, and looked down at him. "You're gonna get yourself killed."

"Trust me."

She laughed softly. "Funny thing is, I do trust you. I guess I *am* scared, Stoney. I want you forever and ever."

"Me, too," he said. He got up and wrapped his arms around her. "It'll be over soon," he whispered into her hair. "I've got to get it done. Okay?"

She tilted her head back, looked at him steadily for a moment, then nodded. "Okay." She kissed his mouth hard, gave him a smile, then stepped back from him. "Just do it, Stoney. Get it done."

Then she turned and walked off the deck. She slid into her old Blazer, started it up, and drove away.

He stood there listening to the rumble of her broken tailpipe fade in the distance. Then he went inside. He had a lot to do, and the sooner he got it done, the sooner he'd see Kate again.

CHAPTER
TWENTY-TWO

AFTER KATE LEFT, Calhoun wandered through his little house in the woods, cataloging his possessions according to whether he'd feel seriously deprived if he should lose them. It was a liberating exercise. He'd left the hospital in Virginia with nothing, and now, after five years of accumulating things, he realized that if he lost everything, he was still better off than when he'd started.

Before last night, he'd felt absolutely secure and private on his property in the woods. He never locked his doors or worried about leaving Ralph.

That's how it was in the Maine countryside. Folks shot deer and ducks out of season and cheated on their wives and their taxes and drove drunk. On occasion, they even killed each other. But Mainers, by God, respected their neighbors' private property. Nobody ever came down his long driveway whom he didn't trust.

But now it had changed. Last night Stoney Calhoun had been invaded. Fred Green had actually snuck onto his property, and it was this more than actually getting shot at that bothered him. There was nothing to stop the man from coming back when Calhoun wasn't home, stealing or trashing anything he wanted.

On the table beside Calhoun's bed in a silver frame stood a five-by-seven photograph he'd taken of Kate two summers ago. She was standing knee-deep in the water struggling to hold up a forty-one-inch striped bass, the first really big fish she'd ever caught on a fly rod. Behind her, the flat water of the half-tide creek reflected orange and pink, and the rich, sharply angled rays of the rising sun glowed in Kate's eyes and on her skin. Her T-shirt and shorts were soaked and plastered to her body from when she'd fallen into the water chasing the big fish up and down the banks of the creek, the same creek where he'd first met her, and there were spots of mud—along with the biggest, goofiest, happiest grin she'd ever given him—on her face.

Calhoun did not want to lose that photograph.

He ended up putting a few things into the truck—his photograph of Kate, his secondhand anthology of American literature, his old Remington 12-gauge autoloader, a box of double-ought buckshot, the aluminum tube that held his favorite Sage six-weight fly rod, his packed fishing vest, and Ralph.

He figured you could learn a lot about a man if you told him he might lose everything he owned except for what he could stuff into the cab of an old Ford pickup truck.

That's how he was feeling.

He had no doubt that Fred Green would be back, and who knew what he'd decide to do next time? But Calhoun was damned if he was going to change his life because of it.

He shoved the framed photograph and the box of shotgun shells into the glove compartment. He slid the fly rod and the shotgun behind the seats and stuck the anthology under the driver's seat. Ralph sat on the passenger's seat with a frown on his face.

"I know you'd rather hang around," he explained to Ralph, "and I know you'd love to bite the ass of anybody who comes trespassing. But

I'm going to need your company today." He didn't tell Ralph that he figured anybody who'd shoot a man in a float tube would have no qualms about shooting a dog. No sense in upsetting Ralph.

It was around nine in the morning when he pulled out of his driveway. He felt calm, ready for whatever might happen. He had his dog and his truck and the only possessions that mattered to him. If Mr. Green came by to trash his house in the middle of the day, he couldn't stop him. He wouldn't like it. But it wouldn't touch his heart.

He drove east until he picked up Route 1 in Falmouth, just outside Portland. He headed north, through Yarmouth and Freeport and Brunswick and the old ship-building city of Bath, and then across the bridge that spanned the Kennebec, still following Route 1 as it wound northeast toward Craigville.

He'd originally assumed that Fred Green was staying in the biggest, most expensive hotel in Portland. When he saw The Lobster Pot Motel, he smiled. It had to be the cheapest, seediest motel in southern Maine.

It looked like they'd run out of money after they built the sign, which towered tree-top high beside the highway. It was surmounted with a big red lobster which, Calhoun assumed, flashed neon at night. The sign itself was in the shape of a lobster trap, of course. On the bottom hung a smaller lighted sign that read CABLE TV. OLYMPIC POOL. ALL CREDIT CARDS. VACANCY.

He turned into the gravel parking area. There were two cars, both with out-of-state plates, parked there. The motel was a single-story rectangular building with eight units in front and eight in back. Its unpainted shingles had weathered silvery, and the white trim paint was flaking and peeling. The Olympic pool was barely the size of Calhoun's living room, and it sat on the edge of the parking lot within spitting distance of the highway.

A sign over the doorway of the front unit on the far left read OFFICE. Calhoun nosed his truck up to the door, told Ralph to behave himself, got out, and went inside.

Nobody was in the office. A table fan sat beside a rack of pamphlets on the counter, rotating back and forth, blowing the stale air around the tiny room. A cigarette machine leaned against the wall, and beside it hung what looked like a paint-by-numbers seascape—surf crashing against rocks and flying into the air, stiff-looking seagulls pasted onto an unnaturally blue sky, a lighthouse on a bluff in the background. A small desk holding a telephone and a pile of papers huddled in the corner behind the counter, and beside it was a half-opened door.

From beyond the door came television noises. A game show, it sounded like, judging by the phony-enthusiastic tone of the announcer's voice and the frequent bursts of laughter and applause.

Calhoun paused for a moment, then said, "Hello? Anybody here?" When there was no response, he spoke louder. "Hello?"

"Hang on," came a woman's voice from beyond the doorway.

A minute later she pulled open the door and came into the office. She couldn't have been much over twenty. A mound of caramel-colored hair was pinned loosely to the top of her head. Strands of it had broken loose and were dangling in front of her face. She wore a shapeless flowered dress that hung to her ankles. Her eyes looked smudged, as if she needed sleep. Her skin was pasty and colorless, and she wore no makeup.

Calhoun noticed that she was pregnant.

"Need a room?" she said.

He shook his head. "No, ma'am. I need some information, if you've got a minute?"

She gave him a wry smile. "A minute? Hell, mister. I got a lifetime. What were you you lookin' for, a *nice* place to stay?" She laughed.

"I believe a sheriff's deputy was in the other day," he began. "Was it you he spoke with? Are you Mrs. Sousa?"

"I sure am," she said. "Mrs. Roland Sousa. That's me. You can call me Amy, though."

"So you were at the desk when Mr. Fred Green checked in a week ago Sunday?"

"The fella that deputy was askin' about? The old guy with the funny ears? Sure. Hell, I'm on the desk all the time. Roland, he's got better things to do than sit around this shitty place all day and night. He says it's the only useful thing a fat old pregnant girl can be expected to do." She patted her belly. "Mr. Green was the fella that deputy was askin' about. He showed me a picture."

"Yes," said Calhoun. "I'd like to talk with you about Mr. Green."

"You bet," she said. "Nail the sonofabitch. String him up by the nuts. I keep tellin' Roland we gotta get one of them automatic credit-card checkers, but he'd rather spend our money on his boat. That guy stayed here two nights, and now they're sayin' they ain't going to pay us. Hell, it ain't my fault that card was stolen." She shook her head. "Well, that's not your problem. What'd he do, anyway? Besides stiff us with a stolen credit card, I mean?"

"He's under suspicion for several serious crimes," said Calhoun. "Not that stealing credit cards isn't serious. So you checked him in, then?"

She nodded. "I guess I told that other deputy everything. He checked in Sunday, early evenin', and he checked out first thing Tuesday morning. Seemed polite enough. Elderly fella, but he had a bounce in his step." She looked sideways at Calhoun. "He gave me the old once-over, he did. Imagine. A fat old thing like me."

"Oh, you can't blame a man for lookin' at a pretty girl," said Calhoun. "Did you have any conversation with him?"

"Well, the usual. TV, towels, check-out time." She shrugged.

"Did he have luggage with him?"

"I don't know. I gave him the key—it was number eleven, out back—and he drove around. I don't carry bags, you know. This ain't a fancy place, in case you didn't notice."

"So other than checking him in and out, you didn't talk to him?"

"Well, he did drop in the office the next morning. Monday, that would've been. Asked where he might get a good breakfast. I suggested a couple places up the road, and that seemed to satisfy him." She hesitated. "Oh, yeah. He asked about fishing."

"Fishing?"

"Well, I don't know if he was interested in fishing, exactly. Said he was lookin' for a guide. Truth is, he didn't actually mention fishing at all. I just assumed. I sent him over to Blaine's. Know where that is?"

Calhoun shook his head.

"Right over the bridge, on the left." She gestured in a vague northerly direction. "Head on into town and just stay on Route 1 where it hangs a right there at the lights. You can't miss it. Sits right there at the marina. Kinda rundown, like most everythin' around here, but Blaine's the only fishin' guide I know of. Couldn't tell you if Mr. Green actually went there or not."

"When he asked about a guide," said Calhoun, "can you remember exactly what he said?"

She shrugged. "I don't know. A guide." She wrinkled her brow as if she was pondering a difficult problem. "Oh, well, now that I think of it, what he actually said was, he needed a guide because he wanted to do some exploring. Whatever that meant. I guess it was me who mentioned fishing. And he said, Yes, that's what he wanted. A fishing guide." She looked at Calhoun with her eyebrows arched. "I mean, what else is a guide for except fishing and hunting? And it sure ain't legal hunting season."

"Did he actually go fishing, do you know?"

She shrugged. "He was gone most of the day. I happened to see him drive in sometime in the afternoon, and I guess he drove out when I wasn't lookin', because I seen him drive in again, oh, sometime in the evening."

"What kind of car was he driving, do you remember?"

She squeezed her eyes shut for a moment, then shook her head. "Sorry."

Calhoun nodded. "Did he use the telephone?"

"We don't have phones in the rooms," she said. "That's another thing I keep tellin' Roland. But no, he needs new brass or somethin' for that damn boat. Guests can use this one here for local calls, or if they got a credit card" —she waved her hand at the telephone on the desk— "but Mr. Green, he didn't use it."

Calhoun chatted with Amy Sousa for a few more minutes, but learned nothing else. So he thanked her and scratched his name and phone number on a scrap of paper.

She looked at it. "Where's this?"

"Dublin."

"Wherever that is." She frowned at the piece of paper, then looked up at him. "That other deputy, he gave me a business card."

"I ran out," said Calhoun.

"Well, that's okay. I'll sure call you if I come up with something. Maybe if you catch that old man, we can get paid for them two nights, huh?"

"We'll sure work on it, ma'am," he said. He gave her a nod and turned for the door.

"Keep me posted, mister," she said. "You come by any time. Any time at all. I'm always here."

He hesitated, then looked back at her. "Good luck with your baby," he said.

Back in the truck, Calhoun blew out a long breath. "I don't know what's worse," he told Ralph. "Not knowing anything about what's happened in your life up to now, or having a clear picture of everything that's going to happen to you for the rest of it."

Ralph was staring intently at a couple of gulls that were pecking at some trash alongside the pool. He apparently had no opinion on the subject.

Calhoun started up the truck, pulled onto Route 1, and headed north. He crossed the long bridge that spanned a tidal river and turned off on a gravel road that curved back down to the river, where a dozen fishing boats were parked at an H-shaped dock and, out in the river itself, several moored sailboats were facing downriver into the flowing tide.

A few picnic tables were scattered in front of a small, square, shingled shack near the water where, according to the sign, you could get fried clams, boiled lobsters, and cold beer. Alongside the paved boat ramp sat another somewhat larger shingled shack—no doubt the work of the same builder. Its sign read BLAINE'S CHARTERS, DEEP SEA FISHING, WHALE WATCHING, BAIT AND TACKLE.

"Sit tight," Calhoun told Ralph, who was peering out the side window, scanning the skies over the river for more gulls.

He got out of the truck and went into the shop. It was cluttered and dirty and dimly lit, and it smelled vaguely of dead fish and wet seaweed.

A middle-aged man with a bushy black beard sat behind the counter reading a newspaper. Without looking up, he said, "Bait's out back. You git it yourself and pay for it here. All we got left is eels and sandworms."

"I need some information," said Calhoun.

The man lifted his eyes. "Mostly what we got is bait and tackle here." He dropped his eyes to his newspaper. "See where the Sox lost another one, huh?"

"Are you Mr. Blaine?"

"Depends on who needs to know."

"Do you remember a man named Fred Green, came in maybe a week ago looking for a guide?"

"Nope."

"White-haired guy in his late sixties, early seventies? Big ears. Southern accent."

Blaine turned a page. "Eels and sandworms," he said. "That's all we got today." He continued to squint at his paper.

Calhoun placed his elbows on the counter and leaned close to Blaine. "I'm talkin' to you, sir," he said.

Blaine glanced up. "I heard you, pal. You're botherin' me. If you don't want to buy somethin', I'm busy, okay?"

Calhoun reached across the counter, grabbed Blaine's beard, and pulled him up from his chair. "I ain't got time to fart around," he said. "A friend of mine got killed and I'm in no mood. Understand me?"

Blaine reached up and gripped Calhoun's wrist. "Let go, man."

"I'd be happy to hurt you," said Calhoun. He gave Blaine's beard a sharp tug.

"Okay, okay. Jesus. Whaddya want?"

Calhoun released his grip on Blaine's beard and patted his cheek. This was the second time in the past couple of days he'd bullied somebody. The other one was the bartender at Juniper's restaurant. He wondered where in his training, or pre-lightning personality, that came from.

"Sorry about that," he said to the bearded guy. "I'm pretty upset, my friend getting killed and all. I just need to know, did you talk to a guy named Fred Green about a fishing guide? It would've been on Monday, a week ago today."

Blaine sank back into his chair and stroked his chin. "I don't know that name"—he glanced up at Calhoun, who was staring hard at him—"but maybe I remember an old guy with funny ears and a southern accent."

"What'd he want?"

"He was lookin' for a guide. Told him we did charters, but that ain't what he was after. He wanted someone to help him find some damn pond. Near as I could figure, it was down around Sebago somewhere. I told him pond fishin' ain't worth spit these days, but he seemed to know exactly what he wanted. So I told him he better find someone else. I even give him a recommendation."

"Who did you recommend?"

"Hippie college kid down in Portland. Works out of a shop down there. Kid name of Lyle McMahan." Blaine peered up at Calhoun. "Maybe you know Lyle?"

Calhoun nodded. "Might've heard of him."

"That boy knows them woods down there better'n anybody," said Blaine. "There's another guy, supposed to be pretty good, works in the same shop. Not as good as McMahan, I hear. Don't know him person-al. Calhoun's his name."

"Did you mention this Calhoun to the old guy, too?"

"Ayuh. Told him either one'd prob'ly suit him." He gazed up at the ceiling for a minute. "Funny thing," he said. "That old fella, he didn't seem much interested in fishin'."

"How so?" said Calhoun.

"Well, I asked him what he was lookin' for, and he kinda shrugged, and when I mentioned brook trout, he got this look on his face, like that was some kind of brilliant idea I had, and he goes, Yep, that's what he's after, all right. Brookies."

"And did Mr. Green indicate he was going to look up Lyle?"

"Oh, sure. I give him the address of the shop down there. Kate's Bait and Tackle." A grin glinted from inside Blaine's beard. "If you ain't done it before, worth droppin' in, just to catch a look at Kate, if you know what I mean."

CHAPTER TWENTY-THREE

THE IMAGE OF BLAINE'S LEERING BEARDED FACE stayed with Calhoun as he drove back down Route 1 to Portland. It made him want to drive directly to the shop, enfold Kate in a big hug, and tell her the hell with all of it, he just wanted to be with her.

What had gotten into him, yanking on the man's beard? He didn't know where that sudden, angry aggressiveness had come from. It made him realize that he was still learning things about himself. He didn't like everything he was finding out.

On the other hand, it worked. The man had talked. Now it seemed clear that Fred Green had come to Maine specifically to find the millpond in Keatsboro. He'd known exactly what he was looking for, but he needed someone to help him find it. He hadn't actually cared about the fishing.

If Calhoun had it figured right, Mr. Green had come to Maine to dig up something beside the Potters' old cellar hole on the hilltop in the woods. It must've been something important and valuable—gold, if Calhoun wasn't mistaken. Green had needed a guide to find it, but he felt he couldn't leave the guide alive afterward. So he'd killed Lyle.

And when Calhoun had persisted in snooping around, Mr. Green came in the night to kill him, too.

Calhoun had been wracking his poor excuse for a brain, trying to think of a jeweler he knew and trusted. The closest he could come up with was Stanley Karp, who owned a pawnshop on Route 9 in the Stroudwater section of Portland. Stanley was an unskilled but enthusiastic fly fisherman whom Calhoun had guided a few times.

Calhoun had begun by calling him "Mr. Karp." It was his rule to address all clients his age or older formally unless they instructed him otherwise, although he didn't remember ever warming to any of the few who didn't quickly correct him.

Mr. Karp had turned to him and said, "For goodness' sake, call me Stanley. How would you like to be called some kind of ugly fish?"

He had insisted on calling Calhoun "Stonewall."

When Calhoun had asked him how much fly fishing he'd done, Stanley had grinned and said, "You'd probably call me an aspiring novice."

It was a little after one in the afternoon when he pulled up in front of Stanley Karp's little shop. When he went inside, Stanley plunked his elbows on the glass-topped counter, leaned forward, arched his eyebrows, and said. "Well, bless my soul, if it isn't Stonewall Jackson Calhoun. I hope you have not come here to transact actual business with me. My clients, unlike yours, are desperate, pitiable souls, for which reason I do not like my friends to become my clients, and I never allow my clients to become my friends."

Calhoun grinned, went over to him, and held out his hand, which Stanley engulfed in both of his. "Actually, I need your expertise, Stanley," he said. "I've got something here I can't identify."

Stanley Karp was a tall, gaunt, absolutely bald man, with a long, beaked nose, pendulous ears, bushy gray eyebrows, and a wide, lopsided smile. He knew very little about fly fishing, but he knew everything about fly-fishing equipment. "You would be astounded," he'd told Calhoun the first day they fished together, "at the wonderful stuff people find in their cellars and attics and garages and closets. They come in here with armloads of bamboo fly rods, and they ask me if I'll give them anything at all for this old junk. They bring me gorgeous Paynes and Leonards, even an occasional Garrison or Gillum, genuine treasures, and when I tell them what they're worth, Stonewall, they laugh at me."

Under the glass counter where Stanley was leaning lay jumbles of gold watches, pearl necklaces, diamond rings. Behind him in a locked rack stood a row of shotguns and rifles. The bookshelves along the walls were jammed with old-looking, leather-bound volumes, and there were tables piled with lamps and vases and crockery, computers and cameras and television sets, bowling balls and ice skates and, yes, fishing equipment.

Every item, Calhoun imagined, told a sad story.

Stanley Karp swept his hand around the shop. "Whatever you have," he said to Calhoun, "I assure you, I've already got ten of them. Here, let's have a look."

Calhoun fished into his pocket and came out with the plastic bag that held the lump of gold he'd found in the ground beside the cellar hole. He put it on the counter. "It looks like a piece of something," he said, "not the whole thing. Something that broke. I'm wondering what it was. It's gold, isn't it?"

Stanley held the bag up to the light and squinted at it. "Hmm," he mumbled. He opened the bag, reached in with a tweezers, and took out the little hunk of gold. Then he twisted a jeweler's loupe into his right eye and peered at it intently. "Huh," he said. "It's gold, all right."

"Well?" said Calhoun.

Stanley was rotating the tweezers, looking at the gold lump from all sides. "Interesting," he murmured. He dropped it back into the bag, removed the loupe from his eye, and looked up at Calhoun. "Have you been robbing graves, my friend?"

Calhoun thought of that foot sticking out of the ground, and he thought of Sam Potter, who'd died up there in the fire almost sixty years ago. He shook his head. "I found that in the dirt," he said. "But I don't think it was anybody's grave. Why?"

"I could be wrong," said Stanley, "but I think you've got yourself somebody's gold tooth here."

"A tooth?"

"Not a whole tooth, of course. A gold crown. Take a look."

Calhoun plucked it from the bag with Stanley's tweezers and peered at it through the loupe. It did indeed look like a piece of tooth, although if Stanley hadn't said it, Calhoun probably wouldn't have figured it out. The top was flat and irregular like a molar, and the bottom had sharp, jagged edges, as if it had broken off.

Calhoun dropped it into the bag, sealed it, and stuffed it back into his pocket. "Thanks, Stanley," he said. "I owe you."

"I suppose it would be impolitic to ask why you are carrying somebody's gold tooth in your pocket."

Calhoun shook his head. "I wish I knew myself," he said.

Kate's Bait and Tackle was less than a mile from Stanley Karp's pawnshop. Calhoun was tempted to drop in. He'd like to talk to Kate about his conversations with Amy Sousa and Blaine up in Craigville, and maybe he'd show her the gold tooth he'd dug up from beside the cellar hole in Keatsboro. He'd tell her that he'd seen Stanley Karp. Kate liked Stanley, referred to him as "that sweet man." She'd have to smile when he mentioned Stanley.

He'd ask her to speculate with him, help him invent scenarios, and maybe he'd tell her about how Ralph had found that foot the other night, but how when he'd gone back there with the sheriff, it wasn't there, so he guessed it wasn't real.

But it had been Calhoun's idea that they stay clear of each other until it was all over with. Fred Green was trying to shoot him. He didn't want Kate involved.

So he headed west and drove home.

About the time he pulled into his driveway, he realized that he was exhausted. He'd hardly slept for the past couple of nights, and now his eyes burned and his head ached and his stomach churned.

He bounced up the rutted driveway, and when he pulled up in front of the house, he sat there in his truck for a minute, looking around.

Nothing looked different.

He slid his Remington out from behind the seat, took the box of shotgun shells from the glove compartment, and loaded up. Double-ought buckshot this time, serious ammunition that could kill a man at sixty yards—the hell with that birdshot that wouldn't even break the skin. Then he and Ralph went inside. Nothing looked different inside, either.

It was a hot summer afternoon, but inside, with the roof shaded by the pines and a breeze sifting through the screens, it was cool and dim.

He found the portable phone, sat at the kitchen table, and called Sheriff Dickman. He told the woman who answered that it was important, and when he gave her his name, she put him through.

"What's up, Stoney?" said Dickman.

"I've got some information for you," said Calhoun. "But you've got to promise me something first."

"Oh?"

"There's something I want to take care of by myself. Promise you won't interfere with that."

"How can I promise that if you don't tell me what it is?"

"I'll tell you after you promise," said Calhoun.

"And if I don't, you'll hang up, right?"

"You got it."

He heard the sheriff blow an exasperated breath. "Okay, Stoney. We'll do it your way."

"You promise?"

"Sure."

217

So Calhoun told him how somebody—Fred Green, he assumed—had come in the night and had taken a couple of potshots at him with a .22. He also summarized his interview with Amy Sousa up in Craigville and his conversation with Blaine. He told him that Stanley Karp had identified the gold nugget as part of a tooth.

The sheriff listened without interrupting, and when Calhoun finished, he said, "I'll send a deputy up there to protect you, Stoney."

"No," said Calhoun. "I can protect myself. I want to handle this. That's your promise. That you'll let me take care of it. The sonofabitch shot Lyle, and now he's coming around here, Sheriff. Do you see?"

"I see that you are pigheaded and stupid, my friend."

"You promised."

Dickman sighed. "So I did." He chuckled. "I assume it would not be breaking any promise if we happen to find the man and take him into custody before he manages to shoot you dead."

"No," said Calhoun, "that would be okay. I wouldn't mind that at all."

"I'll get the word around that he's armed and dangerous. Every state cop and sheriff's department in Maine will get that word."

"Okay," said Calhoun. "Good."

"Stoney?"

"Yeah?"

The sheriff cleared his throat. "Nothing. I just hope to hell you know what you're doing."

"Actually," said Calhoun, "it's funny, but I do. I am pretty confident that I know exactly what I'm doing."

After he hung up with the sheriff, Calhoun went to the bedroom and leaned the shotgun against the wall beside the bed. He picked up the alarm clock from the bedside table. It was a few minutes after three in the afternoon. He wound up the clock and set the alarm to go off at six, to give him time to shower and have a cup of coffee before he had to meet Millie. Then he shucked off all his clothes, threw back the covers, lay down, and pulled the sheet over him. The pillow smelled like Kate.

Ralph was sitting on the floor beside him with his ears cocked, staring at him, wondering what in hell he was doing, going to bed in the middle of the day.

"We're probably going to be up all night," Calhoun explained to Ralph, "so I need to grab a nap. You be sure to bark if you hear anything. This is your watch. I'll take over in three hours."

Then he rolled onto his belly and went to sleep.

The alarm clock in his head went off before the one beside the bed, as it always did. It interrupted a jumbled dream in which Calhoun seemed to be running through a swamp. Children who shouted in some foreign language were chasing him and shooting at him, but in the dream that wasn't what frightened him. He was naked in the dream, and every step he took rubbed him against big scythe-shaped leaves with sharp, jagged edges that sliced his skin. He ran awkwardly with his scrotum cupped in both hands and his feet sinking into the mucky earth while bullets rattled in the canopy of dense foliage overhead and high-pitched children's voices echoed in the humid swamp. He was sweaty and out of breath. His legs and chest and arms were bleeding. Finally he flopped to the ground and slid onto the wet black earth under a bush with leaves as big as elephant ears, and there, lying on her back under that bush, was a woman, also naked, with her arms open to him, smiling and beckoning.

He backed away on hands and knees, somehow knowing that she was more lethal than the armed children who were chasing him.

In the dream, he'd recognized her, and now, in that half-place between sleep and consciousness, he realized that she was someone from before, an actual woman, someone who'd participated in his life. He'd seen her face clearly and had spoken her name in the dream, but now, with his eyes open, he couldn't remember either her face or her name.

He shut his eyes for a minute, trying to recover the memory of her. But she was gone.

He sat up. His sheet was soaked from his sweat. The alarm clock on the bedside table read 5:56. He reached over and turned it off before it jangled, then swiveled around and sat on the edge of the bed, trying to shake off the dream.

Ralph was lying in the doorway with his chin on his paws, facing into the living room, alert for intruders.

Calhoun had had naked dreams in the hospital. They'd usually involved threats to his groin area. The shrinks took these dreams to be a good sign, a symptom of his normality. Basic Freud, was their diagnosis. You have secrets, Mr. Calhoun, and you fear exposing them, of letting others see the real you. Plus, of course, you've got a classic castration complex. Everybody has such dreams, they insisted.

Calhoun didn't know about anybody else's dreams. But his convinced him that he was anything but normal.

The hospital shrinks had gone after the symbolism of his dreams. They'd explained how the unconscious mind assembles disparate images and fragments, mostly events and mind-flashes from the "dream day," distorts and rearranges them, and creates a story that, when taken literally, reveals nothing. The trick, they'd told him, was to deconstruct the dream, to identify its separate parts and to abstract its themes.

Calhoun was a literalist. He wanted to know such things as the location of the swamp, and when and why he'd been there, and who the children were who were chasing him with guns, and the name of that naked woman, and how and when and where he'd known her, and why she frightened him more than bullets.

He had no interest in exploring his psyche, in reading whatever symbolic messages his unconscious mind decided to send him in dreams, the way it sometimes sent him hallucinatory naked bodies in trout streams and feet sticking out of the earth. He already knew he was seriously messed up.

He got up and padded barefoot into the kitchen, where he filled the electric coffeepot and switched it on.

Then he went into the bathroom and took a long, cool shower, and by the time he came out, the dream, and the fear and sadness that it had left lingering in his soul, were all washed away.

He toweled himself dry, detoured to the kitchen to pour himself a mug of coffee, and took it into the bedroom. He pulled on a pair of chino pants and a shirt, picked up his shotgun, and whistled to Ralph. "You're coming with me," he told him.

Ralph stared at him for a moment, then scrambled to his feet and jogged to the door.

Calhoun switched on the outside floodlights. It would be dark by the time he got back, and he hoped—but doubted—that the light might give an uninvited visitor pause. Then he went outside. He unloaded the shotgun, dropped the three shells into his pocket, slid the gun behind the front seat of the truck, held the door for Ralph, and got in himself.

It was quarter to seven. He'd be right on time to meet Millie.

CHAPTER TWENTY-FOUR

CALHOUN PULLED INTO THE PARKING LOT beside Juniper's at five minutes before seven. Millie's Cherokee, a new Toyota pickup, and a rusting old Ford Crown Victoria were the only other cars in the lot.

He took a rawhide bone from his pocket and gave it to Ralph. "Chew on this instead of the upholstery," he said.

Ralph sat there on the passenger seat holding the bone by its end so that it was sticking out of the side of his mouth like a big lumpy cigar, with that so-you're-deserting-me-again look on his face.

Calhoun left the windows open a few inches, got out, and locked the doors. He tapped on the roof by way of saying good-bye to Ralph, who had moved behind the steering wheel and was curled up on the seat with the bone between his front paws, determined to sulk.

Calhoun went into Juniper's. He glanced into the dining room on the right. An elderly couple sat at a table by the window studying their menus. Otherwise it was empty.

He found Millie at the bar talking with the same bartender who'd been there Saturday. Kevin was his name, Calhoun recalled. Kevin was leaning his elbows on the bartop, grinning at Millie under that little Clark Gable mustache of his. Millie was sipping what looked like a gin and tonic, smiling up at Kevin from around the straw, flirting back at him just as hard as he was flirting with her.

Calhoun hitched himself onto the barstool beside Millie. Kevin straightened up, nodded at Calhoun, and moved away.

Millie's hand snaked around Calhoun's neck, and she tilted up and kissed his cheek. "Hey, big guy," she whispered in a poor Mae West imitation.

"Hiya, sweetheart." Bogie, also poor.

She chuckled. "I got here early." She made a show of looking at her wristwatch. "And you, of course, are precisely on time. How terribly Stoney of you." She held up her glass. "My second. Empty." Her eyes darted toward Kevin, who was down the other end of the bar with his back to them. "Oh, Kev-in," she sang.

He turned and came to them with a fresh gin and tonic in one hand and a Coke in the other. "Way ahead of you, Millie." To Calhoun he said, "Coke, right?"

"Right," said Calhoun. "Thanks."

"I'm not drunk," said Millie after Kevin had moved away, "if that's what you're thinking." She was wearing skin-tight blue jeans and a scoop-necked blouse which would inspire any bartender to lean forward on his elbows when she bent to sip from her drink.

"Didn't expect you would be," he said.

"I got what you wanted. About those deeds."

"Good. Don't suppose you're hungry?"

"I am. I told Alice to hold a table for us in the dining room." She smiled. "I don't think we'll have much of a wait."

Calhoun put a twenty-dollar bill on the bartop. Kevin came to retrieve it. "That cover it?" said Calhoun.

"Eleven and a quarter for the gin and tonics," he said. "Coke's on the house."

Calhoun nodded. "Thanks. Keep the change."

Kevin gave him a quick salute, and they swiveled off their stools. Millie held onto Calhoun's arm as they went into the dining room. A round, thirtyish woman appeared with menus, a nice smile, and a little nametag over her left breast that said ALICE. She led them to a table against the wall across the room from the couple at the window. "You okay with your drinks?" she said.

"We're fine," said Calhoun. "Thanks."

"Back for your order in a jif," she said, and moved away.

They looked at the menus. Standard fare—steaks, chops, chicken, seafood, pasta, and the inevitable vegetarian specials. For Calhoun, the choice was easy. On those rare occasions when he ate out, he always had a steak and a baked potato.

When Alice returned, Millie ordered a vegetable-and-tofu stir-fry. Calhoun decided on the porterhouse, medium rare, hold the sour cream on the potato.

Across the room, the elderly couple was arguing in low, tense voices. Millie was staring across at them.

"They're stuck with each other," said Calhoun, "and they both know it's too late to do anything about it."

Millie turned and looked at him. "So how's Kate?" she said.

Calhoun shook his head. "Kate and I are a secret, Millie. Jesus."

"Like hell you are. There isn't a worthwhile secret left in the whole damn state of Maine."

"Well, we're not advertising it," he said.

She nodded. "It just makes me sad, seeing folks who've got each other like those two"—she jerked her chin in the direction of the old couple—"not appreciating it. I hope you appreciate it, Stoney."

"I do," he said. "What about you?"

"Me?"

"You must have somebody, Millie. Fine-looking woman like you, successful business and all."

"Oh, I'm a catch, all right." She smiled and rolled her eyes. "I guess half the guys in York County have taken a swipe at me, one time or another. All the good ones're already married, or . . . or otherwise accounted for. I tell 'em sorry, I'm a lesbian. After a while the word gets around, and now they don't bother me. Of course, now and then one of their wives gives it a shot." She grinned. "Sometimes the idea makes a lot of sense, but I guess I don't have the genes for it. I was married once. Had to get away from him. That's when I came up here." She shook her head. "It was a long time ago. The hell with it. I work hard and I exercise hard, and I get through the day, you know?"

"I figured I'd be alone the rest of my life," said Calhoun. "It's what I thought I wanted. I guess without Kate, that's how it'd be, and I don't think I'd mind."

"Yeah," she said, "you'd mind. After a while, it doesn't seem natural."

Calhoun thought about losing Kate. He knew he could never go back to the way it was before he started loving her. Millie was right. It wouldn't be natural.

The waitress brought their dinners and they ate without talking much. Millie sipped a diet Coke with her meal, and when they finished they ordered coffee.

When the coffee came, Millie reached into her big shoulder bag and pulled out a stenographer's pad. "Okay," she said. "Maybe I was a little drunk back there. But I'm not now." She slipped a pair of reading glasses onto her nose. "I spent the morning in the Keatsboro Town Hall. You wanted to know about that property where Lyle McMahan died."

"Yes," said Calhoun, "where Lyle was murdered."

"Anything particular you wanted to know?"

Calhoun shrugged. "Like I told you, I'm just thrashin' around, Millie."

She cleared her throat. "Well, here's what I got for you. That parcel was originally part of a huge tract that was owned by a timber company. Covered the whole area west and south of Sebago, eight or nine townships now. Several hundred square miles. Granted to them by the state, most likely, though the records don't go back that far. The state, of course, took it from the Indians, but you sure won't find that on any deeds. Anyhow, more than likely they cut it over for ship masts, then for lumber, and then for pulp, and when they wore it out they divided it and put it up for sale. That parcel you're interested in was part of a bigger piece that was bought by someone named Saul Raczwenc in nineteen thirty-six. It was subdivided in thirty-eight, and that seven-hundred-acre piece was bought by Sam and Emily Potter. The town took it in lieu of taxes in nineteen forty-nine."

"They got burned out in forty-seven," said Calhoun. "Sam Potter died in the fire."

Millie nodded. "Yes, I heard that. It's not explained in the official records, of course. Anyway, David Ross, who lives across the street, got himself a bargain. Took it off the town's hands in nineteen fifty-one for the cost of the back taxes. Held onto it until"—she squinted down at the legal pad—"seventy-three." She looked up at Calhoun and smiled.

"David Ross bought that land?"

Millie nodded.

"Then he sold it?"

"Yes. In seventy-three."

"Who'd he sell it to?"

"Something called the A & I Development Corporation."

"Then what?" he said.

"Then nothing. This A & I still owns it."

"Rip off a piece of paper for me," said Calhoun. "I want to write this down."

She tore the top two sheets off the pad and handed them to him. "Already did it for you," she said. "It's all there, including the names of the lawyers who handled the transactions. I imagine most of them are dead by now."

"Thanks." He looked at Millie's neatly printed notes. "So the last time it changed hands was in seventy-three."

She nodded.

"Any idea who this A & I Development Corporation is?"

She shrugged. "Probably one of those real estate speculating groups. A whole bunch of them sprung up in the seventies when they got the interstate up and running. Lot of folks thought southwestern Maine was going to be the next big vacation destination." Millie shook her head and smiled. "Of course, they were wrong."

"Has A & I been trying to sell it, do you know?"

She shrugged. "Couldn't tell you for sure. I mean, you'd think I'd know. Everything in this neck of the woods is multi-listed, so I hear about most of it. But those land-development groups don't usually deal with us little local brokers."

Calhoun leaned across the table and touched Millie's hand. "Suppose you could do me another favor?"

"Now don't you try to sweet-talk me, Stoney Calhoun." She squeezed his hand, then let go. "You don't need to, you know. Guess I know what you want."

"See if you can find out who this A & I is."

She shrugged. "Sure." She cocked her head at him. "What do you expect to get out of all this, Stoney?"

"Hell," he said, "I don't know. Like I said, I'm just doing some snooping. Maybe I'll scare something up." He squinted at the paper. "Wonder who this Saul Raczwenc was," he said. He looked up at Millie. "Any of their kin still around?"

She shrugged. "If I'd known you wanted that information, I suppose I could've done some more digging. But I can tell you with certainty that there aren't any Raczwencs living around here now." Millie sipped her coffee and watched him over the rim of her cup. "You know," she said, "if you want stories, you ought to talk to Jacob Barnes. He's been here all his life. And he must be pushing eighty. You get him started on the fire of forty-seven, there's no stopping him."

"And he'll know about Keatsboro?"

"Back when he was a young man, if you believe half of what he says, it was just one big farm area around here. Cows and pigs and apple orchards, mostly. That general store of his was a feed-and-grain place back then, and I guess folks came from all over. He knew everyone and everything. Still does. I bet he can tell you every night Kate has a sleep-over with you, what time she got there and when she left and what you did in between."

"Jesus, Millie."

She grinned. "I'm just suggesting maybe you ought to treat her to dinner here at Juniper's some night. It won't shock anybody."

"It's Walter—her husband—we're concerned about."

"Folks know that part of it, too, Stoney." Millie reached across the table and took his hand. "And I'll tell you something else. By this time tomorrow, everyone in York County will know that you and I had a cozy dinner together at Juniper's, and that you like your steak medium-rare, and that we held hands during coffee."

Calhoun yanked his hand away.

She grinned. "All I'm saying is, maybe you and Kate will be happier if you don't feel like you've got to sneak around."

"Who said we weren't happy?"

"Are you?"

Calhoun shrugged. "What happened to Lyle's made it hard."

"Sounds like you better get that resolved, then."

He nodded. "That's exactly what I'm trying to do."

When they went outside, the sun had set. The lights from the restaurant bathed the parking area in a dim orange glow, but darkness had gathered under the trees and spread over the fields out back.

Calhoun let Ralph out of the truck. Ralph sniffed Millie's shoes, then trotted off into the shadows, his white legs winking in the semi-darkness.

They went to Millie's Cherokee. She unlocked the door, then turned around and leaned back against it. "Thanks for dinner," she said.

"Thanks for the information," he said.

She reached up and touched his shoulder. "I can't help wondering what you're doing, Stoney. All this thrashin' around."

He shook his head. "Just trying to keep busy, I guess." He bent to her, brushed a quick kiss on her cheek, then stepped back. "Thanks, Millie. Appreciate your help."

Millie's hand went to her cheek. "That was sweet." She grinned. "You know, if you're going to start the gossip flying anyway, you might as well make it worthwhile."

Calhoun smiled, then whistled to Ralph, who came trotting over. "Go on. Get in the car," he said, and Ralph obeyed. He turned to Millie. "I am grateful for this." He patted his shirt pocket, where he'd put the folded-up sheet of paper she had given him. "If there's anything I can do for you . . ."

"Let me buy you dinner sometime, Stoney."

"Sure. I'd like that."

"You and Kate," she said.

"You're a good woman, Millie Dobson," said Calhoun. "Those wives don't know what they're missing."

She nodded, then turned, opened her car door, and got in. She looked up at him. "I'll see what I can find out about A & I Development."

He waved at her as she pulled out of the parking lot, and as she turned onto the street, he saw her hand come out of the window and wave back.

It was a little before ten when he pulled in front of his house. The flood-lights washed the area in bright light. The surrounding woods were absolutely black.

He hesitated for a moment, reluctant to get out of the truck. Fred Green with his .22 could be lurking in those dark woods, centering him in his sights. Then he shook his head. You can't live that way. It pissed him off, this new feeling of insecurity on his own property.

He climbed out and retrieved the shotgun from behind the seat. "Come on," he said to Ralph. "Let's get you something to eat."

Ralph bustled around the yard, lifting his leg several times, sniffing the bushes. If anybody was hiding in the woods, Ralph would know it.

Calhoun fed Ralph and put on a fresh pot of coffee. Then he went into the bedroom and changed into jeans, a dark blue sweatshirt, and sneakers. He found a bottle of Ben's insect repellent in his fishing vest in the living room and stuck it into his pocket, too.

He had a couple hours to kill, so he found the classical music station on his stereo. They were playing Mozart's clarinet concerto.

He sat at his fly-tying bench. Humming tunelessly along with the clarinet, and without thinking much about it, he found himself tying a red-and-white wet fly, a Parmacheene Belle, which had been named after Lake Parmacheene in the northwestern corner of Maine. When he recognized what he had done, Calhoun smiled. Lyle had loved history and had a special fondness for old-fashioned flies, especially those that originated in Maine like the Grey Ghost, the Warden's Worry, and the Nine-Twelve.

Calhoun figured that even when he wasn't aware of thinking about Lyle, part of his mind was doing just that.

Tying flies, like fishing with them, served a double purpose. Both fishing and fly tying gave him something to focus on at one level, while at the same time clearing his mind and allowing it to roam freely, to ponder problems on a different level.

So the front part of Calhoun's brain arranged feathers and bucktail and tinsel, while some darker, deeper part considered why Fred Green had murdered Lyle and now wanted to murder Calhoun himself.

The next time he looked at his watch, it was eleven-thirty. He'd tied nine flies, all of them different. But he had solved no problems.

He pushed back his chair, went to the kitchen, filled a thermos with coffee, and turned off the stereo. He took a heavy army blanket from the bedroom closet, screwed a black baseball cap onto his head, picked up the shotgun, snapped his fingers at Ralph, turned off all the lights, and went outside.

He stood on the porch for a minute, holding the Remington at port arms, waiting for his eyes to adjust. It was a cloudy, moonless night, but after a while he was able to see shapes and textures.

He went over to the truck, took the box of shotgun shells from the glove compartment, and dumped a handful of spares into his pocket. Then he slipped into the bushes along the driveway beside the house. Ralph followed.

He found a big old oak tree to lean his back against. "Lie down here," Calhoun said to Ralph. "This is my watch, so you might as well snooze."

Ralph obediently dropped his chin onto his paws.

Calhoun spread the army blanket over his legs and laid the shotgun across his knees. Then he poured himself a mug of coffee and prepared to wait.

CHAPTER
TWENTY-FIVE

THE TRICK TO STAYING AWAKE ALL NIGHT is to have something on your mind, preferably something to worry about, to mull over, to conduct mental dialogues about. Calhoun had Lyle's murder, and he had Kate, and he had the Man in the Suit—not to mention Fred Green with his twenty-two who wanted to kill him—and they kept him going. He bounced from Lyle to Kate to the man in the suit to Fred Green and back again, and sometimes all four of them managed to get tangled up in each other and he'd find his mind free-wheeling, creating bizarre, nightmarish scenarios. When that happened, he'd stand up and stretch and pour himself some more coffee from his thermos.

The coffee helped, and so did the possibility that Fred Green might show up.

He couldn't see his watch in the darkness, but he had faith in his internal clock. He guessed it was close to four when Ralph, who was lying beside him, snapped up his head and gave a low growl.

Calhoun reached over and tapped Ralph's shoulder by way of telling him to shut up.

The sun wasn't scheduled to rise for another hour, but already the black sky had begun to fade into a pewtery purple. Calhoun leaned forward so he could see through the bushes. He caught a shadowy movement on the far side of the parking area, then made out a dark shape easing along the edge of the opening, just inside the woods.

No. Two shapes.

Without taking his eyes off them, he slowly reached down and picked up his shotgun. Ralph growled again, and Calhoun gave him a gentle slap on the shoulder.

The two shapes slid out of the bushes and into the opening in front of the house.

Deer. A doe and her fawn, moving like ghosts in the semidarkness, not ten yards from where Calhoun and Ralph were hiding. The doe carried her head high and alert, and the fawn—which wasn't much bigger than a long-legged jackrabbit—mimicked her. She'd probably gotten a whiff of the man and the dog and found the mingled scent confusing.

A moment later they melted into the woods and were gone.

Calhoun let out a deep breath and slumped back against the oak tree. He realized that his palms were sweaty and his heart was drumming in his chest.

He reached over and scratched Ralph's muzzle. "Good work," he whispered. "You got the ears and the nose. I got the eyes and the gun. Between us, we're one whole, lethal animal."

He waited another hour or so, and when the birds started chorusing and the daylight began to creep in under the trees, he stood up, yawned and stretched, picked up his gun and his blanket and his thermos, and lugged them into the house.

Ralph trotted to his water dish and lapped it dry.

Calhoun put on a fresh pot of coffee and set the timer for eleven. Then he went into the bedroom, stripped, and flopped down on the bed.

Ralph came in and curled up on the floor. "Your watch," Calhoun told him. "And don't bother waking me up for some damn deer."

He checked his watch. It was ten after five. He instructed his mental alarm to start ringing at eleven, rolled onto his belly, and fell asleep.

He slept badly, with a night's worth of caffeine and adrenaline blasting through his bloodstream, and when he awoke—it was 10:35 by his wristwatch—he felt less rested than before he'd slept. There had been dreams, but they were gone the instant he opened his eyes, leaving him feeling vaguely anxious and disoriented and depressed.

He stumbled naked into the bathroom and started the water running. The cool shower washed some of the cotton out of his head, and he stood under it for a long time, thinking about what he had to do today.

He toweled himself dry, slipped into jeans and a T-shirt, poured a mug of coffee, and went out on the deck. He listened to Bitch Creek sing while he replenished his system with caffeine and resolve.

Then he fetched his shotgun, whistled up Ralph, got into his truck, and headed for Jacob Barnes's store.

Calhoun filled his tank from the pump in front, then pulled off to the side next to a Pepsi delivery truck. Ralph seemed to have resigned himself to spending his days cooped up in the cab of the truck, and he didn't even lift his head when Calhoun got out.

It was musty and dim inside, and Calhoun paused in the doorway and blinked a couple of times. Old Jacob was leaning on his cane talking to the Pepsi guy, who was loading up the glass-fronted cooler against the back wall. Marcus, Jacob's grandson, was behind the counter thumbing through a magazine.

Calhoun went over to him. "Good morning, Marcus."

Marcus looked up. "Mornin'." He was wearing his customary overalls and T-shirt and Mets baseball cap.

Calhoun pulled out his wallet and put two tens on the counter. "It came to fifteen even."

Marcus made change, and Calhoun slipped the five into his wallet. He jerked his head in Jacob's direction. "Your grandpa likely to be tied up for long?"

Jacob looked over at Calhoun. "Be right with you, Stoney."

Marcus returned to his magazine. Calhoun looked idly at the collection of rental videos.

Finally the Pepsi man wheeled his dolly out the front door and Jacob hobbled over and held out his hand. "How's it goin', Stoney?"

Calhoun shook hands with him. "Can't complain, Jacob," he said. "Wondering if I might pick your brain for a minute?"

"What there is left of it—I don't mind. Let's go sit."

Jacob's store did not have the traditional potbellied stove, but there were three rocking chairs in the back corner by the coffee urn where locals sometimes assembled to drink coffee and chew the fat. Calhoun remembered what Millie had said about there being no secrets in Maine. He suspected that a good many local secrets got aired in the back of Jacob's store.

Jacob sat with a soft groan. "This damn arthur-itis," he grumbled. "It don't get no better. Back when I had Ingrid, she used to rub me down. She hit all the places I can't reach myself." He shook his head. "Hell, Stoney. You didn't come here to listen to my complaints." He gave Calhoun a quick grin. "Did you?"

"Nope," said Calhoun.

"Well, that's okay. Personally, I think it's fascinating."

Calhoun smiled. "You remember about me finding Lyle McMahan's dead body over in Keatsboro last week."

Jacob nodded. "Up to Potter's old place. You and the sheriff showed me the picture of the guy who done it."

"That's right. Fred Green's his name. You know Lyle was a friend of mine, and the truth is, it should've been me who took Mr. Green up there that day, not him. It was Lyle's bad luck. Wrong place at the wrong time." Calhoun cocked his head, inviting Jacob to offer a thought.

But all he said was: "Don't know how I'm gonna help you, Stoney. Haven't laid eyes on that Mr. Green. I make sure everybody who comes in takes a look at that sketch. But I ain't heard any useful rumors, if that's what you're askin' for, and I ain't been up to Potter's in a coon's age."

"Actually," said Calhoun, "that property's changed hands a few times since the Potters owned it."

"Oh, sure," said Jacob. "But hereabouts, we still think of it as Potter's. Nobody's lived up there since the fire."

"The name Raczwenc mean anything to you?"

Jacob blinked a couple of times. "Hell, I ain't heard that name in years," he said. "They're the ones who sold that piece to Sam Potter." He leaned toward Calhoun. "You know, Stoney, I can remember what happened fifty years ago as clear as if it was this mornin'. But ask me what I ate for dinner yesterday and I draw a blank. Sure I remember Raczwenc. Come over from Poland or someplace back before the war. There was Saul and his wife—damned if I can remember her name. Anyways, they bought themselves a big parcel up there in Keatsboro and settled right down to farmin'. Saul, he come down here for supplies every couple weeks. We was a feed-and-grain place back then. That's when my daddy was still alive, but I was runnin' the place. That Saul was a funny old duck. Nice fella, though. Worked hard, took care of his property."

"The Potters," Calhoun said, "whose house burned in the fire? I was wondering what you might remember about them."

"They was from down south somewhere. Sam Potter bought that property from Saul Raczwenc, and damned if he didn't built himself a house way the hell back in the woods. Didn't know squat about farming, though he tried." Jacob shook his head. "Sam died in the fire. He was the only one around here, though a lot of houses and barns got burned to the ground. Sam Potter just didn't belong out there in the woods. Didn't understand about fire."

"What happened to the rest of the Potter family?" said Calhoun.

"I heard Mrs. Potter—Emily was her name—I heard she took their kids down to Florida. Can't say I knew the Potters very well. They always pretty much kept to themselves. Sam was kind of a surly fella, actually. Sometimes had one of his kids with him. Girl and a boy. They was surly, too. Folks said that when Sam Potter was in the army, he was one of the first ones to go into the concentration camps, and he wasn't the same afterwards. Always acted like a man who'd seen the devil, I can tell you that."

"After the fire," said Calhoun. "Potter was buried there on their property?"

"Hell, no. Why you askin' that?"

Calhoun shrugged. "I went up there the other day, thought I might've noticed an old gravesite."

"Last I heard," said Jacob, "Sam Potter was resting out behind the Congregational church up to Keatsboro. Unless he got up and moved, I imagine he still is." He narrowed his eyes. "You know, Stoney, some folks think the Potter place is haunted. Dying in a fire ain't a peaceful way to go. They say that burned souls hang around even when their bodies get buried somewheres else. Maybe you ought not to nose around there too much."

"It is kind of spooky, all right," said Calhoun, remembering that phantom foot. "What happened to the Raczwencs?"

Jacob gazed off into space. "Sad story, Stoney. Old Saul, he hung himself. His son found him in the barn, danglin' from a rafter where he jumped out of the hayloft. The missus, she died of the cancer a few years after the fire."

"And what happened to their property?"

"Hell, Stoney. I thought you understood that. You know David Ross, don't you?"

"Well, sure."

"That's David Raczwenc," said Jacob. "The son."

"He changed his name," said Calhoun, feeling stupid.

Jacob nodded.

"David Ross found his father hangin' in the barn." Calhoun shook his head. "That's a tough one."

"I guess to hell it is, Stoney."

Calhoun nodded. "So after the fire, Ross bought back the Potter property, which had originally been in his family. Then—"

"'Scuse me, Grampa."

Jacob glanced up, looking past Calhoun's shoulder, and said, "What's up, son?"

Calhoun turned. Marcus was standing behind him wearing his usual empty smile. "I gotta go," he said.

"You got some pretty girl waitin' for you, boy?"

Marcus shook his head. "Ollie Sorenson wants me to help him truck some firewood."

"Go ahead, then," Jacob said to Marcus. "Say hello to Ollie for me."

Marcus nodded to Jacob, then to Calhoun. Then he turned and left.

Jacob sighed, leaned on his cane, and pushed himself to his feet. "Guess I better get back to work," he said. He began to limp across the floor. "Was there anything else you wanted to know?"

Calhoun followed him, resisting the temptation to hold his elbow and steer him along. "I guess that's about it," he said. "Mainly, just trying to figure out what happened up there, why Lyle got killed."

"Guess when they catch up with that Fred Green you'll have your answers," said Jacob. "Meantime, if I hear anything, I'll give you a holler."

The Congregational church, along with several lovely old Federal Period homes, an antiques shop, and an art gallery, overlooked the Keatsboro village green. The green was a perfect square. It was rimmed with elegant maple trees, and a miniature Washington Monument stood in the exact center, a memorial to the boys who gave their lives in the wars. Four paved pathways led to it from each of the four corners, and a few old artillery pieces—artifacts from the Great War—were scattered around. Bordering the walkways were neatly tended flower gardens, which bloomed with petunias, marigolds, phlox, and impatiens.

Calhoun pulled into the circular driveway in front of the white-clapboard church. He got out and snapped his fingers at Ralph, who looked up, yawned, and climbed down from the truck.

Behind the church, gravestones stood in rows on a west-facing hillside that sloped gently down to a pasture, where a herd of milk cows grazed. In the distance, the hills of New Hampshire bumped against the horizon. The cemetery covered an area about a hundred yards square and was surrounded by a tall black iron fence. The gate was ajar, and Calhoun went in.

There were hundreds of gravestones—some tall and fancy and some modest and plain. Calhoun began walking the rows. Many of the markers dated back to the 1700s and 1800s. A number of them were family plots that told stories of tough old Yankee farmers with a succession of wives, each of whom had given their husbands several children before dying. Many of the children had failed to survive infancy.

Calhoun thought of Lyle. Lyle had probably prowled this cemetery, gathering stories, embellishing them, reading between the lines.

Here and there, a faded little American flag was stuck into the ground, and there were a few pots holding brown sticks that had once been flowers. Memorial Day, Calhoun remembered, was about a month ago.

He found Sam Potter halfway down the slope. A rectangular granite marker read SAMUEL EMERSON POTTER; MARCH 12, 1909–OCTOBER 22, 1947. A VETERAN OF THE SECOND WORLD WAR. LOVING HUSBAND OF EMILY GRAYSON POTTER AND FATHER OF LAWRENCE AND MARTHA. GOD REST HIS SOUL.

A little American flag had been stuck in the ground in front of Samuel's stone, and a cheap plastic flowerpot holding a droopy geranium leaned against the side of the gravestone. Unlike most of the other flowers in the cemetery, these were still alive, although it looked like they hadn't been watered for about a week.

After more than half a century, somebody still remembered Sam Potter, and for some reason, that made Calhoun feel ineffably sad.

He whistled for Ralph, then sat down at the foot of the grave marker. Ralph lay beside him with his chin on Calhoun's instep. He scratched Ralph's ears for a moment. Then he lay back on the ground with his hands laced under his head and waited for Sam Potter to whisper his secrets to him.

CHAPTER TWENTY-SIX

HE ALLOWED HIS EYES TO CLOSE, drifting on his thoughts, ready to receive any messages that Sam Potter might choose to pass along, hints or clues that might help him understand what had happened on his property almost sixty years after he died.

He remembered what Jacob Barnes had said about how the ghosts of fire victims remained behind to haunt the place where they had been burned even when their corporal remains were carted away and buried someplace else. When it came to ghosts, Calhoun was certainly not a disbeliever. He'd seen bodies in trout streams and feet sticking up out of the earth. Visions visited him at night. He wasn't sure where the line between ghosts and imagination was drawn.

He would welcome a visit from Sam Potter—even if it was the product of his own lightning-zapped brain—and he'd be willing to call it a ghost.

But Potter did not speak to him.

After about half an hour he pushed himself to his feet and wiped the grass off his pants. He and Ralph went back to the truck, and ten minutes later they pulled into the barway to the woods road that led through the forest and down the long slope to the milldam where Lyle had died.

It had happened exactly a week ago.

The mid-afternoon summer woods buzzed with the steady drone of cicadas, punctuated by the occasional distant caw of a crow. The lush foliage overhead cast the forest in deep, cool shade, and the grasses and ferns that brushed against Calhoun's legs smelled ripe and spicy. Ralph trotted alongside, stopping occasionally to sniff a moss-covered rock or a rotten stump, but he showed no inclination to veer into the woods, even when a chipmunk darted among the gaps in the stone wall that paralleled the old roadway.

They stopped at the milldam. Calhoun sat down, hugged his knees, and looked out over the pond. Jacob hadn't mentioned anything about the habits of the ghosts of men who'd been shot in the water and drowned, but if Lyle's spirit lurked nearby, Calhoun wanted to give him a chance to speak.

Ralph waded into the water up to his chest, had a drink, and then paddled around for a while. When he hauled himself out of the pond, he came to where Calhoun was sitting before shaking himself dry. Then he lay down and closed his eyes.

Calhoun wiped Ralph's spray off his face with the back of his wrist. "Guess I'm getting weird," he said to Ralph. "Looking for ghosts. Maybe I'm crazy after all. On the other hand, I don't suppose crazy people *know* they're crazy. Maybe the definition of crazy is when you don't think you are. In which case, I ain't crazy. Because lately I've sure been wondering about it."

Ralph opened his eyes and gave him a look that said: "As far as I'm concerned, you are certifiable. But I love you anyway."

If Lyle McMahan's ghost was haunting the millpond, it had nothing to say to Stoney Calhoun, so after fifteen or twenty minutes, he and Ralph got up, crossed at the dam, and walked up the hill to the cellar hole.

He poked around among the scattered fieldstones of the toppled chimney but found no other dug-up places that might yield more gold teeth. He eased himself down into the cellar hole, which grew thick with briar and sumac. Among the weeds and charred timbers and rusted bedsprings he found shards of stained crockery, heat-twisted knives and forks, broken glass, pots and pans, metal picture frames—just what one would expect, and nothing more.

It felt vaguely like grave robbing, and after a few minutes of it he climbed out, sat down, and leaned back against a rock.

He gave Sam Potter's burned soul a half hour to show itself, and when it didn't, he and Ralph got up, walked out to the truck, and drove home.

Calhoun and Ralph took a late lunch—two Granny Smith apples, a can of Coke, and one Milk-Bone—down to the creek. It was about four o'clock, a little early for the trout to start rising, but the music of the moving water soothed him, and he was ready to welcome any apparitions that might decide to come drifting down into the pool.

He'd finished both apples and was about halfway through the Coke when he heard the slam of a car door. His first thought was that his shotgun still lay behind the seat in his truck. Then he figured that if Fred Green had come to shoot him in the middle of the afternoon, he had to be so dumb that Calhoun could handle him without a weapon.

A couple of minutes later Sheriff Dickman appeared at the top of the path that led down to the water. He shaded his eyes for a moment, then lifted his hand in a greeting and came down.

He sat on the rock beside Calhoun. "I was in the neighborhood," he said.

"The hell you were," said Calhoun.

Dickman grinned. "Okay, so I came over special to see you."

"You made me a promise."

"I'm keeping it, Stoney. Just wanted to see how you were making out."

"I'm making out fine. That why you made a special trip? To see how I was making out?"

"Sure. Partly, anyway. Last time I saw you . . ."

"You thought I was crazy."

"Never thought that, Stoney. But I was concerned about you. Hope you don't mind that your friends care about you."

"Well, I'm okay, so why don't you give me the other part."

The sheriff nodded. "Learned a couple things, figured you deserved to know." He took off his Stetson and set it on his knee.

Calhoun said, "I got some stuff, too."

"Oh?"

"You first."

The sheriff shrugged. "Okay. Fred Green. Well, we knew that's not his real name. I sent a copy of your sketch to the Saint Augustine police down there in Florida where the real Fred Green had his credit card stolen, and damned if they didn't ID it for us."

Calhoun smiled.

The sheriff squinted at him. "What, you think you know who it is?"

"I got an idea," said Calhoun, "but I don't want to wreck your story."

"Lawrence Potter's his actual name." Dickman cocked his head and narrowed his eyes. "That what you were thinking?"

"The thought had crossed my mind."

"You might've mentioned it to me."

"It only just occurred to me this afternoon, Sheriff. Go on. Tell me the rest of it."

"Lawrence Potter," said Dickman. "Born 1936 to Samuel and Emily Potter. Graduated from Rollins College in 1958 and has been selling marine insurance in Florida since then. Never married. Lived with an older sister—"

"Martha," said Calhoun.

"Right. Martha." Dickman shook his head, squinted at Calhoun for a moment, then shrugged. "Anyway, Lawrence Potter has been a model citizen. Served two terms as president of Rotary, coached Pop Warner football, stuff like that. About his only vice seems to be boats. Boats and fishing. He likes expensive boats."

"Fishing isn't a vice."

Dickman smiled. "About a month ago sister Martha's Alzheimer's got so bad that her loving brother bowed to the inevitable and moved her to a nursing home."

"The same one that—?"

"Right," said the sheriff. "The same one where a poor old blind guy named Fred Green was staying. In fact, Martha's got the room right next to Mr. Green. I called the company Potter works for. He's on vacation. Goes fishing every June, they said. Travels all over. Montana, Alaska, Iceland. In the winter he visits New Zealand and Argentina. He left a week ago Sunday. Told everybody he was heading for Oregon."

"But he came to Maine instead," said Calhoun.

"Evidently," said the sheriff. He picked up a pebble and tossed it into the creek. "We had a hit on that credit card yesterday."

"A hit?" said Calhoun.

Dickman nodded. "He called the Thrifty car rental out by the airport in Portland on the phone yesterday morning, reserved a mid-sized car, gave Fred Green's name and the stolen credit card number. He was going to pick up the car around noon."

Calhoun nodded. "But he didn't, because if he did, you would've nailed him right there."

"Right," said the sheriff. "When Thrifty ran the number, it came up stolen. They called us right away, and I called the state police, and they were waiting for him. He never showed up. But he's still around."

"He must've sniffed it out," said Calhoun. "I went up to Craigville yesterday. Talked to Mrs. Sousa at The Lobster Pot Motel. She was pretty upset that Mr. Green stiffed her with his stolen credit card. Said he was asking around for a guide. I talked to a guy named Blaine at a local bait shop, who said Green—Potter, that is—was interested in finding a pond down in this neck of the woods, so he recommended hooking up with Lyle McMahan."

The sheriff was shaking his head. "None of this explains why he killed Lyle."

"'Course it doesn't," said Calhoun. "If he did."

"Who else?"

Calhoun shrugged. "I don't know. Him, I guess. I'm just trying not to jump to conclusions."

"We law-enforcement types," said the sheriff, "we're taught that usually things are exactly what they seem to be. We say, 'The commonest things most commonly happen.' We're taught to jump to conclusions, Stoney, because that way we don't waste a lot of time. Any reason why you think this might *not* be Fred Green—Lawrence Potter, that is—who's doing this?"

Calhoun shook his head. "Nope. No reason." He gazed out over the pool. A few mayflies had begun to flutter out of the bushes. They were dipping and darting over the water. Soon they'd begin their swirling mating dance, and then they'd fall into the creek and the trout would lift up from the bottom to eat them.

He turned back to the sheriff. "Lawrence Potter lived up there on that hilltop in Keatsboro," he said. "Would've been eleven years old in forty-seven. His mother must've been off somewhere the day the fire blew through, and he and his sister were probably at school. The Potters came from down south originally, so Mrs. Potter probably took the kids back there after the fire. It's been nearly sixty years, and now Lawrence decides to come back to Keatsboro and visit the site of the family homestead. Needed a guide to help him find it. On the way, he stopped off at the cemetery behind the Congregational church to put a geranium on the graves of his parents."

"Then he shot Lyle," said the sheriff.

Calhoun shrugged. "I guess so. And—"

Dickman held up his hand. "Whoa," he said. "Slow down, Stoney. If Lawrence Potter came up here just to revisit his childhood home—"

"How come he used a fake name and a stolen credit card?"

The sheriff shrugged. "Right."

"And why pretend he wanted to go fishing?"

"You act like you got the answers, Stoney."

Calhoun shook his head. "I don't. But I'm pretty sure of one thing."

"And what's that?"

"He intended to do something immoral or illegal."

"And he did," said the sheriff. "He killed Lyle."

"Maybe," said Calhoun. He shifted his gaze back to the stream.

"Well," said the sheriff, "if it wasn't Green—Potter, that is—who was it?"

"Ghosts," mumbled Calhoun.

"What?"

"Nothing."

The sheriff was frowning at Calhoun. "Stoney, you worry me."

"I appreciate it," said Calhoun. "But no need. And for Christ's sake, don't you forget you made me a promise."

"I won't." Dickman pushed himself to his feet and set his hat on his head. "Well," he said, "I just thought I'd keep you up to speed, and I appreciate you doin' the same." He started to turn away, then stopped. "You take care of yourself, hear me?"

"I intend to," said Calhoun. He got up and slapped his leg for Ralph to follow. "I'll walk you back to your vehicle. Nearly forgot. I got something for you."

When they got to the house, Calhoun went up onto the porch and said, "Look here, Sheriff."

He was pointing at the two bullet holes in the wall beside the door. Dickman went over and squinted at them, then looked at Calhoun. "You mind if I send one of the state guys over to dig 'em out?"

"Guess not," said Calhoun. "Try to let me know when he's coming so I don't shoot him. Come on in. Have a Coke."

They went inside. "In the refrigerator," Calhoun said. "Help yourself."

He went into the bedroom, opened the top drawer of his bureau, and took out the plastic bag that held the .22 cartridge cases that he and Kate had found in the woods.

Dickman was standing at the sliding glass door, looking out into the woods and sipping a Coke.

"Here," said Calhoun, handing him the plastic bag. "See if these tell you anything."

Dickman held the bag up to the light and squinted at its contents, then nodded and stuffed it into his pocket. He lifted his Coke can and said, "Gotta hit the road, Stoney. Thanks for the drink." He hesitated, then came to where Calhoun was standing and held out his hand. "You take care of yourself."

Calhoun shook his hand. "That's exactly what I've been trying to do."

Dickman smiled. "Well, if you find the job too big for one man, don't hesitate to give me a holler."

"Appreciate it," said Calhoun.

The phone rang around eight o'clock. It was Millie. "Did a little more snoopin' for you," she said.

"What'd you find out?"

"Couple things. First off, David Ross—"

"Raczwenc," said Calhoun. "He changed his name."

"Well, shit, Stoney. I thought that was pretty good information."

"It's not bad. But Jacob already told me that."

"Well try this, then," she said. "That company, A & I Development? It's owned by David Ross and Jacob Barnes—jointly. They're the ones who hold that Potter property."

"Ross and Barnes," said Calhoun. "That *is* good, Millie." He thought for a minute. "A & I. Anna Ross and Ingrid Barnes. Jacob mentioned Ingrid. That was his wife, huh?"

"Yes," said Millie. "She died a short time before you came up here. They were very devoted."

"So Jacob and David formed a corporation and named it after their wives. Hmm . . ."

"It worked this way," she said. "A & I was created in 1973. Barnes is president, David Ross treasurer, and Anna's the secretary. Ingrid was one of the directors. They took title to that parcel for exactly one dollar, payable to David Ross, and A & I hasn't done a bit of business since then. They register and file their reports every year, pay the property taxes on that land, and that's it. I made a few discreet inquiries, Stoney, and near as I can figure, Ross came up short of cash in 1973. Instead of selling some of his property, he got Jacob to loan him money in exchange for half ownership of the Potter piece. There is no record of its ever being put on the market since then. No plans to subdivide or develop on record, no proposals to the planning board, no dickering with development companies or construction firms."

"They're just sitting on it," he said.

"Yup."

"Why?"

"I guess that's the question, Stoney. Figure that one out and maybe you'll get some of the other answers you're looking for." She hesitated. "I'm working on a couple of other things, too."

"What kind of things?"

"I'll have to get back to you on that," she said. "I photocopied a bunch of stuff and brought it home with me, and I haven't gone through it all yet. If I'm not mistaken, you'll find it interesting."

"What's it about?"

"That's all I'm going to tell you for now, Stoney."

"Come on. Give me a hint."

She chuckled. "Nope."

"Damn it, Millie—"

"Forget it," she said. "I'll get back to you."

"I was just going to say—"

"You were going to say that I'm the sexiest, smartest, loyalest, most damn interesting woman in the whole state of Maine. Right?"

He laughed.

"Next to Kate, of course," she said.

"Actually, I was going to say you were the biggest damn tease in York County."

"I suppose I could take that as a compliment."

"I owe you," he said.

"Ah, it's my pleasure, Stoney. Forget it."

"No, we'll find us a real expensive place in Portland. You, me, and Kate. Dress fancy. I'll even put on a necktie. Linen napkins, candles on the table, nice French wine, have us some snails and truffles."

"I'd love that," Millie said. "I'd really love that."

CHAPTER
TWENTY-SEVEN

AFTER CALHOUN HUNG UP from talking with Millie, he went out to his truck and retrieved his anthology from under the front seat. He wanted to reread that Faulkner story, "The Bear." He'd been thinking about it since he'd read it the other night, and he felt there was more to it than he'd noticed the first time through. Calhoun had found that simply reading some stories left him feeling uneasy and dissatisfied. Some stories had to be studied. "The Bear" seemed to be one of those stories.

Last night, planning to hide outside all night, hoping to ambush Fred Green, had reminded him of Ike McCaslin, the sixteen-year-old boy in the story, preparing to face the bear. Calhoun had been alert, fine-tuned, jazzed-up, and afraid, too, all at once. He'd felt *alive*. He'd felt the hunt bubbling in his genes, a kind of certainty that he had hunted before, and so had his ancestors as far back as time, waiting in the bushes for caribou to come close, stalking mastodons with fire-sharpened sticks, wondering who was going to kill whom, then recording their triumphs and their disasters on the walls of caves.

He'd always known that fishing and hunting were the same thing, something strong in the blood that was left over from a time when surviving depended on being good at it. Last night, when death was at stake, had felt like stalking striped bass on a sand flat—except more so.

Like many hunts, last night's had not produced a kill. Tonight he would have to hunt again, and he figured he might have to spend many nights out on the edge of the clearing he'd hacked out of the Maine woods, guarding his little island of solitude, his own insignificant place on this earth. But it was *his*, his territory, the place that had drawn him north from the hospital in Virginia. He'd lie in wait every night until Lawrence Potter came again.

He sat in his chair and opened the heavy book on his lap. Ralph sauntered over and collapsed on the floor beside him. Outside, darkness had begun to fall.

Calhoun began to read Faulkner's story, to study it, and as he'd expected, he found echoes in his brain that he hadn't noticed the first time. "It was as if the boy had already divined what his senses and intellect had not encompassed yet," Faulkner had written. "That doomed wilderness whose edges were being constantly and punily gnawed at by men with plows and axes who feared it because it was wilderness." Well, Calhoun had his own piece of doomed wilderness here in the woods of Dublin, Maine, and he'd be damned if men with plows and axes—never mind .22 rifles—were going to take it away from him.

It was close to midnight when he closed the book. He pushed himself to his feet. Ralph lifted his head from his paws and looked up at him.

"It's time," said Calhoun.

Thermos of coffee, army blanket, shotgun, extra shells. He turned off all the lights, and he and Ralph went out onto the porch. He stood there until his eyes adjusted.

Calhoun picked a different place to hide, this time just inside the clearing directly across from the front porch. From here, he had a good sweep of the driveway as it curved up the hill away from the house to the paved road. He found another good tree to lean against, and he settled down.

Reading "The Bear" again had given him new thoughts about Lawrence Potter, and Calhoun decided he had better respect him. Maybe he was old, but he'd managed to kill Lyle. A rifle and a clever brain had a way of neutralizing differences in age and strength and quickness. He might not even come in the night next time. Maybe he'd do it entirely differently. Calhoun could not count on him falling into predictable habits.

Anyway, Calhoun decided that he'd be better prepared if he accepted the possibility that the man with the .22 could be anyone, including somebody from the time in his life that he couldn't remember.

So he could never relax. Not in the daytime. Not when he was away from his house, or in his truck, or at the shop. Not until it was over. The man had certainly meant to kill him that first time, and there was no reason to believe he wouldn't try again. He would keep trying until either he nailed Calhoun or Calhoun nailed him.

And so he sat out the night with his shotgun across his knees and Ralph dozing fitfully beside him, fueled by the caffeine of the coffee and the adrenaline of the hunt. He listened to the night-sounds of the woods and he watched the stars rotate in the sky. Thoughts whirled pointlessly in his head until the sun came up.

He went inside, turned on the coffeemaker, shucked off his clothes, and took a long hot shower. He did not bother dressing afterward. He called in Ralph, told him it was his watch, and went to bed.

His mental alarm clock woke him up at eleven. His mind was clear. No dream-hangover today. Two cups of coffee later, he was ready.

He and Ralph drove over to Jacob Barnes's store. It was around noontime, and the gravel parking area was jammed with pickup trucks and four-wheel-drives.

When he pushed open the door, he saw that the back corner was packed with locals. All the chairs were taken. Several men were leaning against the wall, and a few were squatting on the floor, rocking on their heels, all of them smoking and sipping soda and talking in low voices.

No laughter bubbled up from the group. Calhoun heard none of the usual crude cursing or loud argumentation. Today the voices were subdued—somber, even.

Calhoun had never joined one of these back-room gossip sessions. The regulars were all native-born locals who, even after five years, still regarded Calhoun skeptically. He'd forever be "from away" to them. They were always polite, even friendly, to him. But they'd never quite trust him.

That was okay by him. He wasn't much for gossip.

Jacob was behind the counter loading cans into a paper bag for a woman Calhoun didn't recognize.

The woman hefted the bag in her arms, turned, glanced at Calhoun, nodded to him, and left the store. Calhoun stepped up to the counter.

Jacob nodded to him.

"Marcus abandon you today?"

"I believe he's seein' what he can do for Millie," Jacob said.

Calhoun frowned. "What do you mean?"

Jacob leaned forward, bracing his forearms on the counter. "You didn't hear?"

"Hear what?"

"About Millie's fire?"

"Fire?" Calhoun shook his head. "What happened?"

"Don't know, really." Jacob's eyes were solemn. "Happened in the night. Her house burned down and they took Millie to the hospital."

"Is she okay?"

"She ain't dead."

Calhoun slammed his fist on the countertop. "Jesus," he muttered.

He'd talked to Millie in the evening. She had been fine. Her usual warm, enthusiastic self. He leaned toward Jacob. "What caused the fire? What's the matter with Millie? Tell me what you know, man."

Jacob flapped his hands. "Happened sometime in the middle of the night. They drug Millie out while it was burnin', is what they're sayin'. Clamped oxygen on her face, raced her off to the hospital, sirens a-screamin'. Ain't much left of her little bungalow, I hear. Gutted her right out. Personally, I ain't seen it. Been here since six this mornin'. Folks come in, are giving me the story."

"What hospital?"

"Rochester, I believe," said Jacob. "Closest hospital. Guess they were in some kind of hurry."

Calhoun nodded. "Thanks," he said to Jacob. He went out to his truck and headed up the road to Millie's.

A fire engine was parked out front, and behind it a black Plymouth sedan with a red light on the roof. Calhoun pulled in behind the sedan, told Ralph to sit tight, and got out.

The logo on the side of the sedan read YORK COUNTY FIRE MARSHAL.

The shell of Millie's house still stood. There were big holes in the roof and smoke smudges around the empty windows and along the eaves. The front door had been broken down, and the yard was littered with wet, sooty furniture. Millie's Jeep Cherokee crouched in the side driveway. The paint on the side facing the house was blackened and blistered.

A short, gray-haired man wearing a white short-sleeved shirt and no necktie stood at the edge of the yard talking with a fireman, who was wearing a T-shirt, blue jeans, and knee-high rubber boots, and holding a visored hard hat in his hand. When Calhoun approached them, the man in the white shirt looked up and waved the back of his hand at him.

"Move on," he said. "Git your vehicle out of here."

"Millie's a friend of mine," Calhoun said.

"Millie's a friend of everybody," said the man. "Hangin' around here ain't going to help her."

"Can you tell me what happened?"

The man shook his head and sighed. "We don't need gawkers, friend. We're tryin' to figure out what happened, and you're in the way."

"Can you just tell me if she's okay?"

The man in the jacket turned to the fireman and spoke to him quietly for a moment. The fireman nodded, put on his hard hat, and strode into the shell of Millie's house. Then the short man walked over to where Calhoun was standing.

Calhoun held out his hand. "Calhoun," he said. "I live a few miles back off County Road."

"Chiesa," said the man, giving Calhoun's hand a quick, limp shake. "I'm the county fire marshal. I been here since four AM, Mr. Calhoun. I'm tired and hungry and short-tempered, and I been chasin' folks away all morning."

"What about Millie?"

Chiesa shook his head. "They found her unconscious upstairs in her bedroom. Guess she got a lot of poison in her lungs." He shrugged. "Last I heard, she was holding her own."

"They took her to Rochester?"

Chiesa nodded. "Closer than Portland."

Calhoun jerked his head toward what was left of the house. "Any idea what happened?"

"Not yet. Could be electrical. She had a bunch of overloaded sockets downstairs. Coupla air-conditioning units improperly wired." He shrugged.

"What about arson?"

Chiesa shook his head. "I ain't prepared to say anything about that. That's why I'm here. To investigate. But we only just got the fire put out. Can't rule out arson, but usually these things turn out to be electrical."

"Has Sheriff Dickman been by?"

"He's been notified. At this point, there's nothing for him."

"Millie had two cats," said Calhoun.

"Don't know anything about any cats," said Chiesa. He looked past Calhoun's shoulder. Calhoun turned around. The fireman had come out of the house and was standing there with his eyebrows arched. "What've you got, Eddie?" Chiesa said to the fireman.

"Somethin' you oughta take a look at, sir."

Chiesa nodded. "Okay. Be right there." He turned to Calhoun. "Do me a favor, okay?"

"Sure."

"Don't go spreading rumors. I don't want the word 'arson' being bandied about down in Jacob Barnes's back room. I know there'll be plenty of speculating. But I don't want anyone saying that Fire Marshal Jack Chiesa is talking about arson. You got that?"

Calhoun nodded. "No problem."

"One other thing," said Chiesa.

"Yes?"

"Git on out of here. No offense, but just stay the hell away. Let us do our job."

"You got it," said Calhoun.

He went back to the truck. Ralph was sitting behind the wheel. "Shove over," Calhoun told him. Ralph shoved over, and Calhoun climbed in.

It took about a half hour to drive to the hospital in Rochester. He left the truck in the shade of a maple tree on the edge of the parking lot, cracked the windows, and told Ralph to sit tight. Then he went in.

The woman at the desk told him that Millie Dobson was in Intensive Care and could not see visitors. She knew nothing of Millie's condition.

Calhoun thanked her and went over to the elevators across the lobby. The directory indicated that the ICU was on the second floor. He found the stairway and went up.

Two nurses were seated behind a chest-high horseshoe-shaped counter. One of them was bent over a clipboard. The other had her back to Calhoun and was watching a bank of computer screens behind them, which beeped a quiet, syncopated tune as lines and graphs moved across the screens.

Calhoun leaned his elbows on the counter and said, "Excuse me."

The nurse with the clipboard looked up. "Yes?"

"I came to see Millie Dobson."

She looked to be somewhere in her fifties. She wore a pale blue cardigan sweater over a white blouse. She had iron-gray hair and sharp blue eyes and a soft, matronly body. "No visitors, sir."

"I'm her brother."

The nurse cocked her head. Then she smiled, and wrinkles spread across her face. "Sure you are."

"Can you tell me how she is?"

"She's not out of the woods. Still unconscious. They may have to operate."

"Operate?" said Calhoun. "I thought . . ." He shook his head. "She was in a fire. Smoke inhalation or something."

"It's the head injury the doctors are worried about. She took quite a severe blow."

"Head injury? How . . .?"

The nurse shrugged. "They figure she bumped into something or maybe fell down trying to get out in the dark. They don't know. She has a fractured skull. The doctors're worried about subdural bleeding."

"Jesus," he muttered. "Look. I got to see her."

"And you're her brother."

"That's right."

"Your name Dobson?"

"No. I'm Calhoun. Dobson is Millie's married name."

The nurse flipped through her clipboard. "It says here she's not married."

"She was," said Calhoun. "She divorced. She kept his name."

The nurse grinned and shook her head. "You really want to see her, don't you, brother?"

"Yes, ma'am."

She narrowed her eyes at him for a moment, then nodded. "Come on. Just for a minute."

The nurse came out from behind the counter and led him around the corner. Millie's bed sat in the middle of a small room, surrounded by machines. A bulky bandage covered her head like a turban. A tube was clamped to her nostrils. More tubes snaked down to her wrist, which was taped to a board. Still another snuck out from under the thin blanket that covered her and emptied into a bag attached to the foot of her bed. Wires crawled out from under the blanket that covered her chest and ran to different machines.

She looked small and gray and old and utterly lifeless.

Calhoun blew out a breath.

The nurse touched his arm. "I'll give you five minutes. Talk to her if you want. For heaven's sake, don't touch anything."

He nodded, still staring at Millie.

He was aware of the nurse leaving. "Hey, Millie," he said. "Can you hear me?"

She gave no indication that she'd heard him.

"It's Stoney," he said. "I came to remind you about our dinner date. You better not let me down. I'm really looking forward to it. We'll dress all fancy, have some expensive wine, maybe go dancing afterwards."

Millie's body remained motionless, but Calhoun thought he could see her eyes rolling under her eyelids. He moved close to her. "What happened, Millie?" he said. "Who did this to you? I wish you could tell me what happened. I wish you could tell me if this is my fault."

She gave him no response.

He moved back from her bed, leaned against the wall, folded his arms across his chest, and watched her face. The machines lined up beside her bed ticked and hummed and breathed in the hospital silence.

Then the nurse was at the door. "You've got to leave," she said.

He nodded, went over and touched Millie's cheek, turned, and followed the nurse out of the room.

Back at the counter, he took one of Kate's business cards from his wallet and wrote his phone number on it. "Please," he said. "If there's any change—anything—let me know."

She took the card from him, glanced at it, and said, "Sure, brother Calhoun. We'll let you know. You're her, um, next of kin?"

"Yes," he said. "I guess you could call me that."

CHAPTER TWENTY-EIGHT

First Lyle.

Now Millie.

Calhoun and Ralph were sitting side by side on one of the tumbled-down slabs of granite, formerly the foundation of the bridge that had spanned the little creek behind his house. The brook trout had started sipping mayfly spinners, which were washing down the quickening current where the creek narrowed. Two fish had moved up to the head of the pool where the riffle slowed and flattened. The third trout, the biggest, held himself suspended directly under a tuft of overhanging grass tight against the far bank in a little eddy formed by a submerged rock.

That was the one Calhoun tried to catch mentally. The others were too easy.

He was convinced that what had happened to Millie was his fault, just as he knew that Lyle wouldn't have been murdered if he—Calhoun himself—had taken Fred Green / Lawrence Potter fishing like he was supposed to. Millie had been doing him a favor, and now she was in the hospital.

He got close to somebody, let them into his heart, and then something happened to them. Calhoun suspected that was the story of his entire life, although he did not know that story very well.

"Simplify, simplify," Thoreau had said. Calhoun realized he had let too much complication enter his life. He hadn't intended it. He hadn't wanted it. If he'd been stronger, it wouldn't have happened. But he'd let Lyle become his best friend, and he'd allowed himself to love Kate. He'd guided and worked in the shop. He'd made friends with Millie and Sheriff Dickman and Jacob and Marcus, and recently Anna and David Ross. And nothing good had come of it. Now Lyle was dead and Millie lay in a coma and Lawrence Potter was trying to kill him, too.

Well, he'd have to settle it. Then maybe he would return to the woods and start over. He would concentrate on providing himself with food, clothing, shelter, and fuel, the necessities that Thoreau had correctly identified. He would shun luxuries. He would try to convince himself that love was a luxury, and he'd try to convince Kate of it, too.

He had come directly home after leaving Millie's bedside in the hospital in Rochester. On the drive back to Dublin, he'd made himself a promise: No more snooping around. There'd be no more investigating and asking questions and putting his friends at risk for Stoney Calhoun. He'd already done enough harm.

For the third consecutive night, he prepared to keep his vigil. He found himself feeling almost eager for it. His body had begun to adjust its rhythms to sitting alert and awake through the darkest hours of the night. He'd tuned in to the nocturnal life that scurried and flapped and slinked and buzzed in the dark. He'd heard coyotes howl, and he'd seen the slow-moving shadows of raccoons and opossums in the trees. There were nighthawks and bats and moths, flying squirrels and porcupines and deer. The gurgle of his creek sounded richer and more melodious in the night air, and he knew his trout slurped insects off its surface all night long.

He recalled a fragment of a Whitman poem. It had struck him so strongly when he'd read it in his anthology that he'd stopped to underline the words, and just the act of underlining them had caused him to memorize them:

> *I am he that walks with the tender and growing night.*
> *I call to the earth and the sea half held by the night,*
> *Press close bare-bosomed night—press close, magnetic,*
> *nourishing night!*
> *Night of south winds—night of the large few stars!*
> *Still, nodding night—mad, naked summer night.*

And so Calhoun found himself eager to get on with it.

At midnight, Calhoun and Ralph went outside. He moved to a different location, this time almost directly across the clearing from the house, not far from where the man with the .22 rifle had been standing when he'd fired two shots at Calhoun's chest on Sunday night.

He wore what he'd come to think of as his night watchman's uniform: black baseball cap, dark blue sweatshirt, blue jeans, sneakers. He sat back against a tree and spread the army blanket over his legs. His thermos of coffee stood on the ground by his left hand, his shotgun lay across his lap, and Ralph had coiled up within reach of his right hand.

The moon was a slender comma low in the sky. There were no clouds, and the bright and abundant stars bathed the clearing in pale yellow light.

Calhoun sat and waited. He was relaxed, absolutely comfortable, but alert, not the slightest bit tired despite three nights of very little sleep. His mind was clear and empty, and he thought idly that he probably could just sit out there in the nighttime forever, mindless and comfortable and content.

After an hour, he poured some coffee. Ralph lifted his head, verified that nothing interesting had happened, and dropped it back onto his paws.

After another hour or so—Calhoun checked his mental clock and guessed it was around two o'clock—he reached down for the thermos to pour himself a refill. As he did, he heard a soft shuffling sound down toward the place where the dirt driveway opened into the clearing.

He stared hard in the direction of the noise.

Deer again, probably. Or coyote or porcupine. During the past couple of nights, he'd heard many sounds.

Then he heard it again, and he identified it as a new sound. Not a deer. Not any of the animal sounds he'd been hearing in the woods at night.

In his imagination, at least, it was the sound of a man's boot sliding over damp leaves, a man trying very hard to walk silently, a man who lifted a foot and placed it in front of him carefully, feeling the ground with that front foot before transferring his weight to it, and then slowly lifting his back foot, sliding it across the ground before swinging it forward.

It was the sound of that back foot scraping across the top of last year's fallen leaves that Calhoun had heard.

Ralph sat up quickly. His ears were cocked forward and a low whine came from his throat. He stopped whining when Calhoun put a hand on his back. Calhoun could feel the dog trembling.

Then he spotted the shadow edging through the bushes, approaching his house, moving so slowly that it seemed almost motionless. This was an upright shadow, not the horizontal shape of a deer.

It was the shadow of a man, bent forward, moving carefully, keeping himself screened in the shadows of the undergrowth along the edge of the clearing.

Calhoun touched Ralph's head. "Lie down," he whispered.

Ralph lay down.

He tapped his muzzle. "Stay."

He slowly pushed the blanket off his legs. He held his Remington in both hands and eased himself to his feet, bent forward, crouching, never taking his eyes off that moving shadow that was creeping toward his house.

He began to move to his left. He'd swing a circle around the back of the house and intercept the man on the other side. He had studied this route in the daytime, planned it for the time when he'd need it, and the path was imprinted on his brain. There were rocks and rotten stumps and patches of briar, but Calhoun knew where they were and how to skirt them. He kept to the thick screen of hemlocks, where the shadows were black and a century of fallen needles made a soft soundless cushion under his feet.

Just before he passed behind the house, he stopped and peered out into the clearing.

He could not see the man, who was making his approach from the opposite side, moving as stealthily as Calhoun.

He tried to figure the man's plan. Slip in through the front door? Look in the windows, locate his quarry asleep in the bedroom, and shoot from there?

The only people who had been in his house, who knew the location of his bedroom, were Kate and Lyle and Sheriff Dickman and the Man in the Suit.

He slipped out of the woods and up to the rear of the house. He stopped, leaned his back against the outside wall, and listened.

A footstep, then another, soft but distinct. Close. Right around the corner. He heard the man blow out a quick, soft breath, as if he were winded, or nervous.

Calhoun slipped along the back wall until he reached the corner of the house. Holding the shotgun at port arms, he eased his head around the corner.

The man was there beside the house, bent over with his back to Calhoun. It looked as if he might be tying his shoe.

As Calhoun moved around the corner, the man stood up, and Calhoun knew it was not Lawrence Potter. This was a big man, taller than

Calhoun, with bulky shoulders, heavy chest, thick waist. Calhoun saw that he was holding a container of some kind in his left hand and a rifle in his right. If he turned, he'd see Calhoun.

Calhoun had his shotgun at his hip. The safety was off. He was fully prepared to blast the sonofabitch, no questions asked.

As he moved closer, the man bent over and carefully laid his rifle on the ground. Then he straightened, gripped the container in both hands, lifted it shoulder-high, tilted it, and in the pale light of the stars, Calhoun could see liquid pouring from its spout onto the side of his house.

Then he smelled it. Gasoline.

Calhoun took three quick steps forward, raised his shotgun, and jammed the barrel against the man's neck.

"Don't move," he whispered.

The man froze.

"Throw the can down in front of you."

The man hesitated, then suddenly pivoted and swung the can backward, aiming at Calhoun's head.

Calhoun leaned backward, and the heavy gasoline can missed his face by inches. The momentum of his violent effort caused the big man to lurch and stumble to his hands and knees.

Calhoun stepped forward, raised his shotgun, and smashed the butt end hard into the man's kidneys.

The man grunted, sprawled onto the ground, and lay there on his belly, groaning and gasping.

Calhoun jammed the business end of the shotgun between the man's legs. "Roll over," he said. "Move slow or I'll blow your balls off."

"Okay, okay," grunted the man.

He rolled onto his back.

"Christ," said Calhoun.

It was Marcus Dillman, Jacob Barnes's grandson.

Calhoun took one step back. "Stand up, Marcus," he said. "Go slow and easy. I got double-ought buckshot in this gun, and I won't hesitate to blow a hole in you. In fact, I'd welcome the excuse to do it."

Marcus pushed himself to his hands and knees, took a deep breath, and climbed to his feet.

"Grab the back of your head with both hands," said Calhoun, "and don't let go."

Marcus laced his fingers behind his neck. "Lemme explain, Mr. Calhoun."

"Right now, I really don't give a shit," said Calhoun. "We're going inside and we're going to call the sheriff, and you just better pray that I don't change my mind and blow your nuts away. Because I'm extremely pissed, Marcus, and I really wouldn't mind shooting you. Now move. Real slow and careful."

Marcus, with his hands clasped behind his head, started for the front of the house, and Calhoun kept two paces behind him with the bore of his Remington centered on Marcus's back.

As they approached the corner to the front of the house, something hard and sharp rammed Calhoun between the shoulder blades, causing him to stagger forward. Then it jabbed against his back a second time, forcing him forward onto his knees.

A man's voice behind him said, "Throw the gun away, Mr. Calhoun."

Calhoun tossed his Remington aside. He recognized that voice.

He turned to face David Ross.

Ross was holding a bolt-action .22 rifle. He held it lightly in his left hand, like a pistol, bracing the stock against his side with his forearm. "Marcus," said Ross, "for Christ's sake, you can stop hanging onto your head. Pick up that gas can and finish what you started."

"You going to tell me what this is all about?" said Calhoun.

"Don't see why I should," said Ross. "It ain't gonna matter to you one way or the other."

"I don't understand why you had to go after Millie."

"Felt real bad about it," said Ross. "Always liked Millie."

"And Lyle," said Calhoun. "He never hurt anyone."

"That's the truth," said Ross. He looked at Calhoun and shook his head. "Ain't no sense explaining it to you. But for what it's worth, I'm sorry. Couldn't be helped."

"You're a disturbed man, Mr. Ross."

Ross nodded. "I suppose I am."

Marcus had retrieved the gas can. It looked like a ten-gallon can. He finished emptying it against the side of the house. "All set, Mr. Ross," he said.

"Hang onto that can, son," said Ross. "We don't want to forget to bring it with us when we're done. Pick up your rifle and keep it leveled at Mr. Calhoun, here. Marcus has got a thirty-ought-six there, Mr. Calhoun, and he's damn quick with it, for a slow-witted boy. He's loaded up with hollowpoints that'll make a hole in a man you could drive that old truck of yours through. Okay, now, fellas. Let's go inside and finish this up."

CHAPTER TWENTY-NINE

THEY FORMED A LITTLE PROCESSION as they moved along the side of the house. David Ross, carrying his .22 bolt-action rifle lightly in the crook of his arm, led the way. Calhoun was behind him, followed by Marcus Dillman with his deer rifle.

Calhoun considered his options. He could lunge forward, knock Ross down, perhaps grab his .22. Marcus might hesitate before firing a .30-caliber hollowpoint into his back, and in the confusion, he might miss altogether.

More likely, Marcus would shoot him dead.

Or he could make a backward move directly at Marcus, knock his gun away, and run for the dark woods.

He figured both men were hunters, comfortable and accurate and quick with their weapons. He tried to calculate his chances coldly and rationally. The odds of escaping without getting shot were slim. Too slim.

Part of him was observing his reactions. He was calm. He was thinking, weighing his options, problem solving. He realized that he trusted himself to make a good decision.

Right now, the best decision was to go along. He'd wait for his opportunity.

They were just turning the corner to the front of the house when suddenly Ross yelled, "Ow! *Shit!*" and staggered sideways.

Calhoun stopped and felt the barrel of Marcus's .30-06 jab into the small of his back.

Calhoun heard a low, throaty growl. Then he saw Ralph with his teeth clamped onto Ross's calf.

Ross swung his rifle like a club, smashing the barrel across Ralph's back. Ralph held tight. Ross hit him again, this time on Ralph's shoulder, and Ralph rolled onto the ground. He lay there on his side, panting.

"Jesus H. Christ," muttered Ross. He kicked Ralph in the ribs. The dog whimpered but did not move.

"Now, you just set still, there, Mr. Calhoun," said Marcus from behind him.

"Like hell," said Calhoun. He went over and knelt beside Ralph, who was breathing rapidly. His tongue lolled out of his mouth, and his eyes rolled wildly. Calhoun stroked his head, then moved his hand across his back and ribs. Ralph's little stub tail flickered a couple of times, a feeble effort at a wag.

Calhoun lifted the dog's head onto his lap and stroked it. "I thought I told you to stay," he told Ralph.

"Get him the hell away from the dog," said Ross, speaking to Marcus.

Calhoun felt Marcus's gun barrel on his back. "Come on, Mr. Calhoun," said Marcus.

Calhoun looked up at Ross. "If you killed my dog . . ."

"What?" said Ross. "What're you gonna do?"

"I'll kill you."

Ross nodded. "Guess I wouldn't blame you. 'Course, managing it might be a problem." He gestured with his rifle. "Git over there, Mr. Calhoun."

Calhoun stood up and moved aside.

Ralph lay sprawled on the ground, motionless except for the rapid heaving of his chest.

"Shoot him," said Ross to Marcus.

Marcus frowned. "Huh?"

"Shoot the damn dog."

"Aw, Mr. Ross. I can't shoot no dog. This ain't a bad dog."

"Imbecile," Ross grumbled. He stepped close to Ralph and pointed his .22 at Ralph's head. "Gotta do everything myself if I want it done right."

Marcus moved quickly. He grabbed Ross's rifle and pulled it from his hands. "Don't, Mr. Ross. Please. Don't shoot the dog."

By the time Calhoun realized he could have made his move, it was too late. He'd been thinking about Ralph. Hell, he wouldn't leave Ralph there with those two anyway, not even if it meant he himself could get away.

Ross was holding his .22 again. He glared up at Marcus. "Don't ever do anything like that again," he said.

Marcus hung his head. "I'm sorry, Mr. Ross."

Ross nodded. "Okay. Pick up the damn dog and bring him inside, then."

Marcus laid his rifle on the ground, squatted down, and murmured, "I ain't gonna hurt you, boy." He picked up Ralph and cradled him against his chest. Ralph let out a little yelp, then lay still in Marcus's big arms.

"Move," said Ross to Calhoun, leveling his rifle at him. "Git into the house."

Calhoun went first, followed by Ross, with Marcus in the rear carrying Ralph.

At the doorway, Ross said to Calhoun, "Go real slow. Open the door, reach in, and turn on the lights."

Calhoun obeyed.

They all went in. Ross told Calhoun to sit in one of the kitchen chairs. Marcus laid Ralph on the floor, then went to the sink.

"What the hell are you doing?" said Ross.

"Gittin' the poor dog some water," said Marcus.

"Forget the dog," said Ross.

Marcus ignored him. He found a bowl, filled it with water, and took it to where Ralph lay. Marcus knelt beside the dog, lifted his head, and moved the water dish close to him. Ralph took a couple of slow licks, then let his head fall back to the floor.

Marcus stroked Ralph's back for a moment, then turned. "What now, Mr. Ross?"

Ross had pulled a chair to the middle of the kitchen. He was sitting there rubbing his calf with his right hand and holding his rifle on Calhoun with his left. "Go on back out there and fetch your rifle," he said to Marcus. "I want to git this done."

Marcus went out the front door, and Calhoun sat there facing David Ross, the man who had killed Lyle and burned down Millie's house and kicked Ralph.

He figured he had about two minutes before Marcus returned.

Ross was holding his .22 at his hip. His finger was curled around the trigger. The little bore was a black hole aimed directly at Calhoun's sternum.

There was no way Ross wouldn't get off one shot. But it was a bolt-action rifle, and before he could shoot a second time, he'd have to take his finger off the trigger, reach up to the bolt, eject the spent cartridge, and jack another one into the chamber.

So he'd have to give him that one shot.

Ross was staring at him. His pale eyes were alert and intelligent and calm.

Calhoun stared back at him, holding the man's eyes, controlling them with his own. Then he suddenly turned and shouted, "Ralph, no!"

Ross's head twitched, and in that instant Calhoun threw himself sideways off his chair and rolled onto his feet. He heard the *pop* of the

.22 and felt a hot dart of pain in his left ear an instant before he slammed into Ross.

They both toppled backward and became entangled in the chair where Ross had been sitting. Calhoun grabbed the rifle by the barrel, wrenched it from Ross's hands, and smashed the butt against Ross's head. Then he rolled away and jacked a new cartridge into the chamber.

"Hold it, Mr. Calhoun."

Marcus was standing in the doorway holding his deer rifle at his hip. He wouldn't shoot a dog. But Calhoun wasn't at all sure he wouldn't shoot a man.

He didn't wait to find out. He shot Marcus in the right thigh.

Marcus's eyes opened wide. He looked down at his leg, where a spot of blood was blooming on the front of his jeans. Then he shook his head and looked up at Calhoun with wide, disbelieving eyes. "You shot me," he said.

Before Calhoun could work the bolt of Ross's .22 again, Marcus turned and disappeared out the front door.

Calhoun sat there on the floor for a moment, vaguely aware of a burning sensation in his left ear. He put up his hand and it came away wet with blood.

David Ross was in a half-sitting position against the wall, staring dully at him, holding his hand against the side of his head.

Calhoun wiped his bloody hand on his pants and stood up. He jacked another round into the chamber of the .22, went over to Ross, pressed the bore of the gun against the man's knee, and pulled the trigger.

Ross howled and curled up fetally on the floor.

"You stay here," said Calhoun.

He went to the screen door, then paused. Marcus could be standing outside with his rifle leveled on the doorway. Calhoun would make a big target, standing there backlit from the inside lights. On the other hand, Calhoun figured Marcus was more likely to try to get away. He'd refused to let Ross shoot Ralph, and he had not shot Calhoun when he'd had the chance. Calhoun didn't figure Marcus was a killer.

He slipped quickly through the door and onto the porch, and then he heard the distant sound of heavy, shuffling footsteps heading out the driveway to the road. By the sound of it, Marcus had maybe fifty yards on him. Even with a bullet in his leg, the man was managing to move.

If he got to his truck, he'd get away. All Calhoun could think about was catching Marcus.

He leaped off the porch and began running. He didn't remember the last time he'd tried to run flat out. He was sprinting, moving fast.

His driveway was a quarter of a mile long, and his feet flew over the bumps and ruts. He could hear Marcus ahead of him, and he pictured the man trying to run, a fast hobble, a big dumb man with a bullet in his leg, single-mindedly intent on reaching his truck and getting away.

It seemed as if Calhoun's feet barely touched the ground. He felt as if he could run forever to catch the man who, he figured, had been David Ross's tool, the man who'd whacked Millie on the head and torched her house and who was prepared to do the same to Calhoun.

The end of the driveway was only about fifty yards ahead of him, over the rise and around the corner, when he heard the sound of a truck engine starting up.

Then he heard a loud crash, the sound of heavy steel smashing into metal. Calhoun heard the truck's engine whining, gears grinding, tires spinning and spitting up gravel. And then came that crash again. Headlights flickered and flashed wildly through the trees up ahead.

He topped the rise, and then he saw what was happening, and in spite of the adrenaline that was rushing through him, he felt like laughing.

Ross and Marcus had come in Ross's big pickup truck with the plow hitch on the front. They had backed into the end of Calhoun's driveway just far enough to keep it out of sight from the road.

Now Kate's Blazer was parked in front of the truck, blocking its way, and Marcus was mindlessly ramming the front end of it with the plow hitch, smashing into it, backing up, gunning it forward again. In the truck's headlights, Calhoun could see that Kate's old Blazer was a wreck. But it was a big vehicle, and every time Marcus rammed it, it just skidded backward a few feet.

Then, in one flash of Marcus's headlights, Calhoun saw Kate's face behind the windshield of the Blazer. Her eyes were wide and angry, and he realized that the Blazer's engine was roaring, too, and she was in first gear, trying to drive Marcus back.

Two big four-wheel-drive vehicles going at each other.

Calhoun ran to the truck, yanked open the door, grabbed Marcus's shirt, and hauled him out. They both fell in a heap. Calhoun rolled away, and when he sprang to his feet, he saw that Marcus was grappling on the ground for his rifle.

Calhoun darted in and kicked Marcus in the chest. Marcus tumbled backward, then scrambled to his feet, breathing heavily. His pant leg was wet and shiny with blood. He crouched there glowering at Calhoun, his big arms spread wide, like a wrestler looking for his opening.

Calhoun feinted to his left, took two quick steps, spun around, and kicked Marcus on his wounded thigh.

Marcus howled and managed to grab onto Calhoun's leg. He twisted Calhoun to the ground, and then he was on him, whaling away with his big fists, pounding Calhoun's ribs and arms, heavy sledgehammer blows. One caught him flush, and Calhoun felt the side of his chest cave in and the breath gush from his lungs.

Broken rib, he thought, his mind clear and objective.

He squirmed on the ground and managed to twist his body so that Marcus's heavy fists fell on his back and shoulders. Marcus climbed onto him, forced him flat onto his back and straddled him. His weight was solid and unmovable on Calhoun's stomach. Marcus had both hands on Calhoun's throat. Calhoun was gasping for air. Every time he tried to take a breath, it felt as if someone was shoving a butcher knife into his chest. He felt himself growing light-headed. His arms felt heavy and weak.

An image flashed in his mind, one of those quick memory-flickers, more déjà vu, and he remembered all this from some other time. He'd fought Marcus before. Or a big strong man just like him.

Make a move, he thought. Do it soon or it would be too late.

He worked a hand free, and with all that was left of his strength, he rammed his stiffened fingers into Marcus's solar plexus. Marcus gasped, and his hands slipped off Calhoun's throat and grappled for a grip on Calhoun's arm. Calhoun jabbed him again, and when Marcus tried to move away, Calhoun slammed upward with his knee, caught him flush between the legs, and knocked Marcus off him.

He jumped onto Marcus's chest, made a weapon of the side of his hand, and slashed a hard backhander against Marcus's upper lip, right where it met his nose.

Marcus's eyes opened wide and he said something that sounded like "Huh?" His face suddenly blossomed in blood, and then he went limp. He lay there, sprawled on his back, motionless, with his eyes rolled up into his head.

Calhoun was on his hands and knees, hanging his head, gasping for breath. After a minute, he lay on his back and closed his eyes.

Sometime later—it might've been a few minutes or several hours—Calhoun felt a bright light on his face. He made slits of his eyes.

The sun? Too bright for the sun.

"You okay, Stoney?"

It was Sheriff Dickman's voice.

Calhoun held his hand over his eyes. "Move the damn light, Sheriff."

The light shifted. Calhoun opened his eyes and blinked. Dickman was squatting beside him. "You injured, son?" he said.

"Busted ribs, maybe," grunted Calhoun. He rubbed his throat. "Otherwise, I think I'm okay."

"You got blood all over your face."

"Ross nicked my ear."

"You did a job on Marcus," said the sheriff.

"How bad is he hurt?"

"Pretty bad. You knocked out four teeth, busted his nose. He's still unconscious."

"Guess that's what I was trying to do."

"Don't know where you learned to do that, my friend. You could've killed him."

"I wasn't trying to kill him," said Calhoun. "If I'd wanted to kill him . . ."

The sheriff was looking at him as if he had never seen him before. He opened his mouth to say something, then shook his head. "You are some kind of lethal weapon, Stoney."

"I did things I didn't know I could do," said Calhoun. He took a deep, painful breath, then pushed himself up to a sitting position. He looked around. Kate was standing a little behind the sheriff, hugging herself, looking solemn. She was wearing a long full skirt and a peasant blouse. "Hi, honey," said Calhoun.

She smiled at him and whispered, "Hi."

"Where's Ralph?" he said. "Is Ralph okay?"

Dickman moved aside, and Calhoun saw Ralph lying on the ground beside Kate.

Calhoun held out his hand. "Come here," he said.

Ralph got up slowly, limped over, and licked Calhoun's face.

Calhoun put his arm around Ralph's neck. "Dammit," he said, "when're you going to learn to obey me? I told you to stay put there in the woods."

Ralph kind of shrugged, and then he lay down beside him with his chin on his paws.

CHAPTER THIRTY

THE SHERIFF CAME OVER and squatted down beside Calhoun, who was sitting on the ground patting Ralph with one hand and holding his other arm around Kate's shoulders. "We better get you to the hospital," said Dickman. "Get you an X-ray, patch up that ear."

Calhoun shook his head. "Might've cracked a rib or two," he said. "Not much they can do for that. Guess I can take care of my ear okay. I don't need any damn hospital. I don't care for hospitals."

"How do you feel?"

"I'll live," said Calhoun. "Where's Ross and Marcus?"

"Ambulance already took them away. You mashed up Ross's knee pretty good." The sheriff glanced around. "We got a lot to do. Gonna need to talk to you. You too, ma'am," he said to Kate.

"Right now?" said Calhoun.

Dickman shrugged. "No. Soon, though."

"I'll tell you this," said Calhoun. "David Ross just about admitted killing Lyle and going after Millie. Marcus did the heavy work. But he was just doing what Ross told him. Marcus saved Ralph's life. That means something. Check Ross's .22, Sheriff. He plugged Lyle with it, and he used it to shoot at me the other night, and my guess is, he probably killed Fred Green—Lawrence Potter—with it, too."

Dickman nodded. "I figured out that much all by myself. That foot you saw—"

Calhoun nodded. "It was real. It belonged to Potter."

"What I don't get," said the sheriff, "is why. You got any thoughts on that?"

"I guess Ross has got the answers," said Calhoun. "I figure Potter was his target and Lyle was a witness to it. He left Lyle there, but he buried Potter so everyone'd be thinking it was Potter—Fred Green—who'd killed Lyle. All that time, we were looking for a dead man and thinking a dead man was stalking me. You might want to ask Ross about what really happened to Sam Potter back in the fire of forty-seven. Ask him why he bought the Potters' property. Oh, and see if he's got anything to say about buried treasure."

Dickman arched his eyebrows. "Buried treasure? You mean that little piece of gold you found?"

Calhoun shrugged.

The sheriff grunted and pushed himself to his feet. "We'll talk later. Assume I'll be able to find you here?"

"I'm not going anywhere," said Calhoun.

"I called in a wrecker," said the sheriff. "They'll haul those two vehicles out of your way." He turned to Kate. "Afraid yours is a goner, ma'am."

Kate smiled. "About time."

Calhoun and Kate and Ralph continued to sit there at the end of the driveway while the various official vehicles pulled away. Then they were alone.

The stars were dimming overhead. The sky was turning silvery, and the morning chorus of forest birdsong was starting to get tuned up. Calhoun figured it was about five o'clock. Three hours since he'd first heard Marcus's foot scraping on the leaves beside his house.

"You okay, honey?" he said to Kate.

She smiled. "I'm fine."

"Give me a hand," he said.

Kate stood, bent down, hooked her arm around Calhoun's back, and helped him climb to his feet.

His chest hurt like hell.

She hugged him gently for a minute, then said, "Come on. Let's patch you up."

He hobbled back down the driveway, leaning on her. Ralph shuffled along beside them.

"I thought we agreed that you were going to steer clear of me," said Calhoun.

"I was worried about you."

"You're as bad as Ralph," he said. "Won't stay put when I tell you to."

"Problem is, we both love you."

He turned to her. "You're looking mighty pretty, honey," he said. "I can hardly breathe, looking at you."

"You can hardly breathe," she said, "because you got busted ribs."

Back at the house, Kate washed Calhoun's ear, doused it with antiseptic, and taped a clumsy bandage over it. The bullet had just nicked it, she said. With all the blood, it looked worse than it was.

Then Calhoun went outside, got out his garden hose, and washed down the side where Marcus had drenched it with gasoline, soaking it thoroughly until he figured it was safe.

When he rejoined Kate and Ralph inside, she had the coffee ready. They took their mugs out onto the deck, held hands, and watched the new day arrive.

"Millie says we should go to a restaurant," said Calhoun. "Make a public appearance. Stop sneaking around. Millie says everyone knows about us anyway."

Kate gave his hand a squeeze. "Maybe Millie's right. Walter's been saying the same thing."

"What are you going to do about Walter?"

She shook her head. "Take care of him as best I can, Stoney. I owe him that."

Calhoun nodded. "I guess you do."

"I care about Walter," she said. "He's a good man, and I used to love him." She hesitated. "Guess I still do love him." She lifted Calhoun's hand and held it against her face. "But not like I love you."

"When Millie gets out of the hospital, suppose we go to Juniper's, the three of us? Would that be okay with you?"

"A woman on each arm," she said. "What a show-off. You feel like going to bed?"

"I'm not very tired."

"So?"

Eventually, they slept.

Calhoun woke up sometime in the middle of the afternoon. When he started to roll over, it felt as if Marcus had broken every bone in his body. It took him several minutes to summon up the courage to sit, ease his legs over the side of the bed, and push himself to his feet.

The blankets were all shoved down to the foot of the bed, and Kate was sprawled naked on her belly, hugging a pillow, her glossy black hair fanned out over her back. He looked down at her, admiring the smoothness of her skin, the taper of her waist, the flare of her hips, the length of her legs. Then he smiled, let out a long breath, and pulled the sheet up over her.

He hobbled into the kitchen, put on some more coffee, and collapsed into a chair.

Ralph had followed him out of the bedroom. Ralph was hobbling, too.

Calhoun scratched the top of his head. "We're a pair, aren't we?"

Ralph sighed and curled up beside Calhoun's chair.

A few minutes later Ralph growled, and then Calhoun heard a car pulling into the yard. A door slammed, and he didn't bother getting up when he heard footsteps on the porch. "Come on in," he said.

Sheriff Dickman pushed open the door and stood there holding his hat.

"Kate's sleeping," said Calhoun.

Dickman nodded and jerked his head toward the deck. "Let's talk."

"Pour us some coffee," said Calhoun, "and bring it out."

They sat in the rockers, sipping coffee. Ralph lay on the deck between them.

Dickman held his hat on his lap and propped his heels on the deck railing. "We talked with Ross and Marcus," he said. "They were both cooperative."

"Can you tell me?" said Calhoun.

"Don't see why not. Ross signed a confession. He was full of remorse for killing Lyle and hurting Millie. At the same time, he kept saying he had no choice." Dickman gazed down toward the creek. "As you already figured out, David Ross's name was Raczwenc in nineteen thirty-eight when Sam and Emily Potter bought the property across the street, built themselves a house deep in the woods, and moved in. The Raczwencs were Jewish, and Sam Potter was an old-fashioned southern bigot and a raging anti-Semite to boot. He'd been in the war, and his platoon had gone in to liberate one of the death camps. He saw that horror firsthand and it just made him worse. Sam Potter was a sick, paranoid, haunted man, no doubt about that. Anyway, after the Potters moved in, things began to happen to the Raczwencs. They began to find their livestock dead. Goats and cows with their throats slashed, ears cut off, bellies slit open. Once they woke up in the middle of the night with a cross burning in front of their house."

The sheriff shook his head, glanced at Calhoun, sipped his coffee, returned his gaze to the creek. "David Raczwenc was a teenager. The Potters had two kids, a boy and a girl. The boy—Lawrence—was a few years younger than David, but he still taunted David every chance he got. Told him he was a dirty Jew, a Christ-killer, the usual vile shit. Bragged how his daddy was going to get them, how he'd seen the Jews in the concentration camps. The boy's head was full of all that poison. Lawrence Potter liked to brag how his father had smuggled treasure home from the war. Souvenirs from that death camp, he said."

The sheriff stopped and looked up over Calhoun's shoulder. Calhoun turned. Kate was standing in the doorway wearing a pair of Calhoun's sweatpants and one of his T-shirts.

"Come sit down, honey," said Calhoun. "You might as well hear this."

She hitched herself up onto the deck rail, hooked her heels around the bottom rail, and perched there facing them. "I heard part of it," she said. "I heard the part about treasure."

"Lawrence Potter told David that his daddy had brought home a rucksack full of Jews' teeth," said the sheriff. "Gold crowns and inlays and bridges that the Nazis pulled from the mouths of those poor souls. That was the treasure."

"How horrible," breathed Kate.

Dickman blew out a long breath. "One day the summer before the fire, young David came home from school and found Saul, his father, with a rope around his neck, hanging from a rafter in their barn, blood dripping off him. He was dead, of course. They ended up calling it a suicide, even though the man had cuts on his arms and face. There were a lot of rumors going around about Sam Potter killing Saul, and the county sheriff took the case, but nothing ever came of it.

"David Raczwenc was positive Sam Potter killed his father, not that he wasn't already boiling with hatred of the Potters. So on that day in October of forty-seven, when that fire came sweeping through the woods and looked like it was going to burn 'em all to hell, he saw his opportunity. He snuck over to the Potter's place—"

"And he killed Sam Potter," said Calhoun.

Dickman nodded. "Yes. He shot Sam with his twenty-two, set fire to the place, and went on home. The Potter kids—Lawrence and Martha—they were at school that day, and their mother was off somewhere, otherwise David would've killed them all." Dickman shook his head. "At the time, no one doubted that Sam Potter was the victim of the fire. David Ross was the only person on earth who knew what really happened. He grew up, got married, raised two kids, and got old, and not a day passed when he didn't think about Sam Potter killing his father, and that awful treasure Lawrence Potter had bragged about. He waited close to sixty years for Lawrence to come back. David changed his name to Ross soon as he was old enough. He bought the Potter property when the state took it for taxes, kept watch over it, waiting for the day. Said he never doubted Lawrence would show up. Recognized him the minute he stepped out of Lyle's old Power Wagon. Said it was the ears. Lawrence Potter had funny ears, even as a kid."

"So he snuck down there, killed Lawrence, and Lyle was a witness to it," said Calhoun.

"Yup. When Ross got to the pond, Lyle was fishing, minding his own business, and Potter was coming down the hill with his treasure. Potter had come with Lyle, and he would've left with Lyle. By Ross's way of thinking, that meant he had no choice but to kill Lyle, too. So he did. He killed them both, then called Jacob, said he had some work for Marcus, and the two of them dragged Lawrence down the hill and buried him. They stowed Lyle's truck in David's barn, and the next night Ross drove it to the back of the grammar school in South Riley. Marcus followed along behind and gave David a lift back home. David said he wanted it to look like the mysterious Fred Green had shot Lyle. Keep us looking for Green, knowing we'd never find him."

"Except Ralph found his foot," said Calhoun.

The sheriff looked at him and smiled. "You were right, Stoney. That was a real foot."

"I admit I had my doubts," said Calhoun.

Dickman smiled. "Anyway, Ross saw you come out of there that night with your dog, started to worry about somebody finding the body. So he got Marcus to come over to help him move it. By the time we got back there that night it was gone, and by the next day, the rain had washed away all the scent."

"Everybody thought I was crazy," said Calhoun. "Including me."

"Ross didn't," said the sheriff. "Ross guessed you'd figure it out sooner or later."

Calhoun shrugged. "I would've."

The sheriff nodded. "Ross took that Fred Green's credit card, and he used it at the Thrifty car rental a couple days after you and Ralph found that foot, just to make us believe that old Fred Green was still around."

"Which we did," said Calhoun. "So what did Anna Ross know about all this?"

"Nothing, apparently. We questioned her this morning. She admitted she lied about what happened the night you found Potter's foot sticking up. But she was just doing what her husband told her to do. She didn't know what was going on. The Rosses are from the old school, you know. The husband doesn't tell the wife what he's up to, and she doesn't ask."

"Why go after Millie?" said Calhoun.

"Same reason he went after you," said the sheriff. "He knew she was checking those deeds, snooping around for you. The day before Ross set her house afire, she was at the library looking at microfilm of old newspapers. Ross got wind of it, figured sooner or later she'd read about how somebody, probably Sam Potter, had murdered his father and made it look like suicide, and she'd tell you, and you'd put two and two together."

Calhoun shook his head. "I knew what happened to Millie was my fault. So what about Jacob Barnes? Was he in on this?"

"Jacob claims he knew nothing about anything," said the sheriff, "and Ross confirms it. At one point several years ago Ross was having some financial problems. Got behind on the taxes on that Potter property. He didn't want to lose it, so he asked Jacob for a loan. Jacob's a sharp businessman. Insisted he have some collateral. That's when they formed their partnership. Jacob figured one day they'd sell that land and make some money. He had no idea what Ross was up to, or why he kept needing Marcus. Jacob hired out his big dumb grandson for five bucks an hour to anybody who needed a strong back, and poor Marcus just did what he was told."

"Even burning down Millie Dobson's house," said Calhoun.

Dickman shrugged. "Yours, too."

"And hitting her on the head?"

"Ross did that," said the sheriff. "Marcus wouldn't hurt a woman."

Calhoun nodded. "Or an animal. Ross wanted him to shoot Ralph. Marcus flat-out refused."

"I got a question," said Kate.

Dickman nodded.

"I was wondering about Fred Green." She frowned. "Lawrence Potter, I mean. I understand he needed someone to help him find the place. He hadn't been there for almost sixty years. That's how come he hired Lyle. But why use a phony name?"

Dickman shrugged. "We'll never know for sure, because we're going to have a helluva problem getting answers out of him. Right now I've got some boys behind Ross's barn digging up Lawrence Potter's body from the bottom of the manure pile where Ross and Marcus moved it that night. Ross believes that Lawrence Potter knew his father was shot the day of the fire and that it was Ross who did it, so he came back not only to collect his treasure, but to avenge his father's murder. Ross is convinced that if he hadn't killed Potter, Potter would've killed him. I guess that would account for Potter using a fake name." The sheriff paused to sip his coffee. "No question Potter came back to retrieve those gold teeth. They were his patrimony." He shrugged. "I guess that's the story. Unless you got something to add."

Calhoun said, "I was wondering if you heard anything about Millie."

"She's doing good," said Dickman. "She'll be laid up for a few days, but she regained consciousness last night, and I guess she's raising hell there in the hospital." He stood up and tapped his hat against his leg as if he were knocking dust off it.

"What happened to those teeth?" said Calhoun.

Dickman smiled. "David Ross didn't want that treasure for himself. He says all he wanted was to get it away from the Potters. After he shot Potter and Lyle the other day, Ross poured some of those teeth into his hand, and when he finally saw them, actually held them, he said it felt like he was holding the lives of six million tortured souls in his hands. So he did what he'd always intended to do with them. He threw them all into the pond there on the Potter place. Made me promise not to disturb them, and I don't see any reason to break that promise. He says they should finally rest in peace, and I guess he's right about that."

After the sheriff left, Calhoun reached over for Kate's hand. "Looks like we'll have to get you a new car," he said.

"Good thing I didn't bother getting that tailpipe fixed."

"Might be a good time for us to go partners on the shop," he said, gazing off toward the creek, afraid to look at her.

"Partners," she said quietly. "I like the sound of that."

He gave her hand a quick squeeze. *Partners.* It sounded good to him, too. The word was full of promise. They'd have to discuss it some more.

Not now, though. He knew better than to press his luck with Kate.

The green Audi was sitting beside the house when Calhoun returned from the shop. It had been nearly two weeks since David Ross had come in the night.

Ralph did not come bounding down the steps to greet him when he slid out of the truck. Ralph wasn't doing much bounding lately. Neither was Calhoun, for that matter. Cracked ribs take a while to heal.

Calhoun went in and found the Man in the Suit sitting on the deck sipping a Coke from Calhoun's refrigerator. Ralph, sprawled beside him, lifted his head, gave his stub tail a couple of perfunctory wags, and dropped his head back onto his paws.

"Help yourself to a Coke, Stoney," he said.

"Thanks," said Calhoun. "Appreciate your hospitality."

He got a Coke, went back onto the deck, and took the rocker beside the man.

"I've got to debrief you."

"Figured you'd show up one of these days."

The Man in the Suit gazed off into the woods. "Sometimes," he began, "traumatic events will cause people to remember things that have been buried for a long time. Doors open, lights go on, and suddenly everything is clear."

Calhoun rocked slowly, sipping his Coke, listening to the gurgle of Bitch Creek. He said nothing.

"No doors have opened for you, have they, Stoney?" said the man.

Calhoun shook his head. "Nope. I don't remember anything."

"Good." The Man in the Suit cleared his throat. "I understand you, um, overpowered a much larger and stronger man."

"Just lucky, I guess," he said, remembering how he'd used his feet and his hands against Marcus.

"Did it occur to you that you were taught how to do that?"

Calhoun shook his head.

"Or to register faces so clearly that you could sketch them from memory?"

"I got a weird mind. That's all I know."

The Man in the Suit smiled. Calhoun couldn't remember seeing him smile before. "So nothing's changed since last time we talked?"

"I don't remember anything, if that's what you mean."

"You haven't recollected the man who saved your life or what you were doing with him, then?"

"Nope."

"Good." The man cocked his head and peered at Calhoun. "You keep asking me questions."

Calhoun shrugged. "Sometimes it seems important that I connect my memories. I get flashes. But there are gaps."

"Your life story. Your childhood, your parents."

"Yes."

"Quid pro quo, Stoney. You've got to give me something once in a while, you know."

Calhoun shrugged. "I know how it works."

The Man in the Suit drained his Coke, put the empty can on the table, and stood up. "Well, I'll be back."

"I suppose you will."

They walked down to the green Audi together. Ralph followed along behind. The man started to climb in, then stopped and turned to face Calhoun. "Tell me the truth, now, Stoney," he said. "Just between you and me. Off the record. What do you really remember?"

Calhoun shook his head. "Nothing."

"It's okay. You can tell me, you know."

"I don't remember anything."

The Man in the Suit smiled. "Sure." He got into his car, switched on the ignition, and started to back out. Then he stopped and held his clenched fist out the window. "Here," he said to Calhoun. He opened his hand, which held three 12-gauge shotgun shells. "You better keep these. Shoot all trespassers, my friend."

Calhoun took the shells. Then the man turned around and drove away.

Calhoun rolled the shells around in his hand, then squatted down beside Ralph. "Shoot all trespassers," he said. "That's damn good advice."

Then he went inside to wait for Kate.